A Boy Called Mary

There had been many gay music journalists before Kris Kirk started writing for *Melody Maker* in 1984. But Kris was the first to write as an openly gay man, and to write unapologetically about the music and acts that excited him as such. Kris understood that gay men had always played a crucial role in pop and that "pop has always been the most accurate mirror of cultural change". It was fitting – and not entirely coincidental – that he began writing for the music press at the same time as the first out crop of openly gay pop stars appeared.

Born in Carlisle in 1950, his Roman Catholic parents unwittingly gave him the suitably camp name Christopher Pious Mary Kirk. After reading American Literature at Nottingham University he spent ten years in a variety of jobs (including working as a dresser to Tommy Steele and Benny Hill) before coming to London at the start of the Eighties to work for *Gay News* – it was then that Kris changed his name to "Kristopher with a K". Following that publication's demise he moved to *Melody Maker*, wrote regular features for *Gay Times* and freelanced for a number of publications including *Smash Hits*, *The Face*, *New York Rocker*, *The Guardian* and *City Limits*. A chirpy man who it was impossible to dislike, Kris invariably managed to get the best out of those he interviewed – especially those gay artists relieved to find they were talking to someone "on the same side".

His groundbreaking study of the modern drag scene, *Men in Frocks* (GMP 1984 – a collaboration with his lover the photographer Ed Heath), was a polemic and prayer for the end of gender, uncovering that scene's hidden history from the all-male revues of the war, through the Gay Liberation Front's Rad Fems, to the Gender Benders of the day. A book about gay men and pop – provisionally titled *The Vinyl Closet* was commissioned but never finished. In 1986 Channel 4 broadcast Paul Oremland's drama documentary about Kris's life, *A Boy Called Mary*. In 1988 Kris and Ed undertook what he called their "retreat from

Moscow", moving to rural Wales to open a secondhand bookshop. But when Kris discovered he had Aids in 1991 he reluctantly returned to London for treatment. He went blind the following year. With equipment supplied by the RNIB Kris was able to carry on doing a little of what he liked best – writing. In June 1992 he became one of the first people with Aids to come out in a piece he wrote for *Gay Times* – 'Descent into darkness'; "As long as I have my friends, my family, my fags, my coffee, my opera tapes and my writing I guess I shall tootle along, even though I may not have all my coat buttons done up properly. Life is for living and I am trying to live it as well as I can. But I suppose that I feel that when death finally comes I shall be ready for it. Perhaps that is what life is all about."

Kris Kirk died on April 27 1993.

Richard Smith is the author of *Seduced and Abandoned: Essays on gay men and popular music.* He has written extensively about homosexuality and pop for *Gay Times, Melody Maker, The Guardian,* and *BBC Radio One.* He has also contributed to the books *Drag: A history of female impersonation in the performing arts, Intoxication: An anthology of stimulant-based writing,* and *The Guinness/Virgin Encylopedia of Popular Music* series.

A Boy Called Mary

Kris Kirk's Greatest Hits

Edited and introduced by Richard Smith

Foreword by Boy George

Millivres Books
Brighton

First published in 1999 by Millivres Books (Publishers)
33 Bristol Gardens, Brighton BN2 5JR, East Sussex,
England.

Copyright © The Estate of Kris Kirk, 1999
Introduction © Richard Smith, 1999
Foreword © Boy George, 1999
The rights of the authors have been asserted

A CIP catalogue record for this book is available from the
British Library

ISBN 1 873741 33 2

Typeset by Hailsham Typesetting Services,
2 Marine Road, Eastbourne, East Sussex BN22 7AU

Printed and bound by Biddles Ltd., Walnut Tree House,
Woodbridge Park, Guildford, Surrey GU1 1DA

Distributed in the United Kingdom and Western Europe by
Turnaround
Distribution Ltd., Unit 3, Olympia Trading Estate, Coburg
Road, Wood Green, London N22 6TZ

Distributed in Australia by Stilone Pty Ltd., PO Box 155,
Broadway, NSW 2007, Australia

Acknowledgements

Thanks to the following for their help in putting together this book: Marc Almond, Boy George, Rose Collis, David Fernbach at GMP, Peter Burton, Ed Heath, Carl Loben, Ben Marshall, Sebastian and Simon, Eileen Schembri, David Toop, Val Wilmer and the staff at the National Sound Archive Library.

CONTENTS:

Foreword

BY BOY GEORGE

I have to confess the first thing I did when I received the manuscript for Kris Kirk's book was go straight to the sections on myself. I grimaced and groaned – oh dear, did I really say that? You see a life under the microscope is a scary thing, because one is forced to grow up in public. Thank god this book is by Kris Kirk – a disarming, sweet, intelligent gay man – and not some Fleet Street hack.

The first time I met Kris was right at the beginning of my career in pop. I'd been out of the closet since I was fifteen, but faced with the prospect of becoming a famous pop star I had reservations about revealing my sexual status. Somehow Kris managed to charm me into an interview against the wishes of my manager, my record company and my fellow band members. I somehow knew it was the right thing to do, and Kris made the idea more desirable by simply not pushing the issue. I trusted him. Lord knows why – he just had a kind face. I'm sure most of the celebrities who encountered him felt the same way.

This book is a piece of queer history – and much more. A lot of it made me laugh, especially some of the ridiculous things I had to say back when I hadn't mastered the art of the interview. *A Boy Called Mary* exudes the kind of charm that made Kris Kirk so very popular.

Introduction

SOME HISTORY

"I often get picked up by queers round here. Some of them have very nice places. They must be on quite good money. I've had as much as thirty shillings from some of them. They're not all effeminate either, some of them are really manly and you'd never dream they were queer. Not from the look of them. But I can always tell cause they've *all* got LPs of Judy Garland. That's the big give away."

Anonymous trade to Joe Orton, April 1967.

"I was dragged screaming out of the closet by Kris Kirk in 1986. God rest his soul. He was lovely, but Kris Kirk came to an interview, and I went out of the room for a while and he rifled through my record collection and saw Yma Sumac and Judy Garland albums and just said 'Tell me, tell me, tell me – you are gay!' So I said 'Alright Kris, I'm a faggot, whatever you want to call me. I'm gay, whatever you want to say.' It was almost like just to shut him up."

Marc Almond, March 1999

"Being predictable is a small price to pay for sharing something, for being able to talk."

Neil Bartlett, *Who Was That Man?*, 1988

I often ask if I can have a look through other people's record collections. I think you can tell so much about people from them. Who do you think you are? Who do you like? What are you like? Do you like girls or boys or both? What kind of queen are you? When you were growing up were you a lonely boy or one of the girls? Was it Madonna, Marc or Morrissey who got you through? What are the first and last Bowie albums you own? Or have you just never got him at all? That glut of 12″ singles – is that from when you first went out dancing or from when you finally found a club that you felt you really belonged to? What about all those fucking awful singles you haven't played for years but just can't bring yourself to sling out cause when you were thirteen you thought the singer was The Most Beautiful Man In The World? Sometimes I throw up my arms in disgust – "Opera?! I ask you?" And other times I'll ask "how does this move you?" Is there some secret passion you think no one else will understand – like Yma Sumac or AC/DC? Do you put on Abba records when you want to go out dancing or when you just want to die? What record is so *you* that it's proudly positioned at the front of your collection for everyone to see like some gorgeous new boyfriend? I like someone more if I discover DAF's *Alles Ist Gut* or both Klaus Nomi's albums or a brace by Tom Waits or The Fall or Kraftwerk or The Go-Betweens or Elvis. And if they've got all of them then I ask if I can move in.

I guess you could say that *A Boy Called Mary* is a sort of rummage through Kris Kirk's record collection – you can tell a lot about him from it. Here is a man who first heard pop way back in the Fifties when he was a little bitty kid – and even at that innocent age in those more innocent times he could hear some very queer things going on in its grooves. Here is a man who grew up in the Sixties and swanned out into a queen who was thrilled by the kitchen sink divas of the first wave of Britpop – Sandy, Marianne, Dusty (This book's title, by the way, was a play by Kris on La Springfield's debut album *A Girl Called Dusty*).

Queens like Kris have always been the queer pioneers, the first to take homosexuality out of the private realm and into public spaces. Queens were never able to – or rather didn't want to – hide their difference. But the paradox of pop's queens was that they were often hysterical about concealing a homosexuality that everything else about them seemed to be hysterically revealing. Look at the stars of Kris' essay on the Fifties, 'Sugar and Spice', Liberace and Johnnie Ray – two of the most spectacularly camp interventions ever made on to pop's stage – who denied everything in court. But pre-Wolfenden, it would take a strong, strong man not to.

'Sugar and Spice', like this whole book, also shows the myriad ways that gay men can twist new meanings out of music – and make almost anything mean something to them – and how necessity dictates that gay men learn the art of reading people's surfaces to find out what's going on underneath (on the street such sexual semiotics are called Gaydar), and how important pop's other voices have been in such an otherwise exclusionary culture.

Kris Kirk was also, just as importantly, a socialist. As a gay man writing in the Eighties, he knew pop couldn't help but be political. And if some of these articles read like they were written about a resistance movement during wartime, well that's because they were. Politics in pop is thought to be a little unfashionable these days (even Chumbawamba felt it necessary to give their biggest single an "ironic" title "Tubthumping"), but Kris believed pop should be a place that's as diverse and perverse as possible, and he always embraced what was progressive in popular culture. There's always been two kinds of cultural critics – aristocrats and democrats. And Kris was a democrat who knew that the most important lesson you learn when you look at the history of pop music is how it shows that its audience – ordinary men and women – can be progressive, intelligent and rational. Socialist historian Howard Zinn has argued that with so much stacked against us "even the slightest display of humanity between [different social groups] might be considered evidence of a basic human drive towards community." Meaning pop music proves there's some hope for the world.

Kris also knew that "pop has always been the most accurate mirror of cultural change". And before he begins, I thought it'd be best to foreground his book with a little background. Part of the point of an introduction is to explain why a book exists. That's pretty easy. People create books for the exact opposite of the reason people climb mountains – because they're *not* there. The specific reason why I put this book together was because Kris had spent a long time trying to write the greatest story never told, the history of gay men and pop – *The Vinyl Closet*. He never finished that book. But me and various other people thought these articles sort of told a little of that story rather well. (And, moreover, they remind us how people felt about events *as they happened* – the passing of time can play hideous tricks on the mind). Can you bear with me while I fill in a few of the gaps?

Since the Fifties the world has changed beyond recognition for the people who make up pop's main constituencies; young people, black people, women, lesbians and gay men. Real progress has been made, and pop has played its part; by giving such people a voice which allowed "them" to become "us". The story of pop is the story of how these people have moved from the margins to the mainstream. Sex and desire have always been the motors of pop, and rock and roll began as an affirmation and assertion of sexualities which had previously had no public stage. And nowhere did it sound more fun than it did in Little Richard's glorious camp squeal "Awopbopaloobop alopbamboom!" Little Richard, the self proclaimed "Bronze Liberace", unleashed the

5

Dionysian and androgyne impulses that have haunted rock and roll ever since, and which signalled the dawning of this new era.

By the time rock and roll crossed the Atlantic to Britain, its potential for profit had been made clear, and thus it was incorporated by impresarios from showbusiness (which had traditionally been a gay enclave) like Larry Parnes and The Beatles' manager Brian Epstein. Making what was once dangerous seem safe – a process George Melly called "revolt into style" – was their attitude to both this new music and to their own stable of lads. This "gay mafia" in British management still endures, but it's a relationship that's not as exploitative nor as one sided as popular myth would have it – as is revealed in Kris' interview with Brian Epstein's lover James Rushton (a name that doesn't even feature in Ray Coleman's 500 page Epstein biography). John Lennon and Brian Epstein, Marc Bolan and Simon Napier-Bell, are the two best known examples of how such relationships often extended from the boardroom to the bedroom. This "gay mafia" presented men as objects of desire in a way that only women had previously been. (It's now become a commonplace to talk of pop as homoerotic – it gets a little confusing when people don't specify if the "homo" has a Latin (male) or a Greek (gay) root). Then as now the little girls loved these unmanly boys, revealing a desire in women for men to behave differently which would help to defrost rigid gender polarities over the following decades. In a culture that otherwise exhalts and venerates all things masculine, pop's queens presented an alternative. (However in *The Sex Revolts* Simon Reynolds and Joy Press documented how rock's rebel male has always "dramatized himself against the 'feminine'" – if so, it prompts the question "can a queen ever hope to be cool?")

From this moment on British pop revelled in camp. First in the sense that it was fuelled by a gay sensibility, second because it so often fell hilariously short of its intention (compare Tommy Steele's cheery, cheesy "Rock with the caveman" with the soaring sexual swagger of Elvis Presley's "Jailhouse rock"). Independent producer Joe Meek was the first of what became a gay archetype in pop – the maverick whose marginalised sexuality caused him to cut his own seam outside of the mainstream. Such was the pressure of living in an often terrible present for the then illegal gay man, arguably more so for those in the public eye, that Joe Meek and Brian Epstein killed themselves. Like so many of our "monstrous martyrdoms", we then had to endure having their tragedies retold to us as parables. Books like this redress the balance.

In the mid-Sixties rock and roll grew up along with its audience and its artists. Yet, and not entirely paradoxically, youth itself now seemed more than ever to be a threat to the established order ("There can be no question that part of the revival of independence and dissidence and breaking of constraints, much of which was extremely healthy, which took place in the 1960s, was very closely tied to the developments in the music world, and that frightened people – elites want to put things back in control and order" – Noam Chomsky). The Rolling Stones in particular zoned in on this new sense of social revolution, which increasingly recognised sexual issues as political issues, and utilised camp, drag and androgyny to trouble and to tease – and proved them to be popular with their audience rather than pariah-like.

As pop songs moved on from their formulas of romance to the realism of rock, artists like The Fugs, The Kinks' Ray Davies and The Velvet Underground's Lou Reed began to deal in more "adult themes" – including homosexuality –

in their work. Documenting the rise of once hidden ideas and people who were now being embraced by the counter culture, they found an audience amongst, not just those thrilled by their sheer sense of "otherness", but with those who finally heard a little of themselves. Though this time, explicitly rather than implictly.

Such concerns with appearing "adult" soon led to pop's mid-life crisis. And soon rock got rather boring and "progressive" and pompous. The Seventies were marked by a reaction against the increasingly bland rock-ocracy of corporate megastars. This backlash was really a Back to Basics campaign – a return to the pure pop thrill of short, simple songs, theatricality and thudding beats – which surfaced in three waves throughout the decade; the American underground proto Punk scene, Britain's Glam Rock and finally British Punk Rock. As Ziggy Stardust-era David Bowie made the most abundantly clear, at the heart of all of this was a realisation that rock was not just about sounds, but about sights, stars, shock, spectacle, sex and *performance*. And, perhaps unsurprisingly, it was also pretty queer.

Things had progressed so much that by 1972 David Bowie could come out as a headline grabbing career move. But the oft-heard complaints from homosexual zealots that Bowie was "only pretending" completely missed the point of Glam – and indeed of pop itself. Bowie had really mattered because he came on like a fierce queen who made homosexuality seem unbelievably thrilling at a time when the only other visible options were Larry Grayson and John Inman. And, thanks to a crash course in Andy Warhol's Pop Art ideas, Bowie brought it to an unbelievably large amount of people. Its importance for gay men as an audience was that it could also provide an escape route from the mundane (which was often misread as mere escapism), and a great many heterosexuals found all this just as invigorating and just as liberating.

David Bowie broke open the gates through which would soon slip such campy titans of the Seventies as Elton John, Freddie Mercury and *The Rocky Horror Show*. As well as the first wave of out gay artists; Steve Grossman, Chris Robison, Lewis Furey, Jobriath, Mickey's Seven and Robert Campbell. Most signed to major labels, reflecting an emerging awareness of gay men as a market, but none sold well. More successful in sales terms was the mid Seventies womens' music movement centred on independent labels like Olivia Records and (often lesbian) sensitive singer songwriters such as Meg Christian and Holly Near.

Shock singer Wayne County became Jayne County over these years and played on homosexuality's association with outrage. Here he reveals the interplay and overlap between all three scenes; proto punk, Glam and Punk proper. Punk usually projected a sense of sexual ennui ("Yawn... just another squelch session," Johnny Rotten) – a reflection that the not so long ago secret world of sex was now becoming commodified – but Punk was also concerned with a questioning of relationships that pop had normally perceived to be "natural". Two key Punk players, Tom Robinson and the Buzzcocks' Pete Shelley were able to find a platform within it to come out. Tom Robinson was the first artist to politicise his homosexuality, championing "gay rights" as just one of a number of equally important left-wing causes. Whilst Pete Shelley fitted in more discreetly with his bisexual poetics about failed love. Their interviews here also show that what is sometimes seen as vacillation (or betrayal by really boring people) can be because an individual's own sexuality was in fact in a state of flux (Pete Shelley) or because it simply changed (Tom Robinson).

9

The Seventies were also – more so really – the decade of Disco. Something that's still thought of by many people – be they friend, foe or faggot – as "gay music". Much discophobia showed a latent homophobia ("Disco sucks"), with rock critics judging dance music by rock's standards and finding it lacking. Which makes as much sense as complaining that a hamburger is not an ice cream. Disco was demonised, just as gay men were, as being vacuous, superficial, hedonistic, "inauthentic", and (as if by magic?) somehow not "real" music. But gay men didn't need to read Roland Barthes to understand what a threat such right wing notions of "authenticity" posed to them.

Disco's female vocalists were often as anonymous and yet as pregnant with meaning as a Greek chorus. But soon stars emerged; Diana Ross, Gloria Gaynor, Donna Summer. The latest twist in a long tradition of identification with, and adulation of, women by gay men. Gay men were key innovators in developing the DJs' trade as an art form, and by the mid Seventies had moved into production; making records that musically appealed to and lyrically resonated with other gay men but which were sung by women. A producer/diva divide that's perhaps best understood as a kind of drag of the voice. As Kris Kirk argues, by far the most intriguing of the Disco divas was Grace Jones – who's also the greatest example of a female avant le mot Gender Bender.

By the late Seventies it seemed that the time was finally right to put up "our own" as male divas – Sex O'Clock USA, Poppers, Paul Parker, Sylvester, Boys Town Gang, and, most infamously, Village People. The Veeps were a reflection of the then contemporary obsession in American gay culture with showing that gay men could be every bit as happy, healthy and most importantly, as *manly* as straight men. They took the Clone style, the very antithesis

10

of queenery, into the mainstream. Their songs remain without parallel as (unquestioning) celebrations of the then gay lifestyle, but when an unprecedented cross over success came the Village People's sexuality became somewhat vague in interviews. A process of hokey-cokey-ism pop has excelled at ever since. And something that Kris Kirk was particularly deft at exposing.

Disco had played itself out by the end of the Seventies, but its sounds and sensibility had by then become pop. In the States Prince and Michael Jackson married Disco to rock whilst simultaneously trading on their own sexual and racial ambiguity ("Am I black or white? Am I straight or gay?" Prince "Controversy"). In the UK movements dubbed New Romantic and New Pop were really a new Glam married to a new Disco. But thanks to Punk they now came with extra added sleaze – a sense of grit and glamour, an aspirational realism, best represented by Soft Cell (Marc Almond is – along with Jon Ginoli, Stephin Merritt, Morrissey, Lou Reed and Neil Tennant – one of the few gay songwriters who's built up a really good, really interesting body of work that tells us something about our lives).

These acts paved the way for the Gender Benders; a media invention that forgot that pop had always bended the genders. There were also now a number of women enjoying something which had previously been pretty much an all male privilege; Eurythmics' Annie Lennox, Yazoo's Alf (Alison Moyet), Ronnie (the last was the least known, and a lesbian – go figure). Its biggest star, Culture Club's Boy George, revelled in a childlike asexuality and his main constituency appeared to be pre-teens. But by the Eighties homosexuality had moved from the margins to the mainstream and men in frocks, just like pop itself, had finally lost any pretence they might once have had of innocence. Now Boy George constantly had to justify his

11

cross-dressing-up and the main question being asked about him soon ceased to be "is it a he or a she?" and became "is he or isn't he gay?" With that sense of paradox that's inherent in pop, Culture Club were helped to success in the States by the rise of MTV and a new emphasis on style and on surface – glossy magazines from *The Face* to *Smash Hits* were the new arbiters of musical taste. George was soon joined by Pete Burns of Dead or Alive and the divine Divine – two of the first hit acts from the stable of Stock, Aitken and Waterman.

Just as had happened with Glam Rock back in the Seventies, the Gender Benders raised the question of poofs in pop, and thus unwittingly unleashed the answer. And then came the deluge. Frankie Goes To Hollywood, ten years after Ziggy Stardust, showed that homosexuality – with the emphasis on the sex – was still a shock tactic that could work as a fantastically successful marketing ploy. After the BBC banned their "Relax" single, Frankie became a cause celebre for British youth (and, lest we forget, "Relax" was also a fantastic record). For the first time since the early Seventies' "Bi chic", homosexuality appeared to be fashionable in the real world too. Kris was noting with pleasure that the world seemed to be becoming more bisexual. (In 1984 little queeny me was going off to school with a noticeably decreasing sense of dread.) When Bronski Beat first appeared the *NME* could even accuse them of "jumping on the gay bandwagon". Marc Almond and Boy George soon felt able to come out unequivocally. The love that dared not speak its name was now – to use the most over used press cliché of the time – shouting it from the rooftops. And under the return to sharp ideology and the end to "consensus" politics ushered in by Thatcherism, these out gay acts seemed to be engaged in political warfare by their mere existence. Jimi Somerville proved that an out gay artist could be both popular and political – though he was consistently vilified by the sort of heterosexuals and homosexuals who thought that gay men should be neither popular nor political.

Just as happened with the other members of the big three of Eighties FagPop, the press often tried to reduce Somerville to no more than a one dimensional man. All were most often written about as if they were just new takes on the classic stereotypes of the gay man; the waspish drag queen (Boy George), the sex mad hedonistic pervert (Holly Johnson) and the militant with a chip on his shoulder (Jimi Somerville). The tormented closet case (from Morrissey back to his idol James Dean) is of course just another figure from this gay hall of shaming.

Although Disco was dead as a mass phenomenon, gay men hadn't stopped dancing yet. Building on an electronic template forged by the erotic languor of Giorgio Moroder, the ecstatic urgency of Patrick Cowley, the sheer exuberance of Dan Hartman, the ironic/camp futurism of Kraftwerk and the sexual brutalism of DAF, Hi NRG became the dominant sound of the UK top forty; Frankie Goes To Hollywood, Bronski Beat, Bros, New Order, Pet Shop Boys and Stock, Aitken and Waterman. SAW took Hi NRG out of the gay clubs and into the school disco. But the abundance of half naked dancing boys in the videos for the latter's female acts (Bananarama, Kylie Minogue, Sinitta) suggested that gay men were still seen as this music's target audience by the record business.

But this was the problem. The music industry has always seen homosexuality as something that will either damage sales or work as a marketing ploy. This friction, as Kris documents, caused Bronski Beat to implode after little more than a year of making records. In the wake of the hegemony of FagPop in 1984 – take a look at the singles

13

charts from June of that year if you need reminding – record companies rushed to sign their own little gay – or at least faggy – act; Blue Mercedes, Red Lipstique, White and Torch, Raymonde, Eddy Huntingdon. None of them were successful either musically or financially. The record companies had made the same mistake in the Seventies – and it's a process they repeat whenever a new type of band first breaks through big time. The problem with these acts wasn't their sexuality but their music. They never got anywhere because (bar Raymonde) they weren't any good.

In 'The Vinyl Closet' Kris, writing at the end of 1984, wondered what would happen next and what lessons would be learnt. But the golden age of FagPop proved all too brief, and by 1986 it was coming to an end. As ever, what was going on in the world of pop was dependent on what was going on in the real world; the Right had manipulated the Aids crisis into a moral panic and a desired anti-gay backlash ensued. This was the first time since the Fifties when gay men no longer felt that things would go on getting better and better (Any gay man still intoxicated by things-can-only-get-better-ism would do well to think about how things changed between '78 and '88, as much as how things changed between '88 and '98 – the position of any minority group under capitalism is basically unstable).

In that way that politics and celebrity seem so entwined these days, the usual marker of the beginning of the Aids crisis is normally given as the death of Rock Hudson in October 1985. 1986 was the year of the government's "icebergs and tombstones" Aids TV ads, of Norman Tebbit's "permissive society" speeches, of James Anderton, the Chief Constable of Manchester police, saying that gay men were "swirling around in a cesspit of their own creation", and of the first stirrings of Section 28's eleventh

14

commandment; "Thou shalt not promote homosexuality". In the Eighties pop had become a staple of the tabloids, but by the second half of the decade they no longer wrote about stars like Boy George, Freddie Mercury and Elton John as fascinating and fabulous freaks but as demonised and disgusting deviants (see *The Poofs of Pop*, *The Sun* April 29 1988). Hysteria about stars who were thought to be gay was soon joined by an even more grotesque dirt digging into certain performers' HIV status. Together with the rise of self appointed censors, the Parent's Music Resource Centre, in the States, pop was now being policed as never before. The mood of the times can also be seen in the casual homophobia of many rap and metal acts (Kris' interview with Stryper didn't seem quite so funny at the time), and even that espoused by some pop pin-ups that gay men had helped to keep in gold discs; Jason Donovan, East 17 and Marky Mark. Such was the grim backdrop to the second half of these essays.

Boy George's and Marc Almond's commercial careers may have diminished as they became more sexually upfront, but they didn't completely disappear. Few of the old gay guard did. The Communards had the biggest selling record of 1986 with "Don't leave me this way", Boy George hit number one in 1987 with "Everything I own", Pet Shop Boys were *the* pop act of 1987, just as Erasure were in 1988 and Holly Johnson had a highly successful debut year as a solo artist in 1989.

Madonna further queered pop's pitch over the same period. At a time when gay men were under attack as never before Madonna didn't just defend gay culture but eulogised, for some even came to personify, the then emergent queer culture. Madonna was arguably the most sexually radical mainstream artist of all time, and just as importantly she actually became *more* radical as her career

15

progressed. Proving that if a star is big enough they can pretty much dictate their own terms to their record company. It's just a shame that so few other artists do. (Incidentally I think Kris deserves some sort of award for managing to get through the Eighties *without* writing about Madonna.)

The big question was where were the new gay acts in this period? The late Eighties were a key time for the music business. A time of rationalisation that led to its domination by four supranational corporations. Belts were tightened and the money men took over. In short, record companies were no longer prepared to take risks. And fags were now seen as a (high) risk. (The most FAQ I get from students is "Does the music business exploit gay men?" The FGA; "If the music business didn't exploit people it wouldn't be a business". But pop has never simply been about *either* exploitation or liberation. It's about *both* – that's what makes it so fascinating.)

As the Eighties closed you had to look elsewhere for new blood – to the likes of Diamanda Galas and Momus, two straight-queer artists on the margins (and both on independent labels). Or to the, then, defiantly underground US movements then emerging, House and Homocore. One important question posed by Kris in 'The Vinyl Closet' was answered with the appearance of the first mainstream out lesbian acts. That this had taken so long perhaps only proves the advantages that patriarchy affords gay men over lesbians. (Lesbians had previously been rendered invisible, inaudible, but there had been much gossip on Doris and Dusty, Janis and Janis, Joan and Joan – they were women participating in a man's man's world, especially those making rock music, so we shouldn't be surprised). In the mid Eighties there were folksy indie acts Two Nice Girls and Phranc, and later kd lang and Melissa

16

Etheridge offered a resounding disavowal to the idea that open homosexuality is a bar to success in the States. Though America still has to embrace out gay male stars in the way that Britain has – witness the different responses to George Michael's arrest for cottaging last year. Here he's a hero, there less than zero.

Madonna had been the Ziggy Stardust of Dykepop; tuned to changes going on in the real world, she helped open Pandora's closet. Dyke-esque singers like Michelle Shocked and Tracey Chapman helped further test the water. lang and Etheridge were also seen as part of the vogue for "lipstick lesbians" and "designer dykes" – a cultural approval only granted to "acceptable", feminine lesbians. The later appearance of the crass Fem 2 Fem played on both this and the long tradition of "lesbian" pornography (and it was pornography) as wank material for straight men. Like the song says "it's different for girls". (Anyone wondering if gay porn could be used to appeal to straight women should watch a – Greek or Latin? – Take That video).

Major late-Eighties male stars, like George Michael, REM's Michael Stipe, Morrissey and Pet Shop Boys traded in a new discretion. But, same as it ever was, the doors of their closets were never slammed shut, they were just open at different degrees (and thus few fans are surprised when such stars come out fully). Although the then fashion among pop "theorists" for the apolitical bullshit of post modernism often misread such evasion as an endorsement of the fluidity of sexuality. Conversely, a new wave of gay activism spawned by the Right's moral clampdown, was now arguing for outing those gay stars enjoying the "luxury" of the closet. This argument between making a simple statement of unashamed fact and admitting the existence of a "sea of possibilities" would come to

17

dominate most writing about homosexuality and pop. Including Kris Kirk's. We've moved on quite a bit since then – I read an article about John Waters in *NME* last month, which described him as "openly gay". Those words seem so quaint these days I just couldn't stop giggling.

Tragically Kris Kirk died just as things started getting interesting again. 1990, the year that Kris effectively stopped writing, now looks like the Year Zero of FagPop. In the Nineties we picked ourselves up, dusted ourselves down and started all over again. I take a look at what happened in the last ten years in my own book *Seduced and Abandoned* (as Kris would say "plug, plug"). But all I've ever really done is try to carry on what Kris Kirk started; somewhat spookily, just like Kris, I ended up as the music critic for *Gay Times*, the gayboy at *Melody Maker*, and spent far too long trying to finish a book on the history of homosexuality and popular music. Putting this book together was my way of saying thank you to Kris.

Before you hear Kris Kirk's side of the story (that's one of the great things about pop – it's got so many different sides), I want to share with you two lines that kept popping into my head when I was working on *A Boy Called Mary*. Both neatly sum up why queens like me and Kris and countless others love so much this thing called pop. The first comes from Edward Carpenter who, writing a hundred years ago, was struck by how many male homosexuals were "musical". Trying to figure out some reason why, he unwittingly gave a great description of what we might now call a queeny sensibility; for both music and gay men, Carpenter noted, "share... a certain inclination to indulge in emotion."

The second is the famous last words from *The Rise and Fall of Ziggy Stardust and the Spiders from Mars*, which by managing to speak simultaneously to our sense of feeling

18

different and to our longing for a sense of belonging makes explicit something that's implicit in all the best pop; "OH NO LOVE, YOU'RE NOT ALONE!"

The point of pop music is that it makes people feel a part of something bigger. That's what it does, that's how it works, and that's why it matters.

And Kris Kirk – a boy called Mary – could communicate that better than most.

Now read on...

Peace, love, empathy

Richard Smith
Brighton, March 1999

What a Difference a Gay Makes

CONFESSIONS OF A GAY RECORD COLLECTOR

The late Fifties. Sunday Lunch. Roast beef and boredom and Two-Way family favourites blaring away on the wireless in the corner. I was nine, too young even to know what homosexuality was. But precocious – or devious – enough to get a sudden, inexplicable buzz out of hearing the Everly Brothers crooning a love song to each other. "Whenever I want you, all I have to do is dream". If there'd been a *Top of the Pops* in those days I'd have fully expected Don and Phil to perform the song sitting on high stools, holding hands and gazing into each other's eyes. Boys in love! I was astonished that my family, arguing over the Yorkshire pudding, was totally ignorant of this wonderfully wicked intrusion, this onslaught on everything that I knew we were meant to hold dear. Looking back, it was my first real experience of the subversive. The taste lingers still. Thank you Jean Metcalfe.

I soon learnt about the conventions of duetting, and was bitterly disappointed, of course. But the Evs had sown a seed which, by the time I was gay at fourteen, was becoming a full-blown obsession. Collecting gay pop records became a grand passion for a decade and a half. Quality was never a criterion, nor was the sexuality of the performer. My only rule of thumb was that a song lyric should have at least one reference to a gay situation or character – however peripheral, ambiguous or politically unsound. The result of this very early ghetto mentality of mine is that I'm sitting on two or three classics and some of the tackiest records ever made.

There's never been a shortage of faggots in rock 'n roll from Little Richard on, but it's only recently – after the spadework of Bowie, Tom Robinson, Elton John – that it's become commonplace for people like Boy George and Sylvester readily to admit that they like going to bed with other men. Even now, we still await a major female recording artist's coming out.

In his dreadful but immensely readable paperback *You Don't Have To Say You Love Me*, Simon Napier-Bell has recently blown the gaff about the pop music casting couches of the Sixties. "It was surprising that an industry generating so many millions of pounds was prepared to use little more than the manager's sexual tastes as its yardstick of talent. Most of the managers were men and most of them liked boys". But at the time only the cognoscenti were aware and recorded product was relentlessly heterosexual. Eden Kane singing that "boys cry" (when no one can see them) was about the limit anyone reached in questioning the rigidity of sex roles!

From the mid Sixties on, with the first whiff of civil rights in the air and the semi-legalisation in this country of gay male sex acts, homosexuality began to lose its air of being a dark little secret that nobody talked about. But in music, any references were so discreetly understated that they inevitably shaded into the completely ambiguous. Jody Miller's "Home of the brave" (1965) only has gay relevance by default. But, judging by the number of gay people I know who possess this rather obscure single, it touched a nerve somewhere.

On the surface it's a common-or-garden protest song castigating the hypocrisy and intolerance of Middle America. A WASP boy is sent home by the school board, who will not tolerate his long hair and his "funny clothes". Miller's *angst*-ridden delivery drops the hint that there's more here than meets the eye. The other kids, she whines, are cruel:

21

More than once he's gone home with a bloody nose...
He's not like them and they can't ignore it,
So they all hate him for it.

The ironic refrain "Home of the brave, land of the free/ Why don't you let him be what he wants to be?" seemed to sum up the beginnings of a change in consciousness towards gays. Pariah becomes victim. I guess it was preferable to being ignored.

Otherwise there were very slim pickings indeed in this secret orchard of mine. The only other record to cause a flutter of excitement in those days was "I'll Try For The Sun", a track from Donovan's *Fairy Tale* LP. A soupy little paean of love to a gypsy boy, it includes the classic lines:

And whose going to be the one
Who says it was no good, what we done?
I dare a man to say I'm too young...

No doubt Donovan was only continuing the folk tradition of singing a song written for a woman without altering the gender of the lyrics. But even today it sounds very gay and satisfyingly perverse to these ears.

By 1967, Scott Walker was beginning to have hits with songs by Jaques Brel. Brel is the Genet of popular music, his universe populated by sailors, pimps, whores and "queers" – all rotting teeth and gonorrhoea, creatures rather than people. "Jackie" is the reverie of an ageing heterosexual pimp and Walker's version, with its references to "authentic queers and phoney virgins" has the distinction of being the first UK top thirty record actually to (gasp!) mention homosexuals.

Walker later covered many of Brel's GR (gay relevance) songs, which perhaps encouraged the *New Musical Express's* Alley Cat to start a bitching campaign about the singer's friendship with Jonathan King. Asking ingenuous questions every week like "Does Jonathan eat Scott's porage every day?" and "Does Scott Walker smoke King-sized cigarettes?", the Cat's smirking was a measure of the embarrassment that straight people still felt about the subject at that time. And perhaps the bitching had some effect: you'll find, tucked away on the b-side of a 1971 Jonathan King single a song called "I don't want to be gay".

Attitudes to personal relationships began to change noticeably with the advent of dope and acid. The hippies' delight, Jefferson Airplane, recorded a Dave Crosby song called "Triad" in 1968. It's a reworking of the old "which boy to choose" conundrum, only this time singer Grace Slick *refuses* to choose between:

Me and him, or you and me.
I don't really see
Why we can't go on as three?

The message is "break all the rules", and not only with regard to monogamy. Same-sex love is a natural concomitant too:

Sister-lovers, water-brothers,
And in time – maybe others.

The same year, the musical *Hair* was breaking every convention imaginable and the number most guaranteed to have a respectable audience squirming in their seats was "Sodomy" in which Woof – a gay character – extols the wonders of sodomy, fellatio, cunnilingus and pederasty. Things were changing.

Curiously, British bands seemed far more interested in ambiguity, androgyny and transvestism. By 1966 The Who had already released "I'm a boy", the gender-identity crisis song par excellence. The Pink Floyd's "Arnold Layne" was about a cross-dresser who stole frocks from washing lines. And The Herd's "Something strange" was about, well, something strange... A couple of years later came The Kinks' "Lola".

23

Throughout the late Sixties and Seventies, The Kinks consistently presented their public with unstereotypical and often sympathetic portraits of gays and TVs. Ray Davies' forte is teasing ambiguity – "girls will be boys and boys will be girls" – and the whole point of "Lola" is that the audience never really learns whether the naïve hero succumbs to the charms of the delectable and admirably well adjusted TV.

"David Watts" – recorded in 1967, but never a Kinks' single – is on the surface merely a portrait of hero worship. But the feelings of the self-deprecating "dull and simple lad" are more than platonic for the "gay and fancy free" David who, we learn, isn't interested in his female admirers. Hope springs eternal in the narrator's breast: the final clue is a wilfully and skilfully ambiguous *double entendre*, with our dullard sighing "I wish that his body belonged to me". Few of us have been lucky enough to escape the miseries of calf love and the plight of this spotty creature causes an awful shock of self recognition. And you'll find plenty more gay references by plundering The Kinks' Kanon, particularly on the *Sleepwalker* and *Misfits* albums.

In the States, The Velvet Underground – formed by Andy Warhol – was making music which told what it was like to be a hustler, a transvestite, a masochist and a junkie. The material was too explosive to be heard on UK radio but word was out that the barriers were coming down. Here, the dam broke with Bowie.

His first overtly gay record was "Width of a circle" from *The Man Who Sold The World*, which tells of an encounter in the underworld with a god whose "tongue (is) swollen with devil's love". It's a disturbing picture of a Nietzschean superman subjugating and probably raping the narrator. And it marked the end of the period when you needed to

24

closely read lyrics to find gay references in pop. "Queen bitch", "Jean Genie", "John, I'm only dancing", "Rebel rebel", "Boys keep swinging" helped bring in their train gay songs from some of Bowie's peers like Elton John ("Daniel" is palpably gay; "All the girls love Alice" is palpably anti-lesbian; the *risqué* "Big dipper" is literally *stuffed* with innuendo), Lou Reed (see "Walk on the wild side" and "Make up" from *Transformer*, "The kids" from *Berlin*, etc), and Rod Stewart whose migraine-inducing "The killing of Georgie" reached number two. Lesser luminaries like glam-rockers Jobriath and Starbuck, plus Peter Straker, Tim Curry and Steve Swindells managed *not* to make a career from singing about things explicitly gay.

It seems that as far as hit records go, the party's over now for Tom Robinson, but he's said again recently that the one record he still feels proud about is "Glad to be gay". I wish I could agree. Though I'll readily admit that the record was a trailblazer, hearing it always depresses me into the ground. And not only because of the often ignored ironic lyrics. I can't bear it because it always sounds to me like a big, butch football chant for gays.

To my mind he's made much better records since his fall from grace, like the upbeat giggly and very gay "Never gonna fall in love again" (co-written with Elton John. But when John recorded it he altered the lyrics to make it heterosexual) and his excellent, very gay recent LP, *North By Northwest* – a musically interesting, lyrically revealing collection of songs about loneliness, alienation, and coping with failure.

In mainstream music, lesbian and bisexual female performers have, in general, chosen to be non-gender specific in their love songs. Strangely, there are any number of examples of women who sing about male gays; look at Joan Baez's "The altar boy and the thief", Joan

Armatrading's "Rosie", Nina Hagen's "If I were a boy", Noosha Fox's "Georgina Bailey", Dory Previn's "Michael, Michael", Dusty Springfield's "Closet man", Lynsey de Appalling's "Getting a drag", Suzi Quatro's "Mama's boy" and – particularly – Kate Bush's "Wow" and "Kashkir from Baghdad".

But apart from Gina X's "No GDM" (dedicated to Quentin Crisp, and in which Gina describes herself as a lesbian) the only commercial/mainstream recordings by women that I've come across which manifestly concern themselves with the subject of relations between women are three exquisite love songs, all tucked away as album tracks: "Lady Madelaine" by Marianne Faithfull; "Emmie" by Laura Nyro and "Maria" by Janis Ian.

If you want to stretch things, add a couple of Joan Armatrading's observations in the songs "Back to the night" and "Me, myself, I". And check out "Tell tale" from her new album *The Key* – it's about bisexuality. Independent women's labels are another matter, of course, and I wouldn't presume to pretend that I'm an authority on, for instance, Olivia or Redwood Records.

If you're beginning to get the impression that most gay-orientated music over the years has been of a fairly high standard, let me disillusion you. Much of it has been unspeakably awful. For those of you with a passion for kitsch, there's one absolute monstrosity that I'd urge you to seek out. Written and performed by the dreaded Rod McKuen, "Black eagle" (on DJM) wins my personal Golden Turkey Award hands down.

As the singer sleeps, a black eagle "chained in leather" takes him against his will. He awakes to find a black feather on his pillow and entreats God to rid him of "this vile thing". But the eagle returns, takes him to the woods and "devours (him) as a lover would". McKuen, a born

26

again Christian, obviously has great guilts about certain sexual desires, and he yelps and howls his self hate and anguish as only a tone deaf bad poet could. A five star classic. Buy at your peril.

With *Record Mirror* now running a Gay Disco Chart, I can hardly deny that the tackier end of disco is a genre often associated with gay men. And if at the moment there's any one outfit particularly associated with gay disco, it's Boys Town Gang. Just as the Village People denied their origins after they'd hit it big with "YMCA", no doubt the Boys Towners would now choose to forget their 12" version of "Cruisin' the streets". It comes in a very close second in my personal god-awfulness stakes. The grunts and groans of two studs "making out" on the street to the delighted squeals of a voyeuristic (female) hooker are interrupted by the arrival of two cops who teach "the faggots" a lesson by screwing them against the nearest wall. Next to this, Hilda Ogden's living room looks tasteful.

As to the third stinker to make up this triumvirate of trash, I'll admit I'm spoilt for choice. So let me steer those of you who are interested towards a few random humdingers. If you're mawkishly inclined, try Charles Aznavour's "What makes a man?" or "All the sad young men" by Shirley Bassey – music to commit suicide to. You want a half baked plea for tolerance dressed in mid-Seventies disco bounce? Look out for Valentino's "I was born this way" (on the Gaiee label, licensed by Motown). How about a comedy record that isn't at all funny? "Are you being served?" by John Inman is just for you. Or a record about bitchery that falls flat on its unsophisticated face? Look out for Steve Elgin's "Don't leave your lover lying around, (dear)". And worth its weight in gold as a record made *by* gays *for* gays is "Stand together" on Deviant Records. The group (or collective) isn't named on the label – a wise move. Despite its good intentions as a rallying call to gays it sounds like a parody of "Tomorrow belongs to me", the Hitler Youth song from *Cabaret*.

1983 has already seen a slow trickle of gay records from "Oscar Wilde" by Red Lipstique to "Well fancy that' by the Fun Boy Three. The latter, found on their new album, *Waiting* is the traumatic tale of a young boy seduced by his teacher on a school trip to France. And also worth checking out is Joe Jackson's "Real men" on the *Night and Day* album. But as the number of gay and gay-orientated releases increases, I find I'm less and less interested. That's partly because the thrill of the hunt has gone and those records no longer seem subversive. It's also because I'm becoming increasingly suspicious of that part of myself that stands for ghetto mentality, the ambi/multisexuality of bands like Culture Club, Soft Cell and Bow Wow Wow feels like a much healthier development than the cul-de-sac of separatist music. Besides, I'm convinced I've found the consummate GR pop single. It's the (Radio One-banned) 12" version of "Homosapien" by Pete Shelley and it says everything – musically and lyrically – that I've ever hoped to hear in a gay record. Barring a miracle, things will never be the same again.

An article of this length could not hope to be comprehensive. Artists not covered here who have recorded gay or gay-related material include Lewis Furey (Canadian. Brilliant. Albums available on import only); Sylvester (out gay, but his stunning version of the classic "Lover man" unfortunately leaves out that important word "man"); the under-rated Robert Campbell whose angst ridden 1977 album *Living in the Shadow of a Downtown Movie Show* contains a track called "(Making love to my) Dream boy", and another called "Lions and shadows";

Chris Robison, who issued two gay albums in the States in the early Seventies; Kokomo ("Angel"), Peter Allen; Culture Club; Randy Newman; Paul Simon ("Me and Julio..."); William Burroughs etc.

Singles to look out for; "Johnny are you queer?" by Josie Cotton (*Very* Tony Basil); Ian Matthews' constantly re-issued "Da doo ron ron" – in this version Bill's gender remains intact; "Over the wall we go' by Oscar (AKA Paul Nicholas, song written by David Bowie); and a lesbian version of "Je t'aime" by Butterfly (available on import only). And then of course there's the Rolling Stones' "Cocksucker blues"...but that's a different story.

Collusion, June 1983

Sugar and Spice

POP IN THE FIFTIES

Sugar and spice and all things nice – that's what early Fifties pop was made of. Post-Hiroshima and post-Auschwitz, it's little wonder that in music – as in film – Eisenhower-era audiences looked for escapism, safety, comfort, *niceness*. And make no mistake, UK culture was already well colonised by the US, not least in pop. Sure, we had the likes of Dickie Valentine, Lita Rose and Dennis Lotis as homegrown "stars"; but they mostly recorded note-for-note cover versions of records by US artists like Patti Page, Vic Damone and Kay Starr. And what we mostly heard on the then-Light programme... yep, you guessed it... Patti Page, Vic Damone and Kay Starr. All nice and normal and mainstream. Sex, never mind homosex, was still totally taboo – at the beginning of the decade anyway.

But gay people always have had clever little ways of finding aspects of culture they can relate to, no matter how straight and narrow that culture is. And – though I despised them at the time – in some ways I now find the Fifties an infinitely more fascinating period than the far more libertarian decade they preceded. Because although the gay counter culture and the aesthetic that gays invented – the irony of the camp point of view – were very well hidden, if you look hard enough you can find plenty of examples of the gay/pop/Fifties continuum peeping through. Take Doris Day...

Not that there was ever a breath of sapphic scandal about Doris Mary Anne von Kappelhof from Cincinnati, the nice clean living all-American girl-next-door who swears she "never did like apple pie" and who embodied the decade by always being, as Alexander Walker describes her, "confident, upbeat and absolutely sure of her destiny." And in a sense Doris was some kind of example of the new woman; "To many women in an era when the man was still the boss as well as the breadwinner," says Walker, "Doris looked an ally, a girl who not only wouldn't take their man away from them but was well-equipped to make a man keep his distance till she was ready for him." And therein lies the rub.

For as well as appealing to musical queens, Doris Day was *the* big heartthrob of Fifties dykes. Partly, one presumes, because of that husky voice and the boyish crop she wore so often, and no doubt the tomboy energy she conveyed so well as the pistol-packing, thigh-slapping, two-fisted Calamity Jane. But it wasn't just sex; it was image too. All great icons have a dual personality, and the other side of Doris's homely-as-apple-pie, good sport/perfect wife image was the girl who always says no till the right man comes along, the foremost practitioner of prolonged avoidance of sex. "I knew Doris Day before she was a virgin" was Oscar Levant's best known joke, but it seemed funnier in the Sixties than it does now. Doris Day was a New Woman before even the Old Woman was invented. A potent brew for all those dykes who looked beyond the freckles and saw Sex on Legs.

There could be no greater contrast to the sunniness of DD than the half crazed, part Blackfoot Indian religious alcoholic with a deaf aid called Johnnie Ray. With millions of screaming girls – and not a few boys – forever at his feet, Oregon born Ray was a fully fledged teen idol; the missing link between the urbane macho *shtick* of Sinatra and the sex peddling of Presley. What Ray sold was passion. They dubbed him The Nabob of Sob and The Prince of Wails because his face was always contorted with pain when he wailed his tortured ballads like the eleven-weeks-a-US-number-one "Cry"; on a good night he'd burst into tears on stage, drop to his knees and bang his head on the piano leg in time to the beat. It was something no male performer had done before, it freaked out the oldies – and it sold in bucketfuls.

But behind the tortured young man on stage was a real tortured young man. Ray was gay, and it got him into trouble. Maybe his career would have nosedived anyway with the advent of Presley and co, but being busted for propositioning a plain clothes cop in Detroit in 1959 did his career no good at all. Even though he was found innocent by an all woman jury, Ray got so few bookings in America afterwards that he was forced to move to Europe, where his bust was less publicised; when he died this year, Ray still held the record for the most engagements at the London Palladium by an American artist. But Johnnie died as he lived; a deeply troubled and unhappy man, his footsteps always dogged by a whiff of scandal. In the Fifties gay men really had to watch their backs – which may help explain the hypocrisy of Liberace when it came to *his* law case.

In 1956, the highest paid entertainer in the world was an unctuous piano player from Wisconsin. An arch, self promoting showman with a greased pompadour and an even oilier grin, Wladziu Valentino Liberace specialised in playing truncated *Reader's Digest* versions of Chopin and Liszt and then mistreating them further by playing them alongside the "Beer barrel polka" and his notorious "Ave Maria'. Liberace played onstage under a huge stained glass window of the Virgin Mary with, as a final touch, a kneeling actress wearing a mantilla pretending to pray beneath it.

Liberace's clothes – gold lamé jumpsuits and white mink studded with diamonds spelling his name – were every bit as tacky as his muzak, but they went down a treat with a vast number of late middle aged women. In an age when the word "camp" referred solely to a collection of tents, the rest of the population quite frankly didn't know what had hit them.

It was a macho world in the Fifties, and there were many who were enraged to see an unabashed sissy making millions out of his sissyness. In England, one particularly exasperated man was William Neil Connor, a journalist who wrote pseudonymously under the female soubriquet of Cassandra. In September 1956, just as Liberace was arriving in London to the biggest and most excitable crowds since Chaplin came home in the Twenties, Cassandra emptied his stomach to *The Daily Mirror*'s thirteen million readers. Liberace was "the summit of sex – Masculine, Feminine and Neuter – Everything that He, She or It can ever want", he wrote. "A deadly, winking, sniggering, snuggling, fruit-flavoured, mincing ice-cream-covered heap of mother-love' who played "lilac-coloured hokum".

Liberace sued for libel, accusing Cassandra of inferring he was gay when he said he wasn't. Three years later, when the case finally reached the courts, the thirty nine year old bachelor boy won £8,000 plus costs from the *Mirror*; at the time it was Britain's biggest-ever High Court libel settlement. Now that Liberace is dead (from Aids) we can safely repeat the fact that he was gay as the proverbial coot. Whether one despises him for his gross hypocrisy in denying his homosexuality or excuses it for being about par for the times, there is at least one argument to be made in his defence. In an age of gay baiting, he was one of the first ever performers to expose homophobia. From then on, Cassandra and his cronies couldn't assume they could calumnate gays in the press and get away with it.

Not that everybody hid their light under a bushel; even when the general public hadn't heard the rumours, the gay grapevine – as ever – did its sterling work. Over here, everyone knew someone who'd had Michael "Story of my life" Holliday behind some Butlin's chalet; while over in the US, actor/singer heartthrobs Tab Hunter and Sal Mineo were outrageous enough in their private lives for even British audiences to have heard plenty of homosexy rumours. And a couple of chart topping deep voiced women singers who appeared on prime-time US telly had reputations as notorious as the men.

The conventional pop wisdom is still that for the male pop idol, dependent on his hordes of female fans coming out means the kiss of death to his career. There's no better refutation of this argument than the career of Johnny Mathis, a man voted *Billboard*'s most promising Male Singer as far back as 1957 and who even today is, next to Frank Sinatra, the most consistently charted album artist in American popular music. Looking back now through three decade old press clippings, it's possible to read between the lines. In reviews of his earliest top ten hits (like "Wonderful, wonderful" and his goosebump inducing mega-smash "Misty") there are stirrings of a deep puzzlement among his male critics. "Treacly, unctuous... heartily unmasculine" were some of the codewords sent out to readers by the middle aged men who, weaned on Sinatra and co, found the dulcet tones and sensitive interpretations of this almost androgynous ballad singer too much to take.

As it happens, many years later – in 1982, Johnny Mathis came out, and it caused nary a blink. Telling *US* Magazine of how he first fell in love at sixteen with a baritone sax player who "supported me when everyone else was saying I was too young", Mathis spoke candidly about his two male lovers in LA and Louisiana and told readers "What's the big deal about my homosexuality? Anything as controversial as homosexuality is boring." It's an attitude that has stood him in good stead, because his audiences obviously couldn't give a toss about what he does in bed. If record sales are anything to go by – his *Greatest Hits* album just finished spending ten years on the charts – Mr M is as popular as he's ever been, despite – or perhaps because of – his "heartily unmasculine" persona. Rather than being a truly early Fifties attitude, Mathis had about him some of the gay chutzpah that was to come with Little Richard, Esquerita and all the other great queens of rock 'n' roll.

Gay Times, May 1990

The Nekkid Truth

LITTLE RICHARD

Relaxing in his suite in London's Hilton Hotel, rock and roll's greatest hollerer Little Richard was looking suitably pleased with himself on the day of publication of his no-holds-barred, *très gai* bio *The Life And Times Of Little Richard, The Quasar Of Rock* by Charles White. "It's the nekkid truth about the man who invented rock and roll," the Born Again Bible Basher had screeched the night before in the Hippodrome Club, and indeed there's enough sex here to sink a ship.

Little Richard used to get his sexual kicks from paying men to gang-bang groupies while he watched. It's a fine irony that rock and roll's greatest performer should so appreciate the performance of others. No wonder this eye-popping biography – dismissed by the increasingly puritanical NME as "smut from cover to cover" – is all set to be a massive seller.

Author Charles White (aka Dr Rock, a Scarborough based chiropodist no less) is a world authority on rock and roll but has sensibly failed to deliver the serious critical evaluation that music buffs may have been expecting. The only concession is an exhaustive discography tucked away at the back of the book. Instead, what the Doc provides in great detail is a lurid, full colour, anal-warts-and-all portrait of pop's freakiest faggot turned Bible basher, much of it in the words of the Pompadour himself. And boy, does he dish the dirt! His career has been a lifelong symbiotic struggle between homosexuality and religion that began with singing gospel in the local choir at the same time as being frenched by Madame Oop, a local transvestite, and hanging round the local Greyhound depot for trade.

It continued through to middle age, when he took his bible with him to orgies.

Twenty two is a little old for a megolomaniac to set the world alight. By the time of his first hits, Richard had benefitted from the help of some formidable people: Sister Rosetta Tharpe (who paid him his first pro fee); the legendary Esquerita (who presaged his pompadour and taught him to play); Sugarfoot Sam from Alabam's Minstrel Show (where Richard performed in drag); and – the big break – producer/manager Robert 'Bumps' Blackwell of Speciality Records whose idea it was in 1955 to take the risque "Tutti frutti" from Richard's stage act and clean up the lyrics for the radio.

But nobody ever managed to clean up his fiery stage act or his outrageous image and as Richard began to rack up hit after hit (13 whoppers in four years) so his piano pounding and his mirrored suits, diamond studded capes and *that hairstyle* got wilder and wilder. And so did his audience: rioting was commonplace, particularly when Richard threw his clothes to the crowd.

It's claimed here that Richard was the first performer to begin desegregating Southern audiences, so it's another irony that for most of his career 95% of Richard's fans, on his own estimation, were white: "I didn't record for blacks. Blacks didn't want my sound, you know." But others did, especially fellow performers, from Pat Boone (whose milk sop cover of "Tutti frutti" deprived Richard of a US Number One) and Elvis, through the adulatory Beatles and on to today's Little Richard figure, Prince, another frail black kid convulsed by sex and God, who at least admits the debt.

Today Richard is an evangelical minister. From first to last his story is of a man of capriciousness and extremes, a heap of contradictions. His 1957 religious conversion (due

37

to the sighting of Sputnik) and the decline of his career were simultaneous, but he later happily resumed his love affair with the rock business after being expelled from Bible School for playing around with another male student.

Via more orgies and a thousand-dollar-a-day coke habit ("My nose got big enough to back a diesel truck into") he's now back to Primitive Godliness and, mercurial as ever, putting down homosexuality and pop music as strongly as he once advocated them. It's somewhat dispiriting when, by the end of the book, we hear Little Richard echoing exactly the North Alabama White Citizen's Council (who attacked him in the Fifties for undermining the morals of the nation's youth).

Little Dickie's now a gospel singing evangelical minister who refuses to perform 'Tutti frutti' or any of his standards nowadays, and his book is plenty critical of both rock and roll and homosex, which he describes as 'demonic'. But when he talked to me he laid into the Moral Majority and particularly Donna Summer ("Who told her that God sent Aids as a visitation on homosexuals? She ain't no prophet"), confessed that he always enjoyed being gay ("I've been gay all my life and I really enjoyed it, though I don't do it no more since God filled me with his power. But I loved sex, I *loved* big penises. If there was anything I loved better than a big penis it was a *bigger* penis.") and defended gay people as 'the sweetest, kindest, most artistic, warmest and most thoughtful people in the world. And since the beginning of time all they've ever been is *kicked*. But regardless of what style of life we've chosen we all have the right to the tree of life, the homosexual as much as the hetero."

Richard, now fifty three, was the world's first outrageous pop squealer and it's no surprise to discover he was also the first of the business's Men In Frocks, singing in a red dress as Princess Lavonne in a minstrel show. More surprising are his revelations about his equally egocentric fellow-stars like Jerry-Lee Lewis (who was once so piqued at being given second billing to Chuck Berry that he set his piano on fire at the end of the set) and John and Yoko (who insisted on top billing over Richard at a Rock festival and were such an anticlimax, they were booed off stage).

But it's the steamy stuff that is the most eye-crossing; life on the road was, according to Richard, one big orgy and his own favourite pleasure was hand shandies: "I was pumping so much peter in those days, sometimes eight or nine times a day. I was creaming, steaming and *beaming*," he told me with another beam, presumably at the memory of it. "One time I remember we were playing the Paramount Theatre and Buddy Holly came into our room while Angel was sucking my tittie as I was jacking off. And Buddy put his thing into her and was having sex with her when the loudspeaker announced he was due on stage..."

You want to know more about the pink and yellow cadillacs, the thousand dollar a day drug habit, the mirrored suits, how the infant Richard used to box up his turds and present them as birthday presents, how 'Lucille' was a female impersonator, how Little Richard helped desegregate theatres in the Deep South... and more? Read this trash-with-class bio and learn what it means to be a Living Legend.

Gay Times, May 1985

You've Got to Hide Your Love Away

BRIAN EPSTEIN

James Rushton was a bright eyed, bushy tailed, much chased after twenty year old when he became Brian Epstein's lover. "I'd spent most of my life in Blackburn, and was culturally starved when I first visited London. It was 1965 and I *still* had hardly heard of The Beatles. I think that was part of my charm – I was so naff. When I was introduced by the Musical Director of Glyndebourne to Brian Epstein at a party, I just thought 'Brian who??' But it was obvious that he'd taken a shine to me, and I met him again a week after, at a party he threw at his Georgian country house in Rushlake Green. It was only later that he told me that he'd thrown the party simply as a reason for getting me there.

"We hit it off sexually right away and that night he asked me to give up my job and home and move in with him. I wasn't so sure about that, but when he told me I could be his official PA – and when I heard the salary I would be paid, which was a fabulous amount compared to what I'd been used to – I decided that I would. I was still living at Rushlake two years later when he died."

Fifteen years on James is now living alone – and happily – in Brighton. He himself points out that he's no longer the outstandingly good looking young man he used to be, but he's no pathetic pop casualty with an axe to grind either. Unlike many of those who flirted with (and were later spurned by) the Dolce Vita world of Swinging Sixties pop, James's reminiscences aren't bitter confessions. He talks affectionately and objectively about his relationship with 'Eppy', about what it was like to live on

40

what they then called – and still call now – 'the scene'.

"Brian always had a following of young men who lionised him, and the goings on in the house were hectic. I arrived at the mansion just as the housekeeper was leaving. She had worked for years for the stockbroker who had previously owned it, but she couldn't keep it together when she kept bumping into men screwing away in every room in the house. So I took over the domestic side of Brian's life: I got him a new housekeeper and gardener, paid the wages, organised the food and drink and drugs, and was left to get rid of the one-night stands he got bored with and dumped on me. I didn't complain because I'd very often have his trade after him!

"Brian was very promiscuous. Even when we were 'together' he had a different person every night. I was glad of that – he gave me my freedom but still made me feel I was special to him. Normally Brian would become instantly involved with a boy and go crazy over him for a few days and then become disenchanted very quickly, and that was that. But there were a few individuals who 'stuck', and I was one of them. I'm sure one of the main reasons for that was that he felt he had a responsibility towards me because he'd taken me away from my home and my job. His morality and sense of fair play meant that he couldn't get rid of me. He was a very special man, a bloody nice guy."

Life with Epstein meant "having a ball" in more ways than one. "There were always bands around the house and I used to get to fuck all the guests. People in the pop scene are generally very extroverted, and most of the young men who came to the house weren't averse to playing around. There was one group I particularly remember – there was even talk that I might manage them. They were called John's Children and their prettiest member was called Marc Bolan. Orgies were never planned as such, it just often used to end up that way when six or seven of us were staying there for the weekend. The drugs scene was amazing then – it was the time when they were selling acid is school playgrounds – and *they* used to loosen people up. In those days we bought our joints ready-made; we had silver cigar boxes stuffed full with them."

When the initial ardour cooled and James moved to the mansion's host house (where he continued to be PA and lover, but no longer 'in situ'), he and Epstein continued to have a mutual emotional dependence plus occasional sex. "It's funny, but for all of Brian's promiscuity and his guardsmen and his rough trade – who, incidentally, were always nicking the silver – his sex with me was always very straight and unkinky."

Was he hung up about being gay? "Yes, I think he was – although not as hung up about that as about having no artistic talent. But almost to the end he believed that it was essential in certain circles, to be seen in public with a woman. He once sacked one of his secretaries purely because she wouldn't go to the theatre with him one night to keep up the image. I should add that he reinstated her later, but he obviously wanted to be 'accepted' in society."

James agrees that John Lennon was "almost certainly Brian's real love", but by the time James met him the passion had become "diluted" and The Beatles had become "Brian's surrogate children. The strange thing was that Brian was never really that clever a businessman. He was clever because he got there first, but he loved and coveted the Beatles and wasn't into exploiting them. The NEMS empire was tottering with profits of six to seven million pounds a year when Allan Klein took over the management. Within a year it was around the twenty five million a year mark."

Swanning around in a £28,000 Bentley Continental with

an unlimited expense account might seem an extraordinary situation for any young guy to find himself in, but it was no less extraordinary than any of James's earlier life, which began in poverty in Yorkshire.

His mother, a prostitute, abandoned him at an early age and he was taken into care. Borstal followed and a spell of paid trade ("I was never rent as such, but one had to live") – and then a lucky break, a badly paid job at Glyndebourne, which helped him meet people who helped him on his way. Before Epstein, James had a friendship with Duncan Grant, which lasted until the painter's death.

And then there was Eppy, and being thrown on his own devices after the Carbitrol overdose. There wasn't any provision in the will for James and he'd saved nothing, of course: "But I wasn't in it for the money. I lived the lie, I lunched at the Connaught and went to Mirabelles – I spent my money as I earned it. I could have made a fortune by fiddling Brian, but I'm not like that. Now I do a bit of antique and picture dealing, and make a little bit of money through renovating property. In a way I've opted out slightly, I'm getting on with my own life. I've passed through that stage of seeing wealth as security. I think chattels are more of a burden than anything.

"And I don't regret anything I've done. After Brian I got jailed for eighteen months for receiving stolen paintings. It's not an experience I ever want to, or ever will, repeat – but like borstal, like Brian, I feel it enriched me. Those things have given me an edge on life which I would never have had otherwise. And I'm grateful for that."

Him, December 1983

43

Going Back

DUSTY SPRINGFIELD

Arriving at Dusty's Door, I'm in a state somewhere between excitement and knee-knocking nervousness. The excitement is natural: I'm about to meet for the first time the woman who's generally regarded as the best female pop singer Britain ever produced. But the nerves? I'm not bothered by Ms Springfield's reputation for being 'difficult', having learned to take media hype with a pinch of salt. Why I'm edgy is that though Dusty is renowned for being one of pop's strongest personalities, I've always felt in my gut that she's a vulnerable creature. I presume the last decade or so hasn't been a happy one for her, yet I'd like to know what happened during those lost years.

After all, though her vast legion of devoted (and primarily gay) superfans have continued to chronicle her every move, Dusty has been out of the public eye for a very long time. She may still be a household name and command a genuine widespread affection from the Great British Public, but she hasn't had a Top 40 hit since 1970. Career wise that was the beginning of a bad news decade, an amazing contrast to her Do-No-Wrong Sixties. Then, fresh from a handful of hits with her brother Tom in the folksy Springfields – at the time the country's top vocal group – Dusty plunged into a solo career which netted her seventeen hits with an extraordinary variety of material, ranging from boppy white soul through Bacharach and David tearjerkers to the histrionic Italianate ballads for which she's probably best known.

But the Seventies soon became the wilderness years, with her voluntary exile to America, a run of bad luck with various record companies, the drift into middle of the

44

road soft soul, brain-numbing night club work and eventual silence from 1973 to 1977.

In 1978 the appositely titled *It Begins Again*, a curate's egg of an album, not only failed to stretch Dusty vocally but indicated in the blandness of some of the material (including Manilow) that she no longer had unerring musical taste. Since then Dusty's records have been sporadic and her last album, *White Heat*, an experimental affair which ranged from the sublime to the ridiculous, wasn't even issued in this country. But the spirit is willing – the voice is still very much there, and the long slog towards becoming more than just a household name again has culminated in a return visit to England and, of all things, a contract with Hippodrome whizzkid Peter Stringfellow and his new record label.

From the recent airbrushed images we've had sent to us this side of the pond, I half expected Dusty to look like someone out of *Dynasty*. But the forty six year old ex-convent schoolgirl Mary O'Brien is looking *naturally* vivacious, with tousled white-blonde hair and a toned down version of her notorious panda eye make up, today in purple and mauve. For the sartorially inclined, Dusty isn't wearing the silver outfit John Peel described as making her look like a mini cab driver in Bacofoil, but black tight fitting pants, a polka dot cotton jacket and chic rainbow-pattern stilettoes. She's holding an evil looking, steaming, cayenne drink in one hand (she's dieting) and a cigarette – a new habit – in the other. A couple of kittens play around her feet: "They're on loan from a couple of friends who knew I was pining for my two back home," she grins. "I used to have nine." The husky voice has a slight American burr.

So, has England changed much? "It seems there are a lot of angry people here, but I don't find it depressing because on a selfish level I'm so glad to be away from Los Angeles. It's a sick place, under the cover of everyone being so healthy and sun bleached. Really vapid and so industry orientated; the whole way of life is about TV and records and status and success." It seems like worlds away from her origins – a Hampstead schoolgirl singing in the evenings with brother Tom "in the land of debutantes in their drinking clubs"; in the late Fifties with the sugar sweet Lana Sisters, and those chirpy, cheerful Springfields.

It was on a 1962 visit to New York with the Springfields that Dusty first heard the black music that was such an influence on her and which she did so much to promote in the UK: "I was passing a record shop and The Exciters' *Tell Him*' was blasting out. The *attack* in it! It was the most exciting thing I'd ever heard. The only black music I'd heard in England was big band jazz and Latin music, which I loved. But this was a revelation."

Back in England, and now solo, she spread the word, promoting the then unheard Motown sound in particular by, for example, hosting the *Ready, Steady, Go* Motown Special. "I copied a lot of black music, though I'd say The Exciters and The Shirelles influenced me more than Motown. But I'd copy them all; one day I woke up wanting to be Dionne Warwick, the next day The Ronettes. It took me some time to find my own style – which came with the ballads – but to this day when someone says a new act is copying me, I just don't see it." She's too modest, won't even admit she's the best UK female singer ever. "Maybe when I began I had the gutsiest voice, along with Lulu. But all that has changed; now there's Annie Lennox, Alison Moyet. Particularly Alison. Christ, what a voice. I'd love to duet with her!"

At a time when pop stars didn't make stands, Dusty caused a hullabaloo in 1964 by refusing to play to

46

segregated audiences in South Africa. "I got into so much trouble over having it written into my contract that I would only play non-segregated audiences. There was a loophole in the law that if you played cinemas you could work to non-segregated audiences, so I agreed to go under those circumstances. *Melody Maker* picked up on it and by the time I got there it had been fed to the SA press. The government tried to make me sign a paper saying I'd sing to segregated audiences, but my conscience wouldn't let me so they took away my permit and put me under a form of house arrest. When I got home I was slagged. People like Max Bygraves and Derek Nimmo publicly criticised me as a trouble maker, for making it difficult to go there to work."

By the late Sixties, her reputation began to dog her. "What John Peel wrote about my recent Hippo appearance was hysterical and I'm going to wrap his car in Bacofoil for him! But I don't know how I got my reputation for not showing up; I always show up, except once in Bournemouth. I've got a larger than life reputation and there were times I wanted to live up to it, but most of it's manufactured. If I threw a vol-au-vent at someone, by the time the story reached Australia it was a whole tray. I don't mind; the only bit that hurts is my reputation for being difficult, because I'm not. I can be tough in the studio because it's my duty to put in my best input and if other people aren't 100 percent involved I'm inclined to lose my patience. But I've been very patient with the Hippodrome, under some very trying circumstances." Hmm, more of that later.

Faced with the UK showbiz trail of TV series à la Cilla or endless summer seasons ("I've got nothing against Blackpool, but night after night for twelve weeks?"), Dusty took to the US in the Seventies. So what of the purdah years? "People seem to think that it was a terrible time for

47

me. Some of it was, but most of it wasn't at all. It was the first time I ever stopped and stood still and it scared me at first 'cos all I'd ever done was sing. I stopped singing because I just couldn't hack it; I lost a lot of confidence because each time I made a record for a company it was bought out by a giant conglomerate and I'd get lost in the corporate shuffle. It happened three times and despondency crept in.

"I felt a general disenchantment with myself caused by having a lot of time on my hands. Until then I'd been so very busy, and I went through maybe what a mother goes through when the kids are grown. With me, my kid was my career. Though my heart intermittently got in the way, my career basically always took first place. It was an identity thing: it was all I was. I went straight into singing from school, obviously to get the attention. There's something to be said for the fact that I don't remember much about my childhood; I must have had a sense of not being worth much and the tendency is to invent something to be. And you get caught up in it; the next thing has to be better, better. You start believing your press and become a non-person, the thing you manufactured. I was never a teenager, certainly I stopped growing emotionally in my teens. And suddenly I found myself sitting in LA, a floundering teenager underneath."

She's easy going about it; there's no hysteria. "LA is a strange place, you can feel very alone there. And I'd been backing off from nightclubs, the Vegas thing. I don't like being that close to people. I like concerts, where you have to work, to reach out. I mean, there was no *fun* in it. So I worked less and less. If there's no news people will invent it, and since I have a reputation for drama they're going to say either she's locked up in a mental hospital or she's drinking herself into the grave."

But didn't she get into pills? "If you live in California you're exposed to everything in the music industry and there was a period when, out of sheer boredom, I experimented with all sorts of things. But that wasn't my problem. My problems were about growing up. I was always very uncomfortable being the person I am. I'm still not happy with who I am, but I'm happier than I was."

Though in many ways Dusty is extraordinarily candid, she has always refused to publicly discuss her sex life. This means, however, that she is invariably asked about it in interviews. "People ask all the time. I had a woman the other day who just wouldn't pack it in. It was endless – 'Why aren't you married? Why aren't you married? Why aren't you married?' It's yellow journalism, something you learn to live with. The UK and Australian press are the hardest to deal with, they get much more personal than the Americans, unless there's a big to-do like the Rock Hudson thing. But in England there's a 'We made you, we can break you' attitude; the press were nice to me for a long time and then they got bored and got a jag on trying to cut at me. That was one reason why I didn't want to stay here, there was no privacy. I had everything coming at me.

"Usually I handle it by telling them my private life is none of their business, even though they're going to make it their business anyway, and I've learned to live with that. I don't take stances on anything, which probably irritates the hell out of you! I'm only militant about animals; I've spent a lot of my time over the last few years working for an organisation which rescues abandoned tiger cubs and otters and kodiak bears... Maybe I'm so wrapped up in animals I don't know what's happening to people, I don't know."

Though she's quiet about it, Dusty does a lot of charity work: "Pete Townshend's wife runs a refuge centre for battered women and Pete is organising a charity show which I'm doing because I've been beaten up – so I know how it feels and I know how it feels to be afraid to talk about it. I was beaten up more than once by the same person and the second time I experienced what battered wives often come up against, where they're not only afraid to talk because they'll get beaten up again, but the relationship was so disapproved of anyway that people turn round and say 'We told you so, you should never have married him in the first place.' I've been through it and if I can do anything to help there I will."

So Dusty's back and Stringfellow's got her. "Sometimes like butterflies" is a subtle, tear-you-to-pieces ballad, stunningly interpreted by Dusty. But didn't she come over here to work with Jolley & Swain, the Midas-touch producers of Alison Moyet? "Yes, I did, and they wrote me a really catchy number, very commercial. They weren't ready when I arrived because they were working on Bananarama's album, which was fair enough, but I waited and waited and then I got the feeling Peter (Stringfellow) didn't want that. We had long and fierce battles because I wanted to come back with a funky, hit-you-between-the-eyes number, but Peter had fallen in love with "Butterflies" and from then on there was nothing I could do. It was his personal crusade – there was no listening to anything else.

"It's so ironic that I came back to England for the freedom it has always offered me recording-wise and this is the first time I've ever come across an absolutely adamant attitude from a record company. It wasn't out of bloodymindedness; Peter was convinced it was the right thing. But it was like running into a brick wall – everything's a debate. We had some good old fights, but I admired his enthusiasm. There was a lot of internal politics I don't want to go into, but basically I lost the battle and Jolley and Swain went down with the ship. I absolutely love "Butterflies" and I put all my energies into it, but it's a risky record because it's such a slow developer. It needs a lot of airplay to stick in the mind." Strangely, I never thought I'd accuse the Hippo Kid of excellent taste but, even if the record isn't a hit, Stringfellow has squeezed out of Dusty a classic record which performance-wise surpasses anything she's done in her career.

Finally, Dusty regularly used to go to drag shows; how does she feel about drag queens taking her off? "Wonderful! In fact I want to take some friends to see some British drag, but I'm not sure where to take them because The Black Cap is so busy on Sunday lunchtimes, isn't it? I learned most of my tricks from drag queens... what kind of mascara lasts longest, how to apply eye shadow – very serious decisions. In fact, if the truth were known, I think I'm basically a drag queen myself!"

Gay Times, September 1985

As Years Go By

Marianne Faithfull

"I have *such* a problem with lust. I get along very well with gay men – I always have, because it doesn't put me in that funny position of being a sex-object. Whereas I have awful problems with gay women on that score, and I don't like it. Because nowadays the possibility of being considered a sex object frightens me. It's quite hilarious really that *I* of all people should be saying that. Hysterical, actually..."

That famous chortle of hers is still there, thank Christ, despite all the shit Marianne Faithfull has been through over the years. We are sitting in an office in New York, as she waxes eloquent on the emotional wreckage of her life. Puffing on one of my John Player Specials, her voice is still a husky, plummy rasp and her gestures as *grande dame* as ever. I am in Seventh Heaven, natch. Don't ask me to be objective about a woman I've positively worshipped for nearly a quarter of a century.

It was back in '64 that Marianne Faithfull first hit the headlines as the convent girl pop star, and she's rarely been out of them since. A year after "As tears go by" put her on *Top of the Pops* she left her young husband and baby Nicholas for Mick Jagger, and began living what she now describes as that 'scandalous and sensational life' which led her into a two-decade fling of heroin addiction and alcoholism. Now "clean" of both, she lives in Cambridge Massachusetts, where she has some degree of anonymity, shielded from the UK tabloid press which she reckons has made it impossible for her to live in England ever again. Thanks to a twelve-step recovery programme, she believes that in her forties she has reached some kind of equilibrium. "I now realise I was convinced I was going to kill myself or die at forty," she says. "I got my last big depression around my fortieth birthday, but that was a turning point and I haven't had a serious depression since. Now I feel I'm going to have a very long life, though you've got to keep to the here and now. Take it a day at a time."

Those readers who remember Faithfull the artist chiefly as a lisping seventeen-year-old may be shocked by her latest album, *Strange Weather*, a stark, torchy collection of early blues and spirituals, Thirties ballads and Dinah Washington and Billie Holiday numbers sprinkled with a Dylan classic here and a couple of newies there, including the specially-written Tom Waits title-track, a nod in the direction of Kurt Weill. Delivered in a forty-a-day croak, it's a nakedly honest emotion-baring album that has staggered critics and fans alike. Marianne just puts it all down to a new maturity: "Look, I think if I can find my adult musical self, anyone can. Everything I've done is what any human being can do if they get desperate enough and they really want to do it."

In fact Marianne Faithfull has been making giant strides as an artist since the late Seventies, when she first poleaxed audiences with *Broken English*, a great blast of anger of an album which included "Why d'ya do it", still one of the most explicit portraits of sexual jealousy on record. "I've never been the kind of person who smashes things, which is why *Broken English* was such a huge thing for me because I was finally able to express my anger.

"My primary emotions came out on that record. Nobody ever thought I had those feelings. When you looked at my face, it didn't show except through the wreckage of the years. People knew there was obviously something going on in this woman, but God knows what... If the press always presents me as a victim I guess it's because I've often presented myself as one, and they're more comfortable with that than facing the fact that I'm quite forceful and strong.

"Being a woman and having led a scandalous and sensational life, it's easier to consider me a victim than to accept that I've done what I've done and taken the consequences. Of course I have regrets and I have remorse and, in some ways, I think I've damaged myself irrevocably as a woman and as a human being by doing things high that I might never have done straight. I've brutalised myself by letting people brutalise me. And I'm not talking about sexual slavery and bondage, really – just the wear-and-tear of the situation of a woman who never put any value on herself, who accepted all the put-downs.

"But now I'm beginning to discover that my value as a human being has nothing to do with what I read about myself. That's just my ego-protection; I invented Marianne Faithfull and obviously people will do all sorts of things with that, including making me a stereotype, though it's the stereotype that's so hard to deal with."

The Wanton Woman stereotype which has dogged her life began for real in 1967 with the infamous Redlands drug bust when the police failed to find the Rolling Stones' acid cache they'd hoped for and instead charged Mick Jagger with the possession of four pep pills which in fact belonged to Marianne. The publicity made her into the most notorious woman in the land. While always admitting that she was the legendary 'girl in a fur rug' Marianne dismisses that she was at the centre of a Stones orgy or the recipient of a Mars Bar as "folklore". Nevertheless the image stuck, the legend grew. Even the Archbishop of Canterbury denounced her "depravity", and Marianne feels she's been judged ever since.

"I don't know what to do if people judge me – my character, my morals, my person, my value as an artist, my value as a human being – and, until recently, I've always attracted people like that. I must have a little sign on me somewhere that's invisible to me that says 'I will take emotional abuse – please give it to me!'"

That's why living in America has given her back some self-esteem. "Living here has helped me accept myself, because I've finally found a degree of anonymity and respect for the first time for a long time. Normally one has one's worth and value and other people pick up on that and that's how they treat you. But I didn't have that and I had to look into other people to see what they thought and it was only when I could say 'Oh, they don't think I'm so bad' that I began thinking perhaps I was alright. Whereas in England there's still that resentment people feel when they've created something that they think belongs to them, and when that creature doesn't behave like they think it should, they get pissed off."

After Redlands, Faithfull moved further away from the Virginal Pop Puppet image with which the British public had associated her, and a combination of factors – the death of her friend Brian Jones, her miscarriage of the child she was carrying by Jagger, the onset of her heroin habit – led her to a failed suicide attempt in Australia in 1969. When all that was over she finally left Jagger – "I think the honest truth was that I chose my addiction over Mick. My true master was my addiction" – and became something of a recluse, living in a squat and doing practically anything for a score.

"Did I have relationships with women? I sort of did, and I'm sad to say that I've been particularly abused by my own sex. I didn't really have a relationship with a woman; I had drug relationships. Like any other addict or alcoholic I would do practically anything for dope. I look back on a lot of things that I did in those days and find them very hard to accept; it's painful to think I allowed them to happen. What *did* I think I was doing? Yet I can't blame anyone else for it. That was *me* then."

All the more extraordinary that Faithfull surfaced in the mid-Seventies to get a band together to tour Ireland, where she sang country music and had a number one for eight weeks with the wistful "Dreamin' my dreams". "I love Ireland and I made some really good friends there. I felt accepted by the Irish where I wasn't by other people. I don't know if it's the Catholicism or alcoholism or both, but they don't condemn; it was the first time I truly felt that I wasn't being condemned for my past. I guess they related to the idea of a good girl gone bad gone worse! Sometimes I look at myself and wonder if I'm a recovering Catholic as well as a recovering addict and alcoholic, because when I was younger I swallowed all that dogma and I guess I carried a lot of it into my adult life. Mind you, I don't do guilt anymore. Guilt is a self-serving emotion, just a way of whipping yourself."

Then came *Broken English* and along with it a drug-free period but, after the break-up with ex-Vibrator Ben Brierly in '81, Marianne took up again with heroin and moved to America. Having recorded "Ballad of a soldier's wife" which was a high spot of the Kurt Weill tribute album *Lost In The Stars*, Faithfull began recording an album of her own material in 1985.

"It was extremely traumatic because I was working with a producer who was the most controlling person I've ever worked with. He wanted to put everything through a Synclavier so I couldn't even use the one thing I've always had, which is my relationship with my musicians. I was also in the middle of a sick relationship at the time and, basically, I was just coming to the end of my rope.

"The disease progresses as you go along and I'd been

using heroin for twenty years and it was getting near the end. It was so hard because I didn't know how to ask for help – I was so used to putting up this facade that I didn't know how bad it had got. So I overdosed and broke my jaw in the process by falling down some stairs, failed to kill myself and went into treatment. Oh God, the relief of that..."

During her six months in a Minnesota hospital, her jaw wired shut, Marianne met and fell in love with a fellow-addict Howard Tose, the man to whom *Strange Weather* is dedicated. They moved together to Massachusetts, where Marianne now lives, but Howard committed suicide because he knew he wasn't going to make it. She describes her staying clean when he died as the strongest thing she's ever done. And out of it came the album. "I remember when I did *Broken English* that I felt real rage and though it was cleansing and good to express those feelings, just to splurge out with emotion like that isn't enough. There has to be a building-up after the knocking-down. There has to be growth."

And growth has come in the form of *Strange Weather*. An album which on first hearing takes as its theme regret, remorse and loss of innocence – take a listen to her extraordinary rework of "As tears go by" – further exploration reveals its real subject to be the need for acceptance and, more importantly, self-acceptance. "It was always a great delight to me that my natural sense of irony and amusement kept me going through a lot of shit, but in my last year of active addiction and alcoholism, I really did lose it. That was unbearable. I realise now I've been very, very sick for a long time; I've had a sort of self-obsession and paranoia and a continual feeling of worthlessness that was very sad... What I'm learning to do through my treatment and simple breathing exercises is to let go of ideas good and bad, so that I'm not constantly judging myself all the time – which is what I've always done. No-one was ever a harsher judge of myself than I, but I'm finally learning to give myself some mercy."

Not that she has stopped berating herself altogether for her past. "Remorse is the worst, over things I've done to my family and son – selfish, self-centred acts – things that my disease has allowed me to do that my true self wouldn't have. I've tried to make amends but it doesn't help the attacks of remorse, though the healing thing is that Nicholas doesn't condemn me for any of these things. What I regret most is that I was always so free with my body, and sometimes I feel I'll never really be able to have a normal relationship again.

"I find I'm much more conventional and straight than I ever thought I was, and it's shocked me. I didn't expect it. But I live alone, I don't do sex. It's not something I'm advocating for anyone else, but what works for me right now is to stay away from sex and intimacy. I'm scared, really scared, of sex. Because it has such a lot of personal power things in it and I don't want any longer to live in such a way where I'm either dominated by or I dominate another human being. And it's normally sex that puts me into either one of those situations so, until I've found some way of being true to myself within sexuality, I shall live without it."

Though she has in no way joined the Whitehouse Brigade, Marianne Faithfull nowadays has reservations about some aspects of the Permissive Society for which she was something of a symbol. "I had my Aids test and having the test and waiting for the results really changed me. I'm a prime candidate because I was an IV user and, apart from being gay, being an IV user makes you one of the biggest risks. I knew I had to have the test because

I was convinced I had Aids and I didn't want to give it to anybody.

"I can't explain what I went through waiting for the result and when it came through and it was negative, it felt like a sort of miracle. The whole thing made me realise I had to change my lifestyle because I guess what I realised was that promiscuity and permissiveness didn't really work for any of us. We're all gonna have to change our attitudes to sexuality; something has to happen on this planet of ours. Sexuality is a gift, and I sometimes think I've thrown it away. And I'm not the only one."

A descendant of Leopold Sacher Masoch, the author of *Venus in Furs* and the man who lent his name to masochism, Marianne has mixed feelings about her famous forefather's attitude to sex. "Of course it's important to think about such things – that's healthy – but not, I think, to act on them. I just can't believe that acting out an S&M thing is healthy. Of course relationships are about power and its manipulation, and the tendency of most human beings is to try to abuse that power. The S&M relationship is just another form of dependency and seems to show that human beings are almost addicted to pain and sorrow. But it's very important to try to let go of that pain and sorrow rather than just wallow in it. I've never personally got into S&M, though I think I've been addicted to pain of some kind. I've never needed other people to hurt med – I did a good enough job myself!"

There's that famous chortle again. Marianne Faithfull might be older, wiser and perhaps sadder, but she still likes a good laugh. It's no surprise when I ask this idol of mine if there's anyone she particularly admires and she answers "Quentin Crisp. He's one of the top people I really respect and I feel I've learned a lot from him. He talks a lot about acceptance and self-acceptance; he's really got it sussed.

Because that's what it's all about. After that all we can do is put one foot in front of the other and do the best we can, honey." And with that Marianne Faithfull kicks off a shoe and, with a blissful look on her face, finally gets to rub the bunion that has been bugging her all afternoon.

Gay Times, November 1987

Camp Followers

The Kinks

"I remember distinctly the first time I saw The Kinks on *Ready, Steady, Go* when I was eleven, twenty years ago. I thought Dave was a girl and I was shocked when I found out he wasn't. I thought it was great, terrific."

So says Jon Savage, whose new authorised biography of The Kinks is a timely reminder that gender bending no more began with David Bowie than it did with Boy George. For readers just out of diapers, or older people with shorter memories, Savage's memory of the band in 1965 on the American pop/pap programme *Shindig* gives some indication why those of us with a taste for the perverse had a soft spot for The Kinks: "*Shindig* treated pop as a bit of fluff, but the Kinks were in another orbit: they appeared to be brooding, dark, androgynous mutants leering threats like 'It's All Right' to Middle America while generally posing in the most provocative way possible."

And though Dave Davies *looked* like a real live swishy fag on stage, his outrageousness was nothing to his preening, effete, rubber lipped vocalist elder brother Ray, who acted like one. Little wonder that, as Dave admits to Savage, "we always had a camp following".

"It was something I always picked up off them," says Savage. "They were very effete in a certain Music Hall tradition, and they exploited their effeteness – particularly in the Seventies with "Lola" and their act at the time. I don't think any of the Kinks are homosexual in their sexual practices, in fact I'm sure they're not. But there has always been a camp air about The Kinks and certainly it's something that Dave Davies is entirely blithe about, he doesn't give a shit. And Ray has a distinct appreciation of the camp side of life." An appreciation which – as the book shows – comes out in Ray Davies' lyrics, which are littered with pervy references.

Apart from the hackneyed "Lola" (the top ten's first trannie) fans and non-fans alike will remember the flittering, nylon-pantie-wearing "Dedicated follower of fashion" and the pathetic schoolboy suffering from his calf-love for "David Watts", amongst other Davies' creations. But it is a less obvious song which Savage picks out as special, "See my friend" – the record that Ray Davies told Maureen Cleave in 1966 was about homosexuality; "I know a person in the business who is quite normal and good-looking, but girls have given him such a rotten deal that he became a sort of queer."

"It's an extraordinary record," says Savage. "Apart from being one of the first records to integrate Eastern structures into pop music brilliantly, it also happens to be a beautifully expressed metaphor for a sexual identity crisis. In the end it is actually sexually non-specific. Ray Davies is a perceptive and quite confused man, and it's possible to be confused about one's sexuality and be heterosexual. He actually told his first wife 'If it wasn't for you I'd be homosexual'. But in the end the gay thing is only a small part of what The Kinks say and not worth building up as a major theme. It's a subtext. Ultimately the important point about "See my friend" is that it's a wonderful record which still sounds great today. There's a truth to it. It's up to the individual to work out what that truth is."

So it's not because of the book's picture of Ray Davies' "confused sexual identity" or of his nervous breakdowns that the singer threatened to sue the publishers, Faber, over this 'official' biography? "No, it was basically because Ray Davies is a very difficult man. He has the healthy egotism of any successful artist, but he doesn't like people to know who he is, to pin him down. He's quite entitled to that, of course, but there's a contradiction in him because he also wants publicity. Basically he wants to have his cake and eat it... It's all very much a game with Ray – he's a very litigious sort. He plays games with contracts and lawyers and tests people right up to the limit. After he approved the copy of the book, he threatened an injunction over some of the pictures, and then tried to make us pay £6000 for the use of his song lyrics after he had orally agreed at the beginning of the project that we could use them free, and after that he began making complaints about the accuracy of some of the picture captions, when we had made every effort to check them with him earlier on. The trouble with Ray is that he is used to having control over everything. Here he didn't."

When I suggest that The Kinks were one of the few bands in the Sixties to purvey androgyny, Savage disagrees: "I don't think it's entirely fair to say there wasn't much of it about. I think implicit in the whole of the mid-Sixties wave of pop music there was an androgyny which, though it wasn't as specific as it is now, was nevertheless there. You just need to look at Mick Jagger's pageboy, at the whole image of Brian Jones. That period was definitely the first breakdown of strict gender roles."

Savage has written at great length about androgyny in pop, particularly in a major feature in *The Face* in June 1983, before the word itself was as glib and as over used as it has now become. Out-gay bands and the pop androgynists he sees as inter-connected: "It's very important to understand the current media interest in gaiety in music, particularly with Bronski Beat *ad nauseam* – who I do think should make themselves less available, because they're starting to come over as hysterical and they're going to engender a backlash. With them, and Frankie and Boy George and The

Smiths and Marc Almond – a lot of whom happen to be artists I like and admire – what they are ultimately talking about is the blurring of gender roles. The roles we are locked in are constructs of a particular time in history and for the evolution of the human race they're not relevant.

"So what they're doing, very imperfectly, is pointing to the future. The androgynous principle is constant in many forms of art and behaviour, and it's a very powerful principle. You're talking about different, older rhythms. But that certainly doesn't mean that the music business itself is any more tolerant of homosexuality. It may not be trendy to say you don't like homosexuals, but many people still find homosexuals disturbing. They have the right to that to an extent, but it should be combatted by education and not hysteria. Still, I thought it was quite amusing recently to see Bronski Beat on TV framed by a man and woman dancing. That's what the music industry does."

Pop being something which Savage knows plenty about, having written of what he describes as "the only modern art form worth bothering about" since the *very* early days of punk. Not that he has any illusions about the industry, "Obviously it is a totally exploitative industry – it has to be. It's the last frontier of cowboy capitalism – it isn't unionised, it's not regulated, it's full of young kids who have fame thrust upon them very quickly and it does terrible things to them, often because they are quite insecure when they start anyway. I knocked about during '76-'77 with Poly Styrene of X-Ray Spex and I saw what happened to her and that was pretty awful. She's now obviously found some peace and I'm very glad, but it wasn't very nice to see someone you know and like being broken up like that. Originally at the end of The Kinks book, I said I thought Ray Davies was like the Michael Corleoni character at the end of *Godfather II*, stuck alone in a mansion, cut off from everything. It was cut out, though, and in a way I'm glad. I still have all sorts of conflicting feelings about him."

Savage is presently working for a small production company developing ideas for video TV programmes, including a documentary on Rolling Stone Brian Jones; doing a book with Peter York on their aborted Granada series *Teenage*; is planning a book on the Sex Pistols; and is working on a project to turn *The Face* into a TV series. In many ways he is a far more interesting creature than the subjects of his first book.

Gay Times, January 1985

Frock and Roll

Looking back at the wasteland of the Forties it is highly ironic that male cross-dressing in Britain today is so highly visible, that our greatest danger lies in overestimating its appeal and its ubiquity. Its most visible manifestation at present is amongst what the popular press has seen fit to christen the "Gender Benders": the rather dubious link we began sketching between "youth culture" and dressing up – Teds and Mods to Hippies – finally bore fruit in the Seventies when boys began dressing up *for real*. And the main reason for that quantum jump can be summed up in just two words. David Bowie.

"Mr Bowie started it all. Everybody was influenced by him. We all saw this person and thought: Fuck it, if he can get into it, so can I. That's how I got into this dressing up thing," – post punk drag artiste Colin Swift

We have grown so used nowadays to seeing Bowie as Mr Mainstream Music that we forget what a wonderfully corrupting influence he was in his time. Music was just a part of it, as were the frocks and the platforms and the make-up. Being a Bowie freak was about attitude, and for every Ziggy clone who slavishly followed the Master's latest make-up techniques there was another Bowie freak who was following the Master's dictum: "Explore". And one of the areas to explore was that of sex and gender. Bowie was nothing if not eclectic: as well as spawning a generation of acolytes and imitators, he was an acolyte and imitator himself. And many of his influences were gay, from Kemp to Genet to Burroughs. He was exploring a world that was hitherto unexplored in mainstream pop music and the influences showed from "Width of a circle" to "Queen bitch" to "Jean Genie" to the later "Boys keep swinging"; it showed in his 1972 revelation that he was bisexual (which, according to a *Rolling Stone* interview, he now regrets admitting); and it showed most of all in his public utterances advocating androgyny. Bowie generally used the word in its very limited sense, as it is normally used today, to mean a visual uniting of the physical characteristics of both sexes, though he also used androgynous concepts in his lyrics as part of a futuristic ideal. But what a generation of fans who were both mentally and sexually turned on by Bowie learned was the beauty of physically establishing the perfect mix of "masculine" and "feminine". It wasn't drag and it wasn't straight – it was about confusion.

Always the chameleon, Bowie had moved on by the time that a horde of imitators had latched on to the commercial appeal of selling records through make-up and glitter, and the glam rock overkill had spewed forth Sweet (described by a perspicacious critic as "brickies in drag") and Slade and Alice Cooper. But by then the symbiotic relationship between stage performance and the street performance was established. The message had stuck; the real point was that, although image and style might be superficial, people judged by appearances and the important thing was to confuse them completely. The idea bubbled away for ages amongst individuals and finally surfaced en masse at the end of the Seventies with punk. And though punk men were hardly the most feminised creatures, even here the link with gay persisted. Boy George – who, incidentally, has acknowledged his debt to Bowie for turning his head round – talked to me in August '82 about how London clubs like Chagueramas and Louise's evolved with the times:

"But really it was more of a punk club. When punk rock

started, most of the pubs we went to were gay clubs. You couldn't go to a normal club with spiky hair. So people went to Louise's. Everyone – the Sex Pistols, people like that – used to go there. It's funny to see punks walking about now, thinking they're dead straight. But the whole thing started off with the gay thing."

By the time punk was dead, the New Romantics and the Blitz crowd had started wearing slap and frocks again. However suspicious we may be of the "Gender Benders", George and Marilyn were frocking up well before there were any signs of recording contracts. But we have seen again and again how, as soon as it becomes commercial, the subversive loses its edge overnight: "From art to commerce to corruption – it's always the way" (Robert Altman quoted in *NME*, April 1984), and now that George appears to have lost his capacity to shock or threaten, and dressing up is again regarded as a selling point in music, we can expect a little more in the way of advancement from the icons themselves. There is nothing more capricious than fashion, and now the bandwagon is rolling, the Gender Bender overkill is on its way, if it is not occurring already. The shock of the new has been bought and sold, and there will inevitably be a reaction against the new androgyny, just as there was post-Ziggy.

But we should not underestimate the extent to which the presence of George and people like him may have helped some men to expand their male gender identity. No doubt the Boy George clones – male and female – will soon settle back into conformism, but it will be interesting to see how many of the people who have been encouraged to *explore* the potential in themselves, to find new ways of breaking down sex-role stereotypes, will continue to do so. There is nothing to stop them – having no jobs, they have no bosses to oblige them to dress "sensibly" and they have plenty of free time to experiment with themselves. They have little money with which to create new images, but plenty of creativity and that is all they need. Unlike Bowie, the new icons have only provided them with ideas through their lyrics and have also been very careful to present an asexual image so as not to alienate the granny and kiddy record buyers. But surface and image is a start, and frocking up on the street is still sufficiently controversial to bring them constantly into contact with the unbending ignorance of the "normal" world.

Men in Frocks
with Ed Heath
The Gay Men's Press, 1984

From Wayne to Jayne

JAYNE COUNTY

"The Shangri-las on acid" is how Jayne County describes *AmeriKan Kleopatra*, her new psychedelic elpee for the Eighties. It's also the best description I've heard for the eye popping curriculum vitae of everybody's favourite US trannie, a lady who has somehow managed to be at the centre of virtually every worthwhile cultural shake up of our times.

From the Stonewall Riots to Warhol's *Pork*, from Max's Kansas City and New York's New Wave to the "If you don't want to fuck me, fuck off" days of early English punk, from *Jubilee* to *City of Lost Souls*, from Acid Rock to Hi-NRG and back again, Ms County has been there and survived it all. She may still be as penniless as ever, but the lazy Southern drawl and her legendary sense of humour are still intact. One day someone will write the bio. Meanwhile, here's the next best thing: a snatch of Jayne, who was once upon a time Wayne.

"When I was young in the early Fifties in Dallas, Georgia (pop. 11,000) we had a four room wooden frame house practically in the middle of the woods, with a toilet on the back porch. Most people's out-houses were way down the trail towards the creek! The town's pride was the traffic light; when our country aunts visited we'd take 'em to see it and they's say "Ain't it *purty*! Red and *green*!

"We were five kids and we all dreaded public holidays because mother converted to the Church of God religion which taught that Anglo-Saxon people were descended from the Ten Lost Tribes of Israel and that America was the promised land. They took the Bible literally and celebrated the Old Testament holidays, like Passover, but not the 'pagan' ones like Christmas. My father was a Southern Baptist – a Washer – and when it came round to Christmas or Easter it was a war zone.

"At Christmas my mother'd scream 'Don't you dare bring no Christmas tree in this house, it's pagan! You're celebrating Saturnalia, an ancient Roman feast, and God will strike you dead' and she'd drag the tree out of the house. And my father'd drag it back in again and force us to decorate it, with mother screaming and us all in tears. Every birthday or Easter we'd huddle in horror and beg daddy '*Please* don't buy us Easter eggs 'cos they're a Babylonian sign of fertility and mother'll go *crazy*...'

"In the South they weren't educated to know words like effeminate, never mind transsexual, so I was just a sissy-boy. People were so countrified they didn't have big prejudices. When I was eleven daddy brought the boys home to play poker. I put on a dress and make-up and wrapped a shirt around my head and danced into the room. Daddy was sore but all his friends thought it was fabulous and defended me, especially his bachelor friend Norman, who always took me on his knee and flirted with me after that. Southerners simply treated sissy-boys like they were girls. By third grade all the boys used to carry my books home for me.

"It was rock and roll that pulled me out of Georgia: the radio taught me there were other attitudes out there. In the mid-Sixties I told my parents to fuck off, moved to Atlanta and became a Mod. I hung out with the femme queens and trannies and though there were very few Mods in Atlanta I found myself a Mod boyfriend called Sandy. At the same time as I was wearing bell-bottom hip-huggers, paisley shirts, a big polka dot belt, bleached hair, Cleopatra eye make up and pink lipstick, I held down a job for a while at Lockheed. I wasn't very politically aware at the time and

71

didn't realise the bits of metal I was rivetting were bombers for Vietnam.

"All the queens would go to the park Sunday mornings and party, walking round with their teasing combs, and the Atlantans used to drive over just to gawp at the queers. One time Sandy and I were walking along 14th Street and some rednecks started taking potshots at us with real bullets. Luckily they missed!

"I went to New York by Greyhound in '67. I got off the bus in Times Square and was immediately offered $10 by a guy who wanted to give me a blow job. The first place I went was The Stonewall in West Village where all the drag queens dressed like Twiggy in miniskirts covered in flowers. I hung out with Miss Marsha who didn't take shit from nobody and was always attacking the police. She lived on the street. They were tough girls, the street trannies – it was them who started the Stonewall riots a couple of years later. *They* were wild – I enjoyed jumping up and down on the police car roofs in drag at the height of 'em.

"Jackie Curtis, who my album is dedicated to, was a great influence. She introduced me to the Warhol crowd, but though I did the stage play *Pork* – which brought me to England for the first time – I was never heavily involved in that crowd and didn't want to be. Warhol took away people's individuality, he used 'em. It was a disgrace that Holly Woodlawn was a big hit in *Trash* and she only got paid $100. Warhol sucks people dry.

"We were all hippie revolutionaries. Hippie became glitter and from that came the glitter music thing which evolved into the New York punk scene. Punk is just a prison term for a boy who gets fucked in the jail. In the beginning the New York Dolls wore women's shoes and dresses, but soon as they signed with a record company they began wearing platforms and trousers. Yuk. On the music scene the CBGB's crowd and the Max's Kansas City crowd were like warring tribes. I was a Max's person, though I made my first musical appearance fronting a band as Queen Elizabeth to an audience of Hells Angels in '72.

"The early punk scene was very anti-TV, very homophobic, I was attacked on stage at CBGBs by Dick Manitoba of The Dictators. He was a big fat wrestler and he got up on stage shouting 'queer' at me and was just about to hit me with his beermug. I whacked him with my mike stand and he fell off stage onto a table, concussed himself and broke a leg. I was arrested and whilst I was on bail Blondie, Divine and the Dolls did a big benefit for me to pay my court costs. After a year the case was dropped. Nobody ever called Wayne County a queer again.

"I came to England early in '77, and I was still Wayne County – With The Electric Chairs. The London scene was more showy, less intellectual, which suited me. It was theatrical – all that dyed hair and boys in make up. We played holes like The Nashville at 70p admission. I'd started taking hormones in 1976 and was on my way to becoming Jayne, and though there were some funny digs in the media, they took it pretty well.

"My record company, Safari, got more than they bargained for. They wanted me to play everything down and look like a housewife – drop the huge wigs. But "If you don't wanna fuck me' sold 100,000 copies in the end; it had big sales in crazy places like Japan and Switzerland. They played it on Swiss radio and one time an army major was listening in with his five year old daughter and 'Fuck Off' came on. He went to the studio, broke the doors down and literally tried to kill 'em.

"Wayne became Jayne. People could take me as a homely looking boy with a big nose and too much make up, but when I came back with a new nose and tits and a bit prettier, the straight rock press really had a go at me. But I'm a survivor, I'm strong. I've done some good movies, I'm still gigging and I'm really pleased with the new album. I wrote a lot of songs, picked the musicians and produced it myself and I'm real proud of it. It's very Sixties, it's full of giggles and sparkle. If people don't like it, they're losing their sense of fun.

"I like people to call me 'she' and see me in a woman's role if possible, but roles are changing all the time, so it doesn't really matter. I don't perceive myself as a man or a woman, but as a creature – a special individual. Who wants to be a normal 'real' woman when there are millions of them in the world?"

Gay Times, June 1986

The Greatest Show with the Best Effects

Disco Tex and His Sex-O-Lettes

"They loved me in Mexico, dahling. Of course they're noted for adoring bad acts. The worse you are the more they like it." So breezed Disco Tex, aka Sir Monti Rock III, ex-hairdresser, ex-nude centrefold model and maker of the first truly gay disco record ever, "Get dancing", back in 1974. Never in a million years did I think I'd get to meet this OTT two-hit legend from New York, but here he is – large as life, twice as un-natural and looking every day of his fifty fun-packed years.

Jospeh Montanez Jnr was in London to play the Lesbian and Gay Centre anniversary bash at the Hippodrome and, to be perfectly frank, didn't know whether he was coming or going. "It's hard being who I was, difficult to follow something as good as what I did, so I've had to think of myself as Norma Desmond. We talked about my having a face-lift, but I decided against it because after all I am the oldest living faggot still working. Lee Liberace used to copy me, you know – we had the same management – but I always say that he had a better dressmaker than me.

"I'm not making a sou out of this trip, actually – what with my clothes and my hair it's costing me a fortune dahling. I'm doing this to get a record label – it's the only way to show that I'm still alive and off the drugs. The problem is that everybody is so lacksy-daisy about everything nowadays. You should have heard the two girls I've been rehearsing with this morning – when they started singing with me we had to turn the mikes off, they were so awful. So I'm going to have to go on and do my act alone. If this all had happened two years ago I would have killed the pope, but today I don't give a fuck. Let's face facts – I'm a lousy singer myself. All I am is a show-girl; I'm not a singer, I'm just a happening."

So what has he been doing the last few years? "Oh dahling, I've been the Wayne Newton of Miami. For twelve years I worked a casino doing a lounge act. I tell ya I did the same show for twelve years without changing a fucking lick of a song ' cos it was for tourists. The calls started coming when Liberace died, so my lover and myself decided to try a show in New York. It was brilliant and lots of agents came, but they said I was too chic – I did torch songs wearing a veil – and that I should go back to being tacky, and let them talk about what a bad act I am. Y'see my act is my clothes and my make-up – queens like my guts, they like anything that doesn't work. If it worked, I wouldn't be working."

Tex began life as a chic hairdresser – "I had lots of beauty shops and lots of cash and I was very chic and full of shit" – but always wanted to be a star. "When I was a child – a Puerto Rican growing up in the Bronx – my mom took me to an Amateur Hour audition, but they threw me off the audition 'cos I couldn't sing. So I became a hairdresser. But Mr Monti got drunk one day and gave a lopsided haircut by mistake that caught on and made the cover of *Harper's Bazaar* and suddenly I found myself a Saks of Fifth Avenue hairdresser. But I got tired of doing sixty bitches a day and one time I asked Diahann Carroll how to get into showbusiness and she said 'Here's fifty bucks, get yourself a press agent!'

"I was always very outrageous and dripping in diamonds and emeralds at a time when all the queens were very chi-chi and didn't dare dress up – this was 1959 – but I put on a show at Trudi Heller's and it ran for twenty-five weeks. Even though I couldn't sing a fucking lick there were lines of limos outside the club every night. In the end Johnny Carson had me on his show and I went on dressed in lavender with my long, long hair and sang "I got a woman". I was combing my hair while Johnny interviewed me and he finally said 'So Mr Rock, what about marriage?' And I was looking in my compact and I said 'Marriage? I've been looking for the right man' and he just *crawled* off the stage. The next day there were thousands of letters saying how *could* you put this man on television? It was a big scandal, so of course they signed me up and the next time I went on all in pink with pink bows in my hair and in the end I was on the show eight-four times."

'The first faggot to wear make-up on TV', Monti got his own show on Channel Nine – "Let's face it dahling, all I wanted was attention and I just didn't give a damn" – but then he decided he wanted to be a pop star. "I persuaded Bob Cree, who was the Four Seasons' producer, to do 'Get dancing' with me, but nobody wanted Sir Monti Rock – a thirty-eight-year-old pop singer – so I had the idea to change my name to Disco Tex and the Sex-O-Lettes. Polydor were the only company who didn't see a picture of me and didn't know who I was – they just bought the mast of the record – and of course they *died* when they saw what they'd bought up, this old queen. I was the only gay pop star – I was a plague to them because I was so outrageously honest."

Tex went on to sell seven million records worldwide, but only ever saw "126 bucks in royalties – they call it creative book-keeping. Still, I'm very smart doing hair so I survived – I became the Happy Hasbeen. But now I'm back because I reckon what I could do at thirty-eight I can do at fifty. I've done movies like *Saturday Night Fever* and *Sergeant Pepper's Lonely Hearts Club Band,* but I like being a blond and they kept making me dye my hair brown and as Disco Tex I can be more myself again. I'm a pain in the ass without a little success. It's like I said to Andy Warhol when he came to a party of mine in the early sixties and tried to persuade me to be in one of his films. 'Dahling,' I said, 'I'm not interested in the Underground – Overground is where I always want to be.'"

Gay Times, May 1987

The Gospel According to...

SYLVESTER

The soundcheck at Heaven had taken three times as long as expected, so when Sylvester finally returned home to the Montcalm Hotel for our interview, he was *sore*. "Honey, sometimes I think I had more fun when I was a hairdresser."

Due back on stage in less than an hour and a half, Sylvester – six feet and two inches of manic energy – whooshed a contingent from Chrysalis Records and myself into the lift and bustled us into his hotel suite. A duplex. The Chrysalids deposited themselves on the lower floor with the booze, while the High Queen of Disco and I retreated up a spiral staircase, to squat on the edge of his unmade bed.

Sylvester was in town to promote *M1015* – his most highly acclaimed album in years. Maybe it's because he's had plenty of ups and downs in his career, and is more aware than most of the vagaries of the music business, that he's not afraid to talk dispassionately about his own musical output. He thinks his first world-wide classic 1978 mega-smash "(You make me feel) Mighty real" was a dreadful record. "It sounds really awful next to the rest of my material. There must be three, four, five different tempos in that song. It sounds real tinny. But for some reason it worked. It's a terrible record, and yet it survives. I'm still getting cheques for it.'

"Mighty real" may have opened doors for Sylvester, but he also feels it helped close off a lot of other options. "My training is in jazz and blues and gospel, all that emotional singing. I think I've been completely side tracked and misinterpreted because of the commercial sense of my dance music, which is something I didn't even plan on doing. I was successful and through that I was placed in a space of music that I'm not very comfortable in.

"Dance music has been very good to me and has brought me international and financial success which I would probably never have achieved if I'd stayed with jazz and gospel. But it pleases me that of all the songs I do at the moment it's 'Shadow of a heart' which goes down best on stage. There's no fancy lighting, I don't move, I don't do anything... I just stand there and sing *a cappella*, and suddenly the emotion is there. That's the magic. That's what I live for, my moment of showing there's substance behind the glitter."

The gospel roots grew early. Sylvester was eight when he became known as "the child wonder of gospel", and travelled round the East Coast and the southern States of America with an evangelist choir for seven years. He and his sometime backing singers, Martha and Izora of Two Tons of Fun (AKA The Weather Girls) still sing regularly in choirs. The glitter began in the late sixties around the time that Sylvester started singing blues.

"I was living in San Francisco, and became a member of the Cockettes, who were a crazy theatre group, very revolutionary. It was the start of the hippie period, and a lot of people were being wild, not just me.

"It seemed like the whole of San Francisco and LA was going crazy dressing up. The place was full of mad queens carrying on with glitter on their cocks and beards and dresses. But in all the Cockettes' shows like *Hollywood Babylon* and *Journey To The Centre Of Your Anus*, I was always the serious point of the whole show because I sang blues numbers, sometimes as Billie Holiday, with a gardenia behind my ear, sometimes as Ethel Waters. Out of that developed my own show, *Women Of The Blues*, where I did interpretations of Billie and Lena Horne, Eartha Kitt, Sara Vaughan, Betty Carter..."

It also brought Sylvester his first record contract with the premier jazz label Blue Thumb. And lots of trouble.

"At that time I just went into the studio to sing, and other people controlled everything else. I didn't know a thing about arrangements and though I could write and play piano and violin, I was being very manipulated, I had no control.

"I was being fed drugs. I got very disillusioned with the music business and became a terrible person because I really thought I was a big star. I was living in a Penthouse in Pacific Heights with servants, surrounded by Art Deco and Russian wolfhounds and furs and jewels. I thought everything was being taken care of by my agents, but it wasn't and I had to sell off everything to pay my debts. I did a final concert, to raise the money to go to Europe for a couple of years.

"I lived in Bayswater for six months, and sang jazz in little pubs. As soon as anybody came in who might ask where my work permit was, I'd dash off. I got as down as I could get, even contemplated suicide. In the end I went back home. I'd learned something about humility."

It was disco that saved him, in the shape of Fantasy Records and producer Harvey Fuqua. But after a couple of years of hits during the first disco boom "Fantasy said in 1980 that dance music was dead, the phase was over. They said I was too outrageous and wanted me to change my image so I'd be like Teddy Pendergrass or Luther Vandross, and wear tuxedos and do that Vegas type of material.

"I told 'em 'Get over it'. I knew if I quit it would be a breach of contract. So I'd go in the office in a blond wig and a negligée and roll around on the floor and be the outrageous fag, so they would suspend me. And when they *did* I just sat tight and lived off my savings for a year."

It's only over the last three years, since he moved to a company started by the late Patrick *'Megatron Man'* Cowley, that Sylvester has felt in control of his career. He's now a partner in the Megatone company and can "Pick who I sing for and what the price should be, and if I don't want to do a concert, I don't do it. But I don't always get my way!

"There are a couple of tracks on the new album that I don't particularly like, but they're commercial and I'm not ashamed of them. 'Take me to Heaven', the next single is just so-o-o disco to me, I don't like it. But who am I? I can't be the absolute judge of everything. I have to go along with the people I trust. It's not like I'm compromising; it's more that sometimes I say 'Okay. I don't really think this is right, but if you think it is I'll give it my best shot.'

"But I still don't think my voice has ever been captured on record. The nearest was on my live album. When I sing on stage my mind goes and I'm crazed and obsessed and sometimes I feel I'm being inspired by a higher being, because I sing so loud and so effortlessly."

And what of the rash of openly gay bands and vocalists singing overtly gay lyrics this year in Britain? Has he heard the Bronskis, Frankie Goes? ...and does he approve?

"It doesn't interest me at all. As far as gay politics or the movement is concerned, I think a lot of it is bullshit. I'm not a great advocate of gay rights, though I've done benefits for gay charities, but the majority is bullshit. Lots of queens are full of shit, real fickle, and it's only in danger and adversity and when their whole existence is threatened that they come together."

Over Aids?

"I'm talking about Aids. I'm talking about Mary Whitehouse. They stick together till the trouble's over and then it begins again: the leather queens don't like the drag queens, the black queens don't like the white queens... So though I've been out for years, I'd never limit myself to a song that's specifically gay.

"When I sing 'Lover man', I drop the word 'man'. I won't limit myself – I don't sing to any gender. I want my music to be accepted in the world and not just by one group of people. They say ten per cent of the world is gay, and if every person bought my album I'd be rich. Well, who gives a fuck? I live in *the world*."

And what about the current crop of frock wearers?

"Good luck to them, but *I* was doing it when it was unpopular."

I'd heard Sylvester was going to play in the musical *Cage Aux Folles*. Was he going to let Broadway waylay him?

"No, no. I'm only doing it for ten weeks. I'll make my splash and dash."

And post-election, how did he feel about going back to Jesse Helms's USA?

"If it gets very heavy I'll probably just go to Mexico for a holiday."

And what about those who can't?

"They'll find some place to go. The only ones who are going to lose anything through the Moral Majority are the upper middle class white queens who dictate the political climate for the Third World and blacks and gays. They have all their wealth to lose. We have nothing to lose. But I don't think it's going to be as bad as that.

"I have great hope, there are still many free thinking people. And after all, it's only four years. The worst that can happen is that we'll all be dead at the end of it! I don't want to appear light or frivolous, but with nuclear war... there are some things we have no control over, so why should I make myself depressed?"

Before we leave for Heaven, Sylvester has a two minute fix from a gospel tape he brought with him, and then – *whoosh* – out into the night. If you want to hear that voice – whose power never really *has* been caught on record – he's back in England next month for a handful of live concerts.

Give yourself a treat. Get goosebumps on your goosebumps.

City Limits, January 11th 1985

I Love a Man in Uniform

Village People

Next to Burt Reynolds' first – and last – all singing, all dancing movie *At Long Last Love*, the Village People's *Can't Stop The Music* must be the most dumbo Hollywood musical ever made. Now the boys have produced a new single called "Sex over the phone" which is a strong contender for the title of the Most Embarrassing Record of the Decade. What treat, I idly wondered on hearing it, would the VPs have in store for us next? An underwater ballet? In a bizarre kind of way I was quite excited about meeting the Veeps on the set of the new video for "Sex" they were making with Alan Purnell; I've always been a sucker for a bit of camp and, give the boys their due, they're well on the way to becoming the Uncrowned Kings of Kitsch.

I'd been warned beforehand about the Red Indian's occasional volatility towards reporters, so when I arrived on location at a house in Olympia it seemed inevitable that the first person I should bump into would be Felipe, the Scalp hunter. Needless to say he was sweetness itself, escorting me through the set and into a quiet room to talk, primping his hair in a mirror on the way. We passed the Construction Worker, the GI, the Leatherman; honesty obliges me to admit that seeing them close up was a really good cheap thrill, akin to meeting the cast of *Crossroads* en masse. After all, this manufactured group – brainchild of disco supremo producer Jacques Morali – were megastars for a short period at the end of the Seventies, amassing forty three gold and thirty five platinum records worldwide. And, High Camp or Low, they were the first all gay group to make it. Love 'em or loathe 'em they were "ours". Or were they?

Felipe, a good looking boy with more than a passing resemblance to Tony Curtis, is the longest serving Village Person. Nine years on, he still feels "honoured to have a job like this. It's the longest job I've ever had, and I still get off on performing. Early on, the producers had a strong hold on us, but they realised after a while we weren't puppets anymore and now we have a lot of freedom to do what we want to do."

Like their album of a couple of years ago when they adopted – a little late – a New Romantic look for the cover? "Around then we joined the Blitz movement. If we did that today it would be more acceptable, but it was a little strong for the time. There had been controversy over the movie – the critics hated it – and it was a time when we were trying to search within ourselves as artists to see what makes us what we are. It didn't work. Like, my mom didn't like it. She was into the costume, the Renaissance jackets and all that, but she thought the make up was a little too harsh. The trouble was that we lost our characters, but now we're back as the Cowboy, the Indian etc, which is what people like."

The Veeps play Las Vegas a lot; is that camp? "Pleez, of course. It's hysterical. We have teepees on stage, jeeps driving across it... it's a big show, we have a crew of thirty two people. With an audience like that it gives us a chance to stretch the Village People thing to its limits." Do moms comprise a lot of their audience? "Oh, yeah. We have one devoted, diehard fan whom we call Grandma. She's seventy eight and has literally half the walls in her house covered with photos of us. She even sent me this gold bracelet I'm wearing, as a birthday present. We noticed in Vegas that this little old lady had been sitting at the same table four nights running, so during the show I pulled a feather out of my headdress and presented it to her, and asked what she was going to do with it. I handed her the Mike and, in front of all these people, she said 'I'm going to tickle myself all the way back to Lake Tahoe'. I could have *died*."

I'd heard Felipe wasn't too keen on the VPs being dubbed a "gay group"; was that true? "No. I feel good about that, for the simple fact that we patterned the group on our lifestyle. With our first album *San Francisco*, we did what no one else did, singing all about gay landmarks. It was a big disco hit, though it didn't sell too well, so when we got to our second album we realised we would play the commercial market and we started being a little tongue-in-cheek about it all. If we'd started to come out with the kind of statements that Frankie and Bronski Beat are coming out with today we'd never have got pop crossover, we'd have never had a chance. It would have been too heavy. So we decided to have a laugh about it, and it worked. I really don't know whether Frankie will manage to get pop crossover in the States."

Felipe is convinced that most of the Veepees' audience is a 'family audience'; so doesn't he think "Sex over the phone" is an alienating subject for them? "It's a problem. Most people who buy our records are parents buying them for young kids, and I don't know if they'd like to buy a record with that title for them. But we wanted to come back and the only way to be noticed is to bang the doors down and say 'Look, we're here'. We've always sung about the things that are right in front of your face. Telephone sex is real big in the States, and I'm an advocate of it myself. People today go out to meet the right person and when they meet them they're not right, so they're going to far more outer limits. It's better for them to fantasise what they want it to be. It's quicker, it's not expensive and they don't have to go out of the house." One last question, Felipe. Have you ever had a heterosexual member of the band? "Yeah, all our lead singers have been straight. Like our first one, Victor Willis. And what a monster *he* was."

AN INTERRUPTION...
Mark (Construction worker): "I think we should get rid of the costumes. It's so old hat, s-o-o corny..."
Felipe: "Mark, he's doing an interview..."
Mark: "Oh my God, why didn't you *tell me*??"

Mark has been a VP for four years. "The Village People were the first people to put typical masculine stereotype images into song and dance and make them into a sexual presentation on stage."

And does he feel that they broke barriers by being the first openly all gay group? "We never have been openly gay. I don't know where the press got that one from. The Village People fought the press on that one from day one. We've never come out and made a statement that we're gay. Never ever. Some of the songs have pretty obvious words, but "YMCA" is used at every kid's party; lots of those kids under high school age have no idea what those words mean. I don't know why people think we're blatantly gay because it's never been presented in that way."

But people aren't stupid! "Some are, some aren't. But the people who live in the rest of the US, Middle America, those people still don't know. It's just hysterical. Our Las Vegas show, which sells out consistently, it's all women screaming and carrying on. And they really don't know. They don't catch on."

And now Glenn, the Leather Man with the daft moustache, seven years a Veep. What does he say to people who criticise them for starting off as a gay group and back pedalling when success reared its head? "The group was never openly gay, the group never made any kind of statement. From the beginning it was put together as an entertainment concept. We recognised we had a gay following and said 'That's fine'. We had a straight one too – that was also fine. Anytime anybody has tried to pigeonhole us or force us to make statements we have refused, for the simple fact that if half our audience is gay and half is not, who are we to say they are wrong?"

Ahem. Okay, telephone sex. Why? "Here in Britain telephone sex might seem very outrageous, but it's been there in the States for a long time. It's just over the last two or three years it's become very popular." Why? "Oh, social changes. The Me Generation, everybody's out to do their thing."

On this side of the Atlantic it looks more like a response to Aids; non-physical sex. "I wouldn't say that. For some people maybe. But the majority of people who use it are straight. It's housewives who play cards every Wednesday night and club their money together to do it for a laugh." Is that why it's a heterosexual record, with the fantasy voice at the other end of the phone being a woman? Did you consider a gay version? "That's outside our control. Personally I'm in favour of recognising different markets, of addressing individual markets..."

But as a gay man, don't you feel it strange that the VPs should dial up a woman? Is it not bizarre that the record cover should have a sexy woman in a slip, with the strap slipping off her shoulder, breathing into the phone, with the picture on the reverse of a shirtless man doing the same? "That's the tricky question, you're making assumptions. Some people would see the way it's presented as a man talking to a woman on the other side, but the marketing concept was that each market should refer to itself. So a gay man would see the man on the phone as gay, and think of that as his fantasy. A straight man would look at the woman, a woman at the man."

So the erroneous assumption I made was not about you being gay? "I tell you, you're making the assumption that I'm a gay man."

I must put on record the fact that as individuals the Village People were very kind and helpful to me. Every one of them was a sweet man, and I had a fun few hours watching them put together what looks like a very professional and campy video. But as to the "concept" of the group? Well, what do *you* think?

Gay Times, March 1985

No Regrets

Tom Robinson

"I don't regard myself as a martyr and I don't actually regret any of it from Café Society – the first band – onwards. I think all of my reactions were an appropriate response to the situation, even where there were mistakes and cock ups and unkindnesses and when I did bad – actually evil – things to people. They were the responses that happened at the time.

"I wouldn't go back and say 'Oh, if only I'd done that at that time then things might have been different now'. Because where I've got to now is a good place when you look at it over all. It's a good road to have come along and on the whole I'm glad to be here. I wouldn't say I haven't got problems – like the tax man sending demand letters. But I wouldn't change things at all."

Tom Robinson, sitting in the tiny recording studio in his Shepherds Bush flat, was talking about what he calls his "fall from grace". He's back in the UK for a while, having spent most of this year in Hamburg, writing, recording, experimenting musically. One of the results of this new creative drive is his recent album *North by Northwest,* which I'm delighted to say I admire more on every hearing.

I'm delighted because, as I confessed to him, much of his early music left me stone cold. This was partly because I found the music itself uninteresting but mostly because, in the end, I often felt hectored by it. It seemed to me that Tom Robinson thought he knew all the answers.

But in his recent recordings, particularly *Northwest* – which I'd urge you to listen to – that persona has changed. The new music is more introspective, subtle and varied. There are more questions than answers. Though the black and white of political polemic is still there in places and the 'gay sensibility' is no less evident, the emphasis now is much more on investigating those shades of grey of personal experience.

Would he agree that he's entered a much more exploratory period? "Is that a polite way of asking if I'm lost?" he laughs. But there's so much more depth in the later songs and lyrics, I push. Is it because he's been through trauma that the music is so much richer, more substantial?

There's a long pause while he chews it over. "Goodness. Well, yes, a lot of what I experienced felt like trauma. But on the other hand I can just imagine *Gay News* readers thinking 'what's so traumatic about having a record in the top five and suddenly getting to fly for the first time and meeting lots of different people and getting letters from fans saying how wonderful you are and having a bit of money for the first time in your life?'

"I'm reluctant to sit here and moan about anything bad that's happened to me because so many good things happened at the same time. Things that went beyond the dreams that I'd dared to hope for a year previously. If you get all that fantastic stuff happen to you, you've got to expect the reverse side – the trauma. After all, you know what you're letting yourself in for. You're playing for the highest possible stakes."

But what's it like to be flavour of the month, to have the world at your feet one moment – and then suddenly find it's all changed? I'd feel very bitter about it indeed. Was he? "Yes, in the first couple of years after the fall I *was* bitter. Because – though you try desperately not to believe it – when enough people start telling you you're marvellous for long enough you *do* start believing it.

"And then within the period of a year you actually get

the reverse and you get unjustifiably bad criticism. I'll accept that some of the later records were poor. But just as the music in the beginning wasn't as good as the reviewers were saying, it was never as bad later as they said it was. But I'm many years past that now. We're talking about five years ago."

He's obviously mellowed since then. "Well goodness, yes. I'm thirty two now, I was twenty six when TRB began. And quite a juvenile twenty six at that". And though he still stands by the principles he's always had, he admits he's less judgemental than he was. I'd asked about a song that he and Elton John co-wrote, "Never gonna fall in love again". When Tom recorded it as a single, the lyrics were unashamedly homosexual. But when Elton John recorded the same song later for an album, all the gender references were changed to make it heterosexual. I'd always thought it was a bit chicken-hearted of him. Tom disagrees. Or at least he sees the other side of it.

"I'm going to be an Elton John apologist here. Seven or eight years ago – when I didn't know Elton John and he hadn't come out as bisexual – I was one of the ones pointing a finger at him. I'd think 'here's us – chipping away at the CHE level or working on Switchboard or playing benefits for GLF at The Prince Albert – and if he came out just a *little* it would be a real encouragement to us all'.

"Having got to know him and having seen directly the effect of what just the slightest bit of coming out has had on his career, I'm less inclined to criticise him. You know his support, his record sales, in middle America just went down *whoosh* after he said he was bisexual. Suddenly the chat shows and things stopped coming.

"So it's actually quite courageous of him when, after all that, he puts songs he's written with me on his albums. People know what my lyrics are about, they always associate me with the gay thing. Like "Elton's song" [the video of which has caused controversy recently because it shows schoolboys wandering around Stowe School holding hands – KK] has got a very upfront gay sensibility to it.

"It can't be easy for him when he goes to football matches and the supporters of the team playing against his club, Watford, are singing 'Don't sit down while Elton is around, or you'll get a penis up your arse'. And that's being sung by maybe ten thousand people. Okay, he's happy to face it. He'll say 'I took my decision and I stand by it'. But it can be a source of severe disincentive to go very much further down the road than he's already gone".

Is Tom embarrassed now at the extent he pointed the finger? "No, I very much stand by it. I felt it strongly. But for the person that I am now I find I see things more from Elton's point of view and I'm perhaps trying to put it over to some of his gay public who'd find it hard to imagine themselves in that position. And would probably say in any case 'well fuck it – he should still do it.'

"The part of me that's still a very hardline GLF believer says that as well. But the part of me that's mellowed and softened perhaps... because of all this 'mingling with the stars'... it can perhaps attack your integrity. I don't think it's that, but I'm certainly open to that allegation."

I hadn't expected Tom Robinson's conversation to be so peppered with perhapses, or that he would dig so deep in trying to be scrupulously honest about himself. In fact his political views have changed little – in conversation he's still as concerned about justice and equality, still as sure that it's highly important that gay people, amongst others, should mobilize against the power of the Right. He's just "not so sure now that it's the place of the entertainer to actually issue warnings to the public as if he or she knows better than the audience. Just because you play bass guitar doesn't mean you have the gift of clairvoyance".

A major strength of *North by Northwest* is that the songs, being far more personal than polemical, have a variation in tone and mood which speaks directly to the listener about a whole range of human – and particularly gay – experience.

Indeed Tom's very pleased by a recent full page *Village Voice* review of the album which makes a strong case for it being the consummate gay man's album, the first ever to sum up the everyday experience of Everygayman in the Eighties.

Reworking of older songs like "Martin's gone" (about the traumatic aftermath of the loss of a lover) and "Can't keep away" (the first record *I've* ever heard about compulsive cottaging) are set side by side with songs like "Atmospherics" – which for me is the jewel in the crown of this album – a quirky, moody, mysterious and very insidious number co-written with Peter Gabriel (with a dash of the latter's "Games without frontiers") which was "one of the last songs written" and thus bodes well for the future.

Though there are chinks of light in the album – particularly in the later material ("seems like those happy days are here again") – a lot of the songs are about isolation, the struggle with loneliness. Tom admits that he's been "pretty withdrawn over the last couple of years and I've just sort of entered a phase of being a bit more outgoing again and having a bit of fun".

The *Voice* critic points out that there are references to the singer's lovers scattered throughout all his recorded work. Clues. I asked him if his attitude to relationships has changed at all over the years.

"Yes. I've come to realize that I've been a bastard with

some of the guys I've had relationships with. That the blame laid with me rather than the other guy. I haven't treated the guys I've been out with well. And I regret that. That sounds like a trite thing to say. But now, looking back on the relationships and some of the things we shared at the time... I regret letting it pass too readily, too easily. And not having fought a bit more to make it work. I was often blind to what I was doing to the other guy."

Does he still believe in one-to-one relationships or is he cruisier by nature? "I thought *Nighthawks* was a very skilful dissection of the anatomy of cruising. I can only talk about myself but maybe there's a possibility that I/we've deluded ourselves, thinking of tricking and cruising as a norm. I opted for that after a couple of one-to-one relationships and maybe I kidded myself that it was a satisfactory alternative. And perhaps I'm not alone in that.

"As you get older, you – men anyway – find that you can't go into a gay bar and 'take your pick' as you used to when you were young and pretty. The bars are the same and you go in and you recognize the faces and you see your own face in the mirror on the wall. And you hear remarks like 'Oh, I knew her when she was pretty' and you suddenly realize that a lot of the cruising way of life depends on being able to attract other people just on face value. Which you find after a while – after you get into your thirties – you can't do any more.

"You can either get into an S/M situation, where on the leather scene it doesn't matter really what you look like. It's technique and what you're into that counts. You can go that way, carry on tricking. Or what? Three dots, question mark. The friends I've got who seem to have resolved it have done so by having a stable relationship of a non monogamous nature. They seem to work out some kind of equilibrium".

If I've given the impression that these elements of soul searching indicate that Tom Robinson is now equivocal about being glad to be gay, I should point out that in general his views on homosexuality are as positive as they've always been. And every now and then the passion flared up, as when I asked if he was disturbed by what the *Voice* critic calls "the post-Stonewall masculinity" ie macho.

"I didn't go through that whole exuberant thing of GLF – or just after actually – in order to come along seven years later and start throwing stones at other gay people and saying: 'That's not the way to live your life'. We're not that secure from the likes of *The Daily Star* that we can start bashing each other and saying 'you're ideologically incorrect'.

Similarly, though he sometimes has sexual relationships with women, he'd never describe himself as bisexual. "If you wanted to be strict about it I suppose I could call myself bisexual, but I don't because I have a definite preference for men.

"If you ask anyone on the street out there, they'd say that if you sleep with men you're queer. You could sleep with as many women as you wanted but if you go with blokes that makes you 'a queer'. And why argue with that? Why not say 'Well fuck it. Fuck you. Queer is what I am. And proud of it. So what're you going to do about it?'."

For one dreadful moment at the end of the interview I thought my tape recorder hadn't recorded our conversation. I was seized with panic. As it turned out my fears were unfounded. But at the time I remember feeling how glad I was that it was Tom Robinson. I knew that if the worst came to the worst he'd have patiently given me another half hour. A thoughtful and genuine man whose new music deserves a wider audience than it's getting.

Gay News, September 16 1982

The Bard of Thwarted Romance

BUZZCOCKS

In the big wide world outside, Pete Shelley is best known for having been main man for the Buzzcocks – one of the first and best of the punk bands. *Top of the Pops* regulars from up North whose tunes you could hum and still can, the ones who put out the first punk self-made indie record. In gay circles he's most likely to be known for "Homosapien", the early Eighties gay club floor filler with the naughty words ("Homo Superior/ In my interior") that got it banned by the BBC. Shelley – back with a new recording contract with a major label, a new single ("Waiting for love") and an album in the spring – still remembers his astonishment.

"It sounds really dumb, but both my producer and myself got a real shock when we learned it had been banned for being overtly gay, because we just hadn't thought of it that way. The clincher line was in fact just a nod to David Bowie's "Homo Superior" in "Oh! you pretty things". It was actually never an official ban – they just declined to play it. If they'd banned it I'd have been okay – look what happened to 'Relax' when it was banned. Still, it did get to number one in Australia of all places – I thought they were supposed to be dead macho and homophobic over there. And a friend of mine went to India, to the Himalayas, and when he stopped off at a camp he heard 'Homosapien' playing, so it got around."

Shelley is a soft spoken Mancunian in his early thirties who is often described as 'elfin'. A decade on, he's one of the few punk survivors who hasn't either gone all flash or zonked out completely. He says that "the whole thing started for me when Howard Devoto and I came down for the weekend and we'd heard of this band called the Sex Pistols and thought we'd go and see them because they sounded interesting from the tiny little mentions we'd seen.

"We rang *NME* to see if they were on anywhere, and they didn't know, but their manager was running a shop down the King's Road. So we trundled down and met this ginger haired guy, who turned out to be Malcolm McLaren, in this strange clothes shop that became Sex, and he gave us all this stuff about 'Oh yeah, greatest rock 'n' roll band in the world'.

"We went to some college out in High Wycombe that night and saw what must have been the Pistols' third ever gig or something – they were on with Screaming Lord Sutch – and Howard and I both thought 'Well, fuck me, they're not sitting around waiting till they're good before they do it – they're doing it *now*'. And that's how the Buzzcocks began; not long after that we were playing the now famous Screen on the Green gig with them and a new group called The Clash. It was about then that you started seeing who was who in the audience – Siouxsie Sioux and people like that – and you realised it was becoming a big cult thing."

1986 is that "cult thing's" first major anniversary. A decade ago in London a lesbian/gay club – Louise's in Soho – was the first punk watering hole, the only place broadminded enough not to throw the Pistols and their apostles out. The Buzzcocks stayed in Manchester throughout that scene ("We were always regarded as the weird ones, even by the bands themselves, I think people in London regarded us as Vikings from the North") and the place to go was The Ranch, a "very open" club run by a drag queen Foo Foo Lamar. "It was really tiny and tacky and camp as a row of tents. It was done up like a country and western saloon, but everybody who went there was underage and they played Bowie and Roxy and *Rocky Horror* stuff.

"It wasn't a gay place *per se*, but some of the things that went on there were totally unbelievable... It had all that glam and camp and general ambience that was around at that time. Anybody who was up from London made straight for the place – people like Billy Idol before he developed his sneer – and the thing to do was drink Carlsberg Special Brew through a straw. The whole place was bisexual punk, the two simmered away at the same pace."

Mr Shelley has recently moved to London, where he'll be better able to promote his new material, including his multi-layered new album, *Heaven and the Sea*, a collection of lovelorn songs which will further cement his reputation as the Bard of Thwarted Romance. He's bisexual, though finds even that label trammelling: "I always have trouble with passports, deciding whether I'm English or British and though I don't mind the word 'bisexual' at all I'm aware that to some people it conjures up sex rather than anything to do with feelings. There doesn't seem to be a word for 'having relationships with people'. It sounds bland I know – the obvious retort to that is 'doesn't everybody know?' – my big gripe about society is that it spends all its time looking for difference rather than being happy with similarities. It's such a Western way of thinking.

"I'm not even sure I know what words like homosexual, heterosexual, bisexual mean. There are times of the day when I'm 'heterosexual', when I'm thinking of girls I know and like, girls I wouldn't fancy going to bed with, girls I would, girls in the street... then there are times I can be considered as homosexual. But at those times when I can be considered to be one of the other, I don't feel myself to be that. I'm just solid state me. Emotional feelings, friendship... they're just as important as where you put your dick."

Gay Times, May 1986

Hanging on the Telephone

GRACE JONES

"That night she was singing her song 'I need a man' to a roomful of shrieking gay bobbysoxers. The ambiguity of her act was that she herself looked like a man. No wonder the fruit-bars loved her."

The svengaliesque Jean-Paul Goude talking about his one-time Trilby – Grace Jones.

Loved her? Here was one fruit-bar who wasn't loving Grace Jones to death. After seven hours of wearing a hole in the Axminster waiting for the ill-named Grace to give me a tinkle, I'd already handwashed every item in sight and was now driven to clearing out the fridge for the first time in a year. Whilst excavating the icebox, one's mind begins to ponder. Who *is* this extraordinary, androgynous (and some would say talentless) diva who – aside from keeping *little moi* on tenterhooks all day – had just missed her flight from Paree for a *Dame Edna Show* appearance purely because her favourite shoes had been put on the wrong plane? And why, despite her reputation for the rudeness and aggression – after all, she's only a household name because she bashed Russel Harty over the head on live TV – am I still intrigued by this brazen hussy? How on earth could she still command my begrudging respect? Just who the hell does Grace Jones think she is?

"Grace was born in a log cabin in Missouri in 1963 to a family of poor Russian immigrants. A precocious child, at the age of six she built a raft and floated down the Mississippi to Memphis where her raft was discovered in the reeds by

Pharaoh Sanders, the famous musician who adopted her and took her to New Orleans. There in the French Quarter, she was kidnapped by a troupe of Jamaican sword swallowers who spirited her off to Jamaica and sold her to her parents."

Postmodern icons from Warhol to Terence Trent D'Arby not only reinvent themselves but reinvent their pasts so it's hardly surprising that Ms J's first biographical pop press release was pure hooey. In fact the lady who's known to bare her tits at every possible photo opportunity is the thirty six year old Jamaican born daughter of a clergyman whose family had been influential in West Indian politics for many generations. For some reason that's never been properly explained, little Grace got left behind when the rest of her nuclear family moved to Syracuse, New York and, until she joined her parents when she was thirteen, was brought up by her very strict grandparents: "No television, no radio, no movies, nothing. I wasn't even allowed to straighten my hair or wear open toed shoes... Even when I moved to Syracuse to live with my parents, I had to go by strict rules. I decided when I left home I was going to completely freak out and find who I am. I've been searching ever since. The one thing I told myself: Never compromise."

The other thing she may have told herself was that if looks could kill, Grace Jones was going to be responsible for a hell of a lot of corpses. For even in her teens, when she was seduced away from drama college to New York by the promise of a career as a mannequin, with the world renowned Wilhelmina Modelling Agency, La Jones had learnt to mix her naturally breathtaking looks with a highly androgynous – nay, positively *butch* – image. Here was the beginning of that robot-like, unsmiling aura which was to make her rich and famous.

"I'm a sex symbol in Italy. In America, I'm more this androgyne; we're not quite sure what she is! There's a mystery there. Even if I come out in a dress like Marilyn Monroe, with my physique, the angles of my face, I still look like a male in drag. It's my attitude and I use it to my advantage."

Her looks – and stance – made her the first mega black fashion model, though she was never to climb the heights she later reached in Europe. Maybe it was her (small) role in the early Seventies blaxploitation movie *Gordon's War* which finally drove her to Paris; maybe, as the bios have it, it was to be with her equally androgynous brother, with whom she swapped dollies as a toddler – the one with the huge cock in the notorious Jean-Paul Goude photo. Whichever, she was soon not only grabbing the front cover of *Stern* and *Elle* and *Vogue*, but committing to vinyl some of the arch-nonsense with which she had recently been entertaining her many gayboy amigos.

"What do they call the girls that used to hang around gays a lot? Faghags! Yeah...I guess I was a faghag. Ha ha ha ha ha! I don't know how we survived. I would just dance in a frenzy."

Though Jones is undoubtedly hetero – she confesses that when she used to share an apartment with Jerry Hall the only thing they fought over was a man. "We always used to go for the same type of guy" – she has always been a very visible fixture of the gay world. A party animal *par excellence* (as well as complaining about how little she washed, her lover Goude has often whinged about her predilection for staying out all night and dragging gaggles of gay manicurists back home), Grace Jones loved faggots and – like Midler, like Summer – the faggots bought her her first rush of fame as a performer. That she couldn't sing

105

a note didn't matter a damn ("I find it humorous that finally there's a black woman who sings off key," jokes Jones herself); Our Gracie soon developed her dalek like rasp first on a couple of camp disco queen singles for a French label and then, quintessentially, on her first clutch of recordings for Island Records where she talked her way through classics like "I need a man", "La vie en rose" and the seminal *Nightclubbing* elpee.

"*My first idea had been to work outdoors in the West Village on the waterfront, in the heart of 'fag heaven'. She would perform in the trucks where most hardcore homophiles copulate. But it was too late in the season.*" (Goude again.)

Grace was never a singer but, boy, did she know how to perform; "I entertain myself, and they get off on it. It's like masturbating in front of everyone else." Sex was always very much an ingredient in her act (the first time Goude saw her she was "wearing just a prom skirt and nothing else. Her tits were bare." and so was the art of posing; "A lot of people thought Grace Jones was just a big gimmick. Me being carried on stage like Cleopatra. Me singing in a wedding dress with a garter belt and all underneath. But I knew what I was doing. I knew how to use a room. I knew about clothes. I knew about lighting. I came on raw and crude, and people were hungry for it."

Well, yes, but it took Grace quite some time to realise that the *less* she performed, the more of a performer she became. The egomanical Goude is not necessarily the most reliable source of truth, but it's difficult to dispute his claim that by the time he came to mould, manage and mother her in the mid-Seventies the Jones career appeared to be in steepish decline. "Instead of using her rawness (clubs like Studio 54) packaged her in an ordinary disco format. By presuming to refine her, they threatened to destroy her... Some silly columnist wrote in his paper the next day that he wouldn't want Grace Jones even to wash the windows. It's funny because the same guy is the fickle fairy who in the beginning was actually one of her most enthusiastic fans." (Goude again.)

"I always have this idea in the back of my head of using Grace as the ideal vehicle for my work... I decided deliberately to mythologise Grace Jones."

Fathead that he is, Jean-Paul Goude must take a lot of credit not only for turning GJ's career around, but for creating that threatened mystique which has helped this not-greatly-talented diva to feed well on that thin border betwixt cult and mainstream far longer than she herself probably ever dared to expect.

Painter, photographer, sculptor, stage director, set designer and self confessed "heterosexual sissy", Goude has never been renowned for his anti-sexism, as a quick blink at his autobiographical photo-book, *Jungle Fever* proves. The book – whose title comes from a phrase used by a friend to describe Goude's predilection for black women – is as repulsive as it is compulsive. It's disturbing not so much because of the sweaty minge shots and public sexual gymnastics portrayed therein, but for Goude's decidedly questionable attitude to sex ("Pornography...it's like a morbid, slumming obsession to me.") and to women.

"I was an art groupie before I even started singing" – GJ.

For Jones truly is Goude's "vehicle" and, like the rest of his other black women ex-loves portrayed in the book, one wonders if she's being taken for a ride. Of course the bold

107

geometric designs of his high surrealist epic portraits of Grace as gorilla, or as one of an army of Jones-clones, or as a nude caged animal surrounded by dead flesh are breathtaking in their sheer audacity and wit. But isn't this just a return to upmarket mannequinism? And what to make of the curious lengthened legs, distorted limbs and anatomically impossible cut-up photo-portraits of the woman? Homage? Or something less salubrious?

Puppet or poppet? There's a kind of bravery about her, but something else too. When the GJ who disrupted a Grammy Award ceremony by complaining loudly and publicly that MTV weren't showing videos by black artists like herself, is the same GJ who describes herself as a "prancing nigger" or names a portrait of herself "Nigger Arabesque", you begin to wonder where she's coming from. Perhaps, like Julie Burchill, she's one of those people who can't help saying provocative things that they either don't believe or don't really mean in order to get attention. But sometimes irony can leave a nasty taste in the mouth.

"I was born to be different." – GJ.

Jones disputes that she's ever been a pawn, tool or cipher. Working with ace producers Sly and Robbie on the groundbreaking minimalist *Warm Leatherette* was "collaboration", she says, as was her work with Goude. It was her choice to become a nihilist icon; the absolute subordination of content to style was as much her baby as theirs. The apotheosis of this artistic *zeitgeist* was in her work with Frankie Goes To Hollywood producer Trevor Horn on *Slave to the Rhythm,* when they literally stretched one single over both sides of an LP. Is Grace Jones being used, or is she using us? And if it's mutual is that okay?

The intervening years have not necessarily been kind.

Co-starring in Arnold Schwarzenegger's *Conan the Destroyer* and playing the Amazonian hench woman May Day in a James Bond film (*A View To A Kill*) do not a movie career make, and the new album for a new record company – *Bulletproof Heart*, which she co-produced – is as dead as a doornail. Or perhaps not dead enough, as *Melody Maker*'s Steve Sutherland would say of a woman whose work he once saw as a strategic extension of punk boredom.

"If there's one thing we want to hear less than that Grace Jones is a singer," he argues, "it's that Grace Jones is a human being, just like you and me. But that's about all *Bulletproof Heart* is telling us. It's too full of personality when it was her lack of character and absence of moral fibre and conventional feeling that intrigued and beguiled us. She was monstrously attractive when she was product but, ironically, out on her own, trying to be somebody, Grace Jones is nothing. Nothing at all."

"Someone told me recently that I do a lot of hitting, and I said 'Sure I do. I got hit a lot as a child'."

Of course, Grace never called. Weeks later I switched on the box, intrigued to see how the woman who bashed Harty got on with the loud mouthed arch-insulter Everage. Very well, of course. Grace came over as nice and cute and funny, with a good line in jokes about her own nipples and a good attitude to her parents and her kid. A human being just like you and me. And yet so very beguilingly handsome.

Gay Times, February 1990

Extra Ordinary

Culture Club

I'd grown used to seeing his public image staring at me from every magazine cover in sight – the alabaster foundation, the Clara Bow bee-stung lips, the plucked eyebrows, the nipple length dreadlocks, the multi-coloured funeral shroud – that it came as quite a shock to see George O'Dowd bounce into the Virgin Records' office sans make up, like the ordinary, giggly twenty year old bloke that he is.

I'd met him a week earlier at The Embassy Club and already learned that the Culture Club singer wasn't the icy poser I'd assumed him to be. He'd been warm and friendly – despite the expressionless mask, the enigmatic smile – agreeing to talk to *Gay News* "even though everyone's warned me against it". Now I saw the big grin.

Who warned you off talking to *GN*, George – and why? "Well, the rest of the band wasn't too keen. But not because of the gay thing. Even though most of them are straight, they don't give a damn about that. It's just because of all the things that have been happening in the press lately." Like you telling London's *Standard* that you're multi-sexual, that the person you're going out with is neither a boy nor a girl, that you'd love to give birth to a baby? "Yes, I think everyone in the band is worried about me not being taken seriously. But that doesn't bother me at all."

It's not often that a male pop star admits that he likes going to bed with other men, particularly when the band they're with is very near the big time. But Boy George – as he likes to be called – does so readily. Though he's no Tom Robinson, waving the flag for gay solidarity. "Look, I fancy women and I fancy men. I'm free to do whatever sexual things I want to do. The whole reason I don't go to gay clubs regularly is because I don't fit in, I don't feel like I want to be a part of that. Like, my idea of being a free person is to do what you want to do and be what you want. And the fact that I might do it in Tescos or in Bang – be *me* – is beside the point.

"A lot of people really need to be part of a movement. I don't. I'm quite happy. I'm not saying it's wrong, but to me a group of two hundred skinheads is the same as two hundred gays. It's a one dimensional thing, it doesn't go any further. There are a lot of individual gay people who've got a lot of character and are very interesting. But you get all these people who are trying to be the same. The whole idea of saying 'I am gay' is like saying 'I am normal', like saying 'I am the same'.

"I don't want to be normal, there isn't any such thing as normal. But people who go to gay clubs, they all dress like construction workers and try to adopt what they consider to be a heterosexual appearance and they end up looking really bent. They look twice as queer as a man in a pair of stilettoes and a dress. It's such a caricature of all those things that you know are really tasteless."

For all his individualism and his capacity to outrage, George is a romantic, with inclinations towards monogamy. "I'm not a highly sexed person. I like having sex but I never think 'God, I have to have sex'. A lot of straight blokes have to fuck women every night and a lot of gay blokes are the same with men. The fact that they're gay doesn't make any difference, they're exactly the same as the normal bozos down the pub, looking for a bird. When you go to a gay club it's like a meat rack, it's horrible. I like to go to clubs where there are both sexes.

"If you're going out with someone and you're in love with them and you're having sex every night, it's great. It's

111

much nicer to make love to someone you really care about. I like emotion. When I was younger I used to sleep with a lot of people, girls and boys. And then suddenly you think 'I'm not really meeting people, I'm not connecting.' I prefer to have a relationship."

I asked him if he thinks the human race is gradually allowing itself to become more bisexual, if young people are now becoming more open minded. He's not so sure. "The most important thing about being young is that you should forget about other people's prejudices and investigate yourself. With racism, sexuality, everything. But it's different. Like we were never told about homosexuality at school, even though one of my teachers was a lesbian. Most people have a tribal mentality, they stick to the pack. Lots of kids that went to my school are probably married now – and have adopted the same mentality as their parents – like sheep".

George says that in his early years at his comprehensive school he was "shy. I had no character. And I was ridiculed because I had a high voice then". He reacted by being more outrageous, dying his hair bright orange, telling everyone in sight that he was gay. Eventually he was sent to the school psychiatrist and then finally walked out of school.

But he's not anxious to encourage others to do the same. "It's a bad thing for someone like me to say to kids 'You should be gay'. It's a big decision for a young kid. I was an ahead child. But a lot of kids aren't and they shouldn't be rushed. I don't even think the age of consent should be lowered. If it were to be, I think a lot of young kids could be exploited". But does the age of consent have any affect on anyone? "No, maybe not. Maybe it's irrelevant. But I still think it's important that it's there".

Such conservatism fits with the complete individualism that Boy George espouses. I'd heard that he'd had kind things to say about Margaret Thatcher. Where does he stand politically? "There's no such thing as a good government, they're all out for themselves. What I said about Thatcher is that she's a snob, but at least she's an honest snob. But I think Tony Benn's a complete tosser. Labour is supposed to be the people's party. They built thousands of lousy council flats and they're all empty and decayed. There's shit in the lifts, rubbish everywhere. And you show me one Labour MP who lives on a council estate".

We argue for a while. I point out that the semi-legalization of male homosexuality came under a Labour government. "Yes, but every government is run by straights – and I don't mean in a sexual sense. If there were queers in a Labour government, they'd throw them out". There's a hardness there that I find disturbing, particularly when George talks about "people fighting for survival, like animals, even in relationships. That's what makes people what they are... to assume that people are equal is ignorant".

He takes me next door to hear the next single "Do you really want to hurt me?". The sweetly-spiced Culture Club sound is fuller, richer – George's voice more soulful, emotional. "Well, I *am* emotional. I love to cuddle, hold hands – silly things like that. I suppose at the end of the day I could sit in all the time and watch the colour tv, happy to be a housewife. If I wasn't how I am".

Gay News, August 5 1982

The Filth and The Fury

FRANKIE GOES TO HOLLYWOOD

"Bow Wow Wow and Echo and the Bunnymen had just played a free gig in a park in Liverpool, and they left the stage up afterwards so that all the local bands could show what they had to offer. I watched the Bow Wows and you've got to hand it to that one Anabella – she's sex on legs. And I thought 'What can we do to top it? We've got to make an impact.' So we lived out our fantasy, that's Frankie Goes To Hollywood's thing. We had the Leather Pets – two girls in leather – writhing about in a cage, and the rest of the boys were giving strap and bondage in leather knickers and half t-shirts, and I wore leather chaps and a g-string and my arse was hanging out, with one cheek painted pink and the other one blue. Maybe that's no big deal to a Heaven audience, but in Liverpool the reaction was *fierce*. They talked about it for weeks after..."

FGTH have come a long way since Larks In The Park, their summer 1982 first public appearance. Signed to Paul Morley's prestigious Zang Tumb Tuum label following a propitious appearance on *The Tube*, Frankie's debut single "Relax" is sniffing the rear end of the chart as I write and is poised, Holly Johnson hopes, to go all the way up. Holly – vocalist, writer and creator of the Frankie-style monster – is giggly and garrulous and still enthusiastically upfront about the delights of wild gay sex, despite having just been knocked sideways by an extremely puritanical put down interview in the oh-so-hip *NME*. Gavin Martin, I suggested, sounded like he felt dirty just *talking* to Holly. "I only read it once," says Holly, "'cos it really hurt me. Especially the final quote about him wanting to take us to a bar where there were no faggots allowed. He was a little

Irish lad and he was a bit curious about the gay thing – you know what they're like. Paul (Frankie's other singer) and I were dead nice to him and we took him to the Coleherne at about five o'clock at night, when it was dead quiet. He wasn't nervous or intimidated, in fact he loved the attention. But afterwards he made it sound like we forced him to go. We opened ourselves up to him – we're like that, we gab – and he took what we said and really twisted it. It was just scandal, scab..."

Talking of which, The IBA had just banned the "Relax" video on the day I met Holly. The saga of how virginal young Frankie – drawn into a night club by a leatherman – finds salvation in a Babylonian court populated by tigers, girls in iron maidens and an Emperor Nero with a shaving cream fetish is, it appears, a bit near the bone even for a media and a music scene seemingly saturated with gay and sex product.

"In all forms of entertainment you get gay people, because basically we're the best at doing it because we've been repressed so long. It just shows a bit more now, 'cos people are a bit more open about it. But though Boy George and Bowie are gorgeous boys – if you like that sort of thing – they're working in a grey area, they're playing with androgyny. But we're black and white, there's no pussyfooting with us. We are into PLEASURE and we think that what has been regarded as sexual perversion should be brought into the open."

Is that why you made a record that is so manifestly music-to-have-sex-to? "As far as I was concerned," says Holly, "in the song "Relax" the word 'come' wasn't only meant in a sexual sense. It's a philosophy for the whole of life, but that's what people clicked onto immediately." But the slurping sucky noises must be some of the sexiest ever recorded? Doesn't it just reek of amyl? "I can tell *you've*

115

been listening to the sex mix. I think quite simply we've made a classic disco record without being tame."

As to the semen-soaked sex sleaze private life that Gavin Martin found so repulsive, Holly says his taste isn't "only and totally S&M. I like the image, and they're good guys to meet. Six years ago in Liverpool – and before all that Village People crap – we got into the Tom of Finland image, leather caps and leather chaps. The band I was in started to attract the MSC leather faction, we were doing something they were attracted to. We were aware of what we were doing, and we were aware that people were into fistfucking and slings, but we hadn't realised there was a proper scene. They were good guys to meet – dead normal, all working in Fords or in offices, and most of them were in their forties. I was only seventeen and I thought it was fantastic – they were doing what they wanted to do, and it's really great that they can do that."

The other three non-gay members of the band are, though, "a little vaped out by the gay thing 'cos we all reckon it's been getting too much attention. As far as sexuality is concerned, homosexuality is not the only thing. There are loads of things you can dabble in...whatever takes your fancy." Holly admits to having been a little phased himself recently, when he found that he greatly enjoyed having a relationship with a woman: "For someone who regarded himself as gay, it came as a bit of a shock. But I think we're all brainwashed into fitting ourselves into categories, and I don't think it's a good thing."

One of Frankie's real strengths shows through on the twelve-inch's b-side. Holly's moody, spooky vocal on "Ferry cross the mersey" shows that he has a voice to be reckoned with. "I was dead made up with that. We knew we had to come up with a hot version, 'cos it's a Liverpool anthem and you don't meddle with things like that. But yeah, I think it's quite respectable. That's the only thing I stand on, anyway, my voice. I'm not particularly stunning looking and those other boys are. That's not why I'm here. I'm here because I can sing. The next record "Two tribes" – which is our ace in the pack – will prove that."

And one last sex question before we part: Do you ever feel like doing a Jim Morrison and flashing yourself on stage? "If I had twenty three inches I would, child," he laughs. "The way the show's going it could turn into actual sex on stage anyway. No, I don't mean it – *honest!*"

Him, January 1984

The Boystown Gang

Hi NRG

Ten years ago before promoters fully realised how much gold could be made from gay discos, the majority of gay men danced in tiny clubs to whatever was on the national chart, just like everybody else. Since then the phenomenal rise of the gay disco has brought in its train a new type of dance music which, like it or not, is now regarded as ours – the ubiquitous Hi NRG. And out of this has emerged an entirely new breed of performers, ninety nine per cent of them women, who are stepping out of the closet of the recording studio and onto the stages of gay clubs. Say hello to the Disco Divas.

You know the type – or at least you think you do. You see the girl on stage, vigorously miming or singing along to a backing track of her latest single, and usually acting sexy to a wildly enthusiastic all male audience who would run a mile if approached by a 'real' woman. Now put yourself in her position. What is it like to trudge around the national gay circuit doing endless PAs? What does she think of the audiences? Does she actually *like* the type of music she's performing? And is she – as women performers in the music business have often tended to be – the puppet of her management and/or her record producer and totally dependent on the machinations of the men who surround her? Or does she know exactly what she's doing and where she's going? I went to meet a cross section of Disco Divas and some of their Svengalis. And I'm delighted to report that I met a pretty shrewd bunch of women.

Laura Pallas hardly conforms to the Hi NRG stereotype sexy image, and there's no way you could describe her as anyone's puppet. The ebullient Laura ("Call me Mama

Pallas") has built up a steady gay following over the last year through a mix of professionalism and enthusiasm that would confound even the most hardened cynic, plus a readiness to trudge around the country – which in 1983 meant a gruelling schedule of 125 gigs and twenty five PAs. Towards the end of last year, she released her own Hi NRG single, a remake of the old Northern Soul favourite "Skiing in the snow". But she's not too keen on being too strongly associated with the Hi NRG boom. "Skiing" wasn't a project that was actually put together for me. I was pulled in at the last minute because the girl who was originally going to sing couldn't do it. I said I would do it, on condition that the record went out under my name – sometimes in this business a girl records a song under another name and somebody else goes out and promotes it. In fact I schlepped round the country doing a lot of promotion on it – twenty four gigs and nine PAs in December alone – because I wanted it to do well.

"But I don't intend continuing my career solely in the Hi NRG vein. If you like, I'm using Hi NRG not in an exploitative way, but as a stepping stone in my career. I'm frightened by being stuck in one section of music. I'm a gutsy, emotional singer and I'm versatile enough to carry off a vast amount of different material and confident enough to think that when I start to do other things my gay audience will come with me."

And does she actually like Hi NRG herself? "Well, if you're pushing me, I must be honest and say I don't think it's good music. I think it's a cheap way of making quick money. Let's face it, you can take any singer and put her on a Hi NRG record and shove her on the gay scene. There are lots of Philadelphian housewives standing up and miming to their pre-recorded voices on the gay circuit." And are they being exploited, to be washed up without a career in a couple of years? "Well, if they're being taken advantage of I don't blame the producer – I blame the artist. Unless you're involved in your career you're going to get trodden on from the start. I did a gig recently with a couple of Hi NRG female singers and I was totally shocked at their attitude. They turned up not knowing the words of their songs, not knowing what the hell they were doing. I just can't understand how they don't take an interest in their own careers."

Laura admits she's lucky with her managers, "Gorgeous George" Gillet and Kendo Nagasaki – the latter being the famous Masked Marvel ex-wrestler, the former his ex-manager. "There are lots of sharks in this business," says Laura, "and I was bitten a few times before I met the boys. But we've built up a good working relationship because we trust each other – they wouldn't do anything without my approval and vice versa. Everybody needs someone behind them, looking after their interests."

And what about the future of Hi NRG? "Some people think that it's going to burst wide open in 1984 and will really start selling outside the gay market, but I can't see it. I haven't yet seen one Hi NRG record in the Top 30. I've signed to Record Shack, which is *the* Hi NRG label, but it's gonna change by the time I'm finished with it. I don't think they've seen their potential as a label yet, but Eartha Kitt's "Where is my man?" has given them the opportunity of moving up into the top bracket and I'd like to help them get a top thirty hit. I'd also like to record material that my gay following will actually want to *listen* to at home." One last question: What's your definition of Hi NRG? "Oh no! I was afraid you'd ask that. I think it has something to do with the number of beats per minute, but I've honestly never been able to fathom it myself."

Someone who *is* ready to define Hi NRG is Jeff Weston,

the driving force behind Record Shack, co-owner of both the label and the record shop which spawned it. "Hi NRG is music over and above 125 beats per minute (bpm) on the backing track. Eartha Kitt's record, which is our biggest seller so far, is *not* Hi NRG – it's pop stroke gay. "So many men, so little time" was Hi NRG stroke pop. On other labels, "I am what I am" is pure pop, but "Maybe this time" is pure gay. Two thirds of the people who buy our records are gay, but we don't see ourselves as a gay label. If other people describe it as Boystown music it's up to them, but the music Record Shack created is called Hi NRG."

He describes Record Shack as "An *artist's* label. We nurture our artists. Eartha Kitt's record was licensed to us, but with the artists we record ourselves we have minimum two year deals and we take responsibility for the people we sign. We organise tours for four different artists, including Miquel Brown." So why does Record Shack specialise in women singers or, more properly, why are most Hi NRG singers female? "Well, we did have a joint distribution with London Records for Sylvester's "Do you wanna funk?" but he wouldn't come over here to promote it, so we're never going to handle any more of his stuff. But yes, we specialise in women – in fact, my partner and I have a standing joke. If either of us sees a black girl with braids in the street, one of us always says to the other 'Can she sing? Sign her up!' But I think one reason is that they're mostly love songs or raunchy songs, and women sing them better; gay men can relate to a woman singing about a man. Anyway, I like women. Men are too moody, too independent. Women are more amenable to being guided."

One woman who doesn't seem so amenable to guidance is Earlene Bentley, singer of "The boys come to town". Earlene sings opera, jazz, gospel and soul – "anything from Billie Holiday to Handel's *Messiah*" – and is also an accomplished actress who's presently appearing at The National Theatre. But she just *hates* gigging around. When I ask her about her couple of PAs she's done recently I'm greeted with a lovely dirty laugh, somewhere between a guffaw and a cackle. "Oh my, I really wished I hadn't done them. I did two PAs at Heaven and I really didn't like the atmosphere, it was crowded and huge. One time I got up to sing along to my own voice on the backing track and I didn't remember the little things I did on the record and I got my words mixed up. It was awful."

Earlene has recorded in the past – "but more poppy stuff. I prefer not to remember them. I can hardly even remember what I did for Record Shack!" But don't you want to have a big hit record? "No, no thank you. Ian Levine, my producer, says I won't get a hit 'cos I won't promote the records, but I don't want to go round the clubs saying 'Here's my record, please buy it'. If the record's good enough then people *will* buy it. And *then* I'll promote it. But meantime I don't really feel like pushing around all over the place. I've done a lot of travelling in the past... I always think of that film *The Rose* and there's no way I want that kind of pressure that Bette Midler had behind me, all those people depending on me. I used to be ambitious but now I've grown older I realise the more successful you are, the more problems you get. Right now my biggest problem is where to put my little doggie, Timbi, when I go on tour. I don't want to have to give him up. It's a small problem, but it is a problem and I don't really want bigger ones than that."

Earlene is bemused by the Hi NRG recording process. "First they put the orchestral arrangements together, then they put instruments on top and then they call me in and put on my voice. And I go out of the studio and they stick all this other stuff on top of it, stick echo on the voice. And every time I hear what they've done afterwards I go 'Uuuuugh!'" After mentioning her new single – whose title I could not remember, and neither could she – I asked Earlene what she thought of Hi NRG. "Some of it's okay," she said diplomatically. "But it's not really my type of music so much."

Someone whose type of music it definitely *is* is the aforementioned whizz kid Ian Levine, Heaven's DJ and *the* hot-shot UK producer and mixer of Hi NRG. He scoffs at Weston's 125 bpm definition of Hi NRG. "That's rubbish, absolute garbage. He would say that because he doesn't understand it in musical terms. Hi NRG is a fast type of music, but there are lots of exceptions like the new Eartha Kitt, which still has that joyous, uplifting Hi NRG feeling." Ask Levine about his beloved Hi NRG and he gets carried away: "It's a very unusual musical form with a very unusual set of roots. It's been shaped by the Motown sound of the Sixties and the Philly sound of the Seventies, with various other elements like Northern Soul mixed in. It *is* soul music, but the end result is much whiter – it's blacks singing white music. Hi NRG has been around for ages, but modern Hi NRG has a straightforward non stop metronomic beat." Ah, so that's the technical explanation for the repetitive sound which a close friend recently described as "sounding like somebody has just walked into a synthesizer and pressed the button which says 'DISCO AUTOMATIC'."

I asked Levine, as a gay man, what he thought was the appeal to other gay men of a Disco Diva who does a sexy act. "Gay men love to be turned on by outrage. It's not sex, it's just very high camp. There's a certain type of female who doesn't appeal to a gay audience, like the blonde haired Page Three girl, the ultra-hetero dream. Gays like the outrageous tarty type, with a bit of raunch." I ask if he means someone like Ruby James, whose appeal puzzles me. "Yeah, she's wonderful, they love it. She comes on stage like a slut with torn clothes. She looks like a wonderful faghag, the way she gets down and grovels her hips and everything. She's doing an over the top sexist act, and the queens love it. But of course she'd have to change her act for a straight audience.

"When females over emphasise that sex element, it's great – they're giving out pantomime sex without being filthy. It's like my Miquel Brown record "So many men so little time". It's a tongue in cheek record about a gay man sung by a woman. The lyrics are saying 'I can't get enough men to satisfy me, I want a different man every night, I want to wake up every morning and not know the name of the person sleeping next to me'. In England, the lyrics were too overtly gay to cross over, but in the US alone it has sold three quarters of a million copies. Lots of people there don't think of it as a gay record, don't realise that the record's idea was taken from a gay slogan I saw on a t-shirt in LA."

It's ironic that the singer of that number, the serene and very beautiful Miquel Brown, is herself celibate. "You see," she laughs, "first of all I'm a lady, so I just treat it as comedy. In fact when I first recorded it, I had no idea what the record was about, it never occurred to me what it was really saying because I didn't bother to listen to it close. I didn't know it was aimed at a gay audience, I thought it was aimed at women. Though it was big on the gay circuit here, it didn't really sell too well. But in the States it has sold three quarters of a million, and is still selling three or four thousand a day seven months after release, which is unheard of. And I've got a totally different audience over there; many of them are eight and nine year olds. One woman brought her little boy backstage to see me and I was really shocked. I said, 'What is this child doing in this club? I wouldn't let a child of mine buy this record! Have you listened to the lyrics?' They thought I was crazy over there, when in radio interviews I actually condemned my own song. But it's saying 'Promiscuity is great, go out and do it', and I have to say 'I don't think that's nice'."

Miquel reckons that a major part of her US sales have been to "middle aged women. It's their theme song. You know, women who have been divorced two or three times, and are maybe aged forty five to fifty five. They're into the song, they just live it – it's their fantasy." What? The type of women who go to see Tom Jones? "Exactly... and throw their underpants on stage", she giggles. Now I wonder what that says about gay men...

I'm surprised when Miquel tells me she's an actress first, a singer second. "I'm an actress who sings in tune, and I'm good and loud." A veteran of stage shows like *One Mo' Time* and *Mardi Gras*, she nevertheless found it "frightening and hair raising" at first to perform alone with backing tapes, "but now it's fine. Basically I'm a fairly introverted person but on stage I use a character. A drama background helps with things like that. But it's not a sexy act and I think I'm getting better at conveying the real me. Me is very frightened, very vulnerable – but me can get through it."

And her definition of Hi NRG? "To be truthful, I suppose I'd have to say disco junk. It always uses that same beat and you think 'Oh God – there's got to be something more.' Even Michael Jackson's "Thriller" without the video is just another Hi NRG dance song. That's not to say some of them aren't good – "So many men" was a good record. It's just not music I'd go out and purchase. My favourite track on my album is a slow song "Maybe he forgot", because it gives me the opportunity to act through the lyrics. It has guts to it. I should be content to stay with Hi NRG because that's what feeds me and it's nice that my record in particular seems to have brought the record scene round again to Hi NRG after it died for a time. I'm quite content because people are dancing to it and it's keeping them off the street."

Eartha Kitt, happy enough that Hi NRG had brought her first UK hit record in eighteen years, didn't even consider her record as disco. "I didn't think of doing a disco single. Disco, pop, jazz – as far as I'm concerned it's just Eartha Kitt with a beat behind it. When I first heard it, it was on cassette – in this supposedly progressive civilisation we have become a push button world – and it was just an arrangement of the lyric, I didn't hear any beat behind it. Jacques Morali, my producer, went into the studio with it and because studio time nowadays is so expensive he put down the violins, then the basic track for the rhythm section, then another section, all the way down the line and then on the last day when he was putting on the string section I thought 'Maybe I'd better go in and see what it's all about.' He called a rehearsal, I sang the track, he recorded the rehearsal and, before I knew what was happening, that was it. Things have certainly changed."

Hazell Dean was different from our other Divas for three basic reasons – she writes some of her own material and for other people, she's not with Record Shack, and she's a Hi NRG fan – "I love it, I play it all the time." Twenty five year old Hazell has been in the business a long time, moving from local jazz bands to session singing, from vocals in an MOR group to an entry in *A Song For Europe*, from a 1979 contract ("that didn't really happen – wrong song, wrong producer") to her present status as a Hi NRG artist, who has shifted 300,000 units of "Searchin" worldwide.

It must be a relief for someone who has obviously gone

through hard times in her career to find a niche: "I've done supper clubs, I've done cabaret, but I prefer doing this because we're talking records. It's not that I wouldn't do it again, it's just that I don't want to spend the rest of my life going round England doing Working Men's Clubs. It's not a pleasant life. I prefer this – it's hard work, it's long hours, but at least you're promoting something." She's quite content to stay with Hi NRG while it lasts: "Things take their own course, I can't tell you what direction my career is going to go in. Who knows? I just want to sing good songs."

Hazell doesn't even mind singing to backing tracks – "All I have to worry about then is me. In some places the sound is better than others, but that's the only difference." And what about performing for gay audiences? "I must say the gay clubs opened my eyes. The first time I played one was Heaven on a Saturday night, and I was a bit surprised. Not shocked – nothing really shocks me – but I kept thinking 'I've got to stand up there in front of all these men, gay men' and I wasn't really sure how they'd react to 'this woman' sort of thing. But when it began I realised you can be quite outrageous, you don't have to worry. Because they like it, they like looking at a woman. Once I got over that, I was fine."

Of all my interviewees, Hazell seemed least forthcoming until I asked her about her manager, a woman called Meg. "Even though I've always known that I wanted to be one thing – a recording artist – there have been times in the past when I have been very insecure. In this business lots of people give you spiel, and sometimes you believe them and you get disappointed. It isn't someone you can trust and believe in. I'm a singer and I'm no good at the other side of the business. But I know that if Meg goes off to arrange something for me, she's in there representing my interests. I know she believes in me as an artist, and she's the only person I can look to, because she knows me inside out.

"In the early days she had to struggle really hard. She's Dutch, she didn't know anyone here, she had to start from scratch. She'd ring record companies and they'd say 'We like the song but not the singer,' or 'We like the singer but not the song' or 'We like the singer and the song, but not the image'. She only told me these things recently – at the time she kept them to herself and I'm grateful for that. It's funny, it started with a tiny little empty contact book and now it's huge and bursting! She has always believed in me and we have both stuck out for what we believe in for a long time. And now hopefully we're beginning to see some reward for that effort."

Maybe Hi NRG isn't the perfect genre for these artists to show what they're capable of. But they're singers and if you're a singer, unless you're very lucky, you give people what they want and hope that some day they'll want what you'd like to give them. Perhaps some day people will want to hear real soul again. See the girl on stage. You know the type – or at least, you think you do.

Him, March 1984

And the Beat Goes On

BRONSKI BEAT

In a dark corner of Stoke Newington Town Hall all hell has broken loose. The occasional wedding feast provides the most excitement this North London municipal building normally ever sees, and the caretaker and maintenance workers are aghast at the noise and confusion involved in setting up the hall for Bronski Beat's benefit in aid of the miners.

The cleaners predict the floor will cave in under 1,300 pairs of dancing feet and the Hackney Miners' Support Committee are worried about the crowds of ticketless people they may have to turn away. The show has sold out within two days of a discreet announcement in the music press; three weeks on and the committee's phone still hasn't stopped ringing. Bronski Beat, unknown a year ago, are hot property.

Their sound engineer puts it simply: "They've avoided the usual route of playing shitty holes or the pub circuit, so they're still fresh to it. They've become successful amazingly quickly." And so they have. Maybe too quickly...

I first met the group almost exactly a year ago to the day, in Larry and Steve's high rise hovel in Camberwell. They were so broke they were having to share the same bus pass and – to quote Jimmy, who lived in an adjoining bleak tower – were "running around in rags".

February 7, 1984. Camberwell is one of London's poorer areas and the dilapidated tower block was in the grimmest part of the borough. You reached the sixteenth floor by holding your nose in a urine-filled lift. It was here that three scruffy, affable guys in their early twenties lived,

129

surrounded by a jungle of synthesizers and amps, and framed by a wallful of Catholic kitsch, including a large 3-D picture of the Pope on The Vatican balcony lugubriously blessing the heads below.

"We're a bunch of tack queens," laughed synth player Larry Steinbachek, who had moved up to London from Southend a couple of years before with the band's manager Anthony Kawalski. Fellow synth player Steve Bronski, and the larynx of the outfit Jimmy Somerville, both of whom had independently fled from Glasgow (Jimmy five years before, Steve more recently) dissolved into giggles. No they hadn't signed a recording contract but Anthony – introduced as "the fourth Bronski" – admitted that the companies he was negotiating with were "beginning to talk telephone numbers".

Amused by the excitement they were just starting to cause, they boasted that they had no thoughts of forming a band during their endless days on the dole. "It was just messing around, with me screaming into a mike and them plonking away on Larry's synths," is how Jimmy put it in his impenetrable Glaswegian brogue.

What forced the issue was an event called September In The Pink, the GLC-funded 1983 gay arts festival. Jimmy, who'd only started singing a few months earlier, persuaded the others to do a live set for their friends at what was becoming *the* watering-hole for London's young 'alternative' – and mostly poverty stricken – gay crowd, Movements disco at The Bell pub in Kings Cross. "We only had six songs," said Jimmy. "But we had six encores. We had to play them all again."

Word of mouth publicity soon spread the group's name. Their first non-gay gigs were at Brixton's Fridge and a performance at The ICA. By the time they supported Tina Turner at the beginning of 1984, Bronski Beat couldn't get friends onto the guest list because it was full of record executives. Everyone was talking about the new electronic dance trio and, in particular, the vocalist with the pitch of an angel.

Fame seemed imminent. Had they considered how they were going to handle big money? "Oh, I think we're going to be pretty realistic," said Larry. "We're not going to get into champagne or Mercedes" And though they wouldn't label themselves a gay band – "We're just three gay men who are in a band" – the Bronskis were determined to continue singing about men loving men "Our lyrics are about human politics," piped Jimmy. "But the music we're making is fun. That's what we came into this for. And that's why we want our careers to be slow and manageable."

So Bronski Beat were going to stay ordinary, unaffected. Only Anthony seemed to realise how tough the music business could be.

Before I left they played me a tape of a song they'd been working on: "A wee number called 'Smalltown Boy'. It's about us." Within a month they'd not only signed a contract with London Records but, thanks to Anthony Kawalski, had their own label, Forbidden Fruit, which gave them a larger degree of control over their product and careers.

By the end of the year they had effortlessly had three monster singles throughout Europe and an album that went gold on release. And, astonishingly, they still appeared to be hanging on to their integrity. What storms they'd had, they appeared to have weathered.

February 1, 1985. Back in Stoke Newington streams of people visit the dressing rooms asking Bronski Beat whether they'll do a miners' benefit for *their* local committee. The group patiently explain that it's impossible to do them all. Awkwardly they refer the supplicants to their booking agent. Apart from the fact that Jimmy has swapped 'rags' for a crisp Nike shirt, Larry has treated himself to a "new pouffy £12 haircut" and Steve has put on a deal of weight, they appear to have changed little. The music goes down a storm, though Jimmy is late on stage as usual.

Despite a recent arrest on a gross indecency charge, Jimmy is as chirpy as ever. In a couple of days' time Bronski Beat are going to the glitzy, star studded San Remo Song Festival. Jimmy turns up his nose at the idea of a big pop bash with Frankie and Duran Duran in attendance but says "I'm going to take COAL NOT DOLE stickers and plaster them everywhere!" A futile act, you might think, but one which illustrates the pressures at work. Within a month, these pressures will have resulted in a major trauma.

Larry Steinbachek got out of Camberwell as soon as he could. He now lives in the Hackney house of London Records' marketing manager Colin Bell. It's comfortable, verging on smart. Just the place for the Bronski who used to spend his spare time building synthesizers from kits. It's the first time for a long while that this twenty four year old with a reputation for being a stay-at-home has had a bit of peace and quiet; the only time he was "errant" in the past, according to Anthony, was when his privacy was disrupted. Now he's happy twiddling knobs and teaching himself how to structure the perfect pop single. It goes with his reputation as the boffin of the band.

"It's true! Since I was eleven the tape recorder has been my best friend! Anthony and I moved up to London because of our jobs, but I soon chucked mine in when I'd saved enough to buy my synths. All the songs on the album were written when the three of us were either living

132

together or living a couple of tower blocks away from each other. And being on the dole we spent all day fiddling around, doing a bit of recording, nibbling away at ideas, condensing them into a song, experimenting.

"Now that we live apart and rarely socialise when we're not working, we find it a bit difficult – very difficult – to cope musically. We have to plan everything, putting one or two days aside and saying 'that's for writing a song'. We've had to be businesslike and efficient and we've never worked in that way before.

"In October after the album had been such a smash we went through a real crisis, musically and emotionally. It just hit us – 'we can't go on, we can't keep on producing records like this.' We were all very nervy and edgy, hardly speaking to each other – totally paranoid about what was happening and how people were seeing us.

"We were recording a new song called 'Close to the edge' and Jimmy's lyrics were "If I fall will you catch me? If everything finishes, will you be at the end?" It was the perfect song to record at the time – it was so much about what we felt emotionally about walking on a tightrope. After we heard the playback we went away and had a long talk about why we were doing it at all, where it was taking us. Incredibly it was the first time we'd ever discussed the implications of what was happening – it was a really intimate experience, discussing things we'd never really talked about as friends and lovers. It was a testing point and we got through it."

So were they really the eponymous, naive Smalltown Boys wandering into a grown ups' world? Yes and no. Larry was the only literal smalltowner and probably had a more introverted life than the others. He came from a working class family living in a council house near Southend, the kind of place old people move to "to die of bungalow disease". He says he was drawn to the big city like the others.

"The record ('Smalltown Boy') says a lot about the band – it's very simplistic, which at the time we were. Every day was a new joy then. It sounds like children experimenting in a studio. Jimmy's vocals are very tiny, very fragile. I was used to recording him and I knew what he was capable of. But all the aggression went out of it in the studio, simply because it was his first single and he was shit scared."

But if they were so starry eyed, how come they got a record contract most people would give their eye teeth for? Forbidden Fruit brought them not only a good financial deal but also a large – indeed final – say in the promotion of themselves and their music and even a power of veto over the packaging of their product. If the group don't like a record sleeve, the record will go out in a brown paper bag.

"Anthony knew what we wanted and he got it," says Larry. "Maybe if we hadn't been so successful from the start we'd have had companies saying they couldn't take risks. But we were lucky when we signed because it was obvious they were onto a winner. There was no question ever of our being 'closet'.

"We're not the type of people who could go out in front of an unwilling audience and desperately try to entertain them. We never started with a career in mind, we were always in it to have fun. We've never had a goal, ever."

"It was Holly's birthday during the Song Festival and we all went out to a club to celebrate together. Sade was there, and Chaka Khan and the Frankie boys. But those Bronski boys didn't go. They're not like everybody else, they don't socialise with other pop stars." Red Indian Village Person Felipe Rose

134

Their self sufficiency has given Bronski Beat a reputation for being stand offish. How do other bands see them? "I've no idea," shrugs Larry, "they probably think we're a joke – three nelly queens. When we're with them we giggle at all the ultra-macho bands, the Flash Harries, posing and strutting about. A lot of them are camper than we are. We just stand there slagging them saying; Look at the amount of make up on *her!*"

That's a far cry from the sober Bronski image that comes across to the media. "You should have seen us in the studio with Marc Almond when we were recording 'I Feel Love' with him for the next single. We had a real scream in the studio. Some of the tapes got so *rude...*"

So how come they always sound so serious in their interviews?

"We're always asked why we make a point of our homosexuality and we don't, it's the media that make a point of it. The media always seem to consider us gay men first and musicians second. We might touch on something in a line of our songs and they think it's a heavy thing. The intellectualising comes from without rather than within." Not from *The Sun* though; the Bronskis won't speak to any Fleet Street reporters. "We don't want to be condensed into one line – a line we probably never said anyway."

Anthony once described the group as a support system for Jimmy. Is that true?

"I'd pull the plug if I ever thought that. Of course he's the singer and singers are always picked out. It's quite funny nowadays when we do TV shows, especially abroad – Steve and I get shoved further and further into the shadows, there's no lighting on us. And there's Jimmy bopping away in a blazing white spotlight!"

"It all happened so quickly I was left in sheer

bewilderment...Suddenly you see your own face and hear your own songs everywhere. It was really disorientating. I burst into tears in New York. I couldn't take it, I wanted to come home. I'd only ever been in Glasgow and London. I felt high and dry and I started crying like a baby. Mike Thorne, our producer, really helped me out. He explained what was happening." Steve Bronski

February 6, 1985. There are gold discs stacked against the wall in Steve Bronski's small flat in Ealing where he lives with his boyfriend Mike. Steve's favourite colour is pink, and there's enough here to drown in, including a bright pink bathroom with a Mickey Mouse I Speak Your Weight scale, a Christmas present from Larry.

Steve, who's now twenty five, had occasionally been down to London when he was younger and in the past had been involved with both the Hare Krishna sect and a country and western band. he finally came to London for good after an argument with his flat mates about being gay. "I saw the south as freedom," he recalls. Steve was a guitarist until Anthony introduced him to Larry, who in turn introduced him to the Joy of Synths. Like all the others he just drifted into Bronski Beat. He doesn't miss Camberwell, but of all of them, it's he who most misses the nearness: "I do find myself feeling lonely. My musical inspiration was always Jimmy and Larry. They seem to be fine, they get on and do things themselves, but I love working with them and I'm used to us all working at home, with Jimmy singing away. It's dead difficult to work in a rehearsal studio and we don't get much time to jam. Sometimes it seems there's no time for anything at all..."

Steve remembers the "Close to the edge" crisis very well, but unlike Larry doesn't think anything was resolved: "We'd been friends until then, but it became just a thing of our working together. We hadn't talked about any of the implications of the group getting big and the strain really showing.

"Jimmy hadn't been talking to me for six weeks or so, and I really didn't know why. We began talking about who had the control, whether the whole thing was taking us over despite ourselves. But we didn't really work out our priorities. We might try and tell you that, but we constantly change our minds.

"We're due to go to Italy tomorrow for this San Remo Festival, and I'd like to go because I've never seen Italy, and Larry's quite keen too. But Jimmy really, really doesn't want to go at all – he's fought so hard against it. He says it'll just be a load of pop stars acting grand, but I think it could be a hoot.

"But you get wiser, you really do. Anthony shielded us from a lot of the shit that record companies get up to, the way they try to shove you around. We were so naive. We were really shocked for example about how they break records in America – some bands bribe DJs with cocaine and money. Some of them spend $100,000 on bribes!

"We opted for the Forbidden Fruit label here so that in time we can help other young artists, regardless of their sexuality, by putting out their music.

"That was another thing we were so naive about – sales. We've sold over a million albums worldwide now, which is over a million pounds between us. We've got it, so what do we do with it? Lie in the sun and become clichéd pop stars with nothing to write about because we don't experience anything real? We want to pump the money back into community based studios – somewhere where we can record all our new demos and other people can use the facilities and make music.

"Personally I enjoy not having to worry about being

broke, but I do worry about people getting friendly with me just because of who I am. I've had friends in the past who have used me, and I had to move away from them. Mind you, having money has done wonders to my waistline – I've put on nearly two stone in a year. One reporter said I looked like a sausage bursting out of its skin, which I thought was really funny. Nearly as funny as when Boy George said he thought Jimmy looked like a potato!"

Though he's normally a gentle fellow, Steve was brought up in a large housing estate in Glasgow and dealing with gang violence "has been pretty helpful to me in this business; I've had no trouble telling certain promoters that I don't trust them. I might have been a bit wild to say the least when my temper went."

Perhaps that's why he so appreciates his alter ego, Stella Hellbelly, who recently turned up to play synth in a pink frock and silver wig at a miners' benefit at the Electric Ballroom, and has occasionally surfaced – masked – in some of London's drag venues. Stella might have had her panics in the past, but it looks like she may be settling down to seeing life as a hoot again. Like Larry, Steve seems to have found some new equilibrium in his life. If anyone was having real trouble it was Jimmy.

Bronski Beat appeared on the BPI Awards Show on February 11. I had fixed to interview Jimmy the following day. He rang me a few hours beforehand, sounding distraught, postponing the interview to some future date. Within hours he disappeared, leaving a message for the rest of the Bronskis that he needed to "sort his head out". A projected appearance on *The Tube* was cancelled and four days later the tabloids and Capital Radio announced that Jimmy had left the group.

February 15, 1985. Anthony Kawalski has always seemed cool and businesslike, but tonight he's ashen faced. He doesn't know where Jimmy is and is having to deal with London Records who are "very understanding".

Bronski Beat are the first band he has managed. Pre-Yazoo, Alison Moyet asked him to be her manager. He had to turn the offer down because he didn't know what management meant. Before Bronski Beat existed Larry wrote electronic music for Anthony's video tapes. Anthony was the catalyst that brought Larry and Steve together, and was the first to meet Jimmy; indeed there was talk at one time of Anthony and his videos being a part of the Bronski set-up but Jimmy – a lifelong socialist – vetoed the plan when he learned that Anthony had voted SDP at the last election.

He became their manager after the third or fourth gig, on his own suggestion. There can be few who envy his job of looking after these three likeable but wilful individuals. Anthony says he realised the band was going to be big well before they did: "I wanted to organise their thoughts about what direction they wanted to take. They were very naive, particularly with regard to business and even now there's a resistance to accepting hard facts." He learned to play the record companies against each other, using the same tactics they'd used on him, and things ran smoothly for a while.

Anthony persuaded the band that any pressures over promotion et cetera would diminish once they got on to a certain plateau, "Getting there buys you time later. I've been through a lot of torment praying I can keep them on an even keel, trying to make sure they had time to write. But by the time of 'Close to the edge' the individual conflicts were nagging away, because none of them could accept the reality of the situation that they were enormously successful and that they were in a position of power to affect the way the rest of the community perceives gay people."

The real conflict came over possible success in America and Anthony admits that "perhaps I used the wrong criteria by saying that it meant the difference between thousands and millions. The word 'millions' really upset Jimmy, he felt I couldn't divorce success from money. But I totally believe the value of their stance, their opportunity for getting people to reassess their opinions far outweighs the financial rewards even we are making.

"I really hope Jimmy appreciates *that* rather than the problems that getting money creates; because that's been the main problem – his conflict between hanging onto his socialist ideals and coping with the fact that a successful band automatically generates wealth.

"He's desperately trying to hang on to his socio-political roots, which is why he's determined to stay in his Camberwell high rise."

The following day Larry, Steve and Anthony leave for America to mix their new single, a version of Donna Summer's "I feel love". On February 18 Jimmy telephones from Paris. He is taking ten days off to think things over.

What triggered off the trauma? "The BPI awards – it was the last thing I needed to think about. I hated the idea of having to sing in front of people like Holly Johnson and George Michael. I got drunk, it was the only way I could handle it. I hated the whole thing; the awards are just a tribute to the promotion machine. They're not about talent, they're about product. Immediately after it I had a fight with Steve. Then there were other pressures like the court case preying on my mind and wondering how my family had reacted. And I was so frustrated because we'd done nothing new for ages, and because we don't communicate in the way we used to."

Jimmy Somerville came to London from Glasgow for a weekend in 1979. He and a friend "decided to sell our bums" in Piccadilly on their second night in town, and Jimmy has lived in the capital ever since. For a while he was a disco queen with "a wee wedge" until he discovered the Hemingford Arms – a disco run by some gay socialist men – and decided he preferred dancing to the B-52s than to Diana Ross.

"They were brilliant days – we all had the same tendencies to the Left and liked the same sort of music. I spent my life dancing."

While squatting with his radical friends, Jimmy tagged along to the making of a video that the Gay Video Project was putting together. To save money on copyright, requests were made for original contributions to the soundtrack. Jimmy pulled a few phrases out of the 'Thought Book' he always carried with him and... "over a tacky drum-box I wailed my song 'Screaming'." From then to now was a dream come true. But dreams are sometimes uncontrollable, and have a nasty habit of flopping onto the floor."

After the sojourn in Paris, Jimmy is back in his Camberwell high rise flat, perky again and ready to "lay down the law even if it means my being a *prima donna*. If they don't like what I'm going to suggest they can either fire me or I'll leave the band. But I'm not planning to leave Bronski Beat. I did consider it when I was at my lowest, but I feel very positive about the way we work together and the music we make. But there will have to be big changes."

There are two separate traits in Jimmy Somerville which people often confuse. There's the stroppy bugger with the big mouth who is always making trouble ("I'm always getting into fights. I had two in Paris while I was away! I provoke fights with my big mouth, it's disconnected from my brain. The first time I met Anthony I got into

141

a fight with him.") And there's the political animal who is strongly anti-materialistic and who kicks against all forms of social and political control. Although all three Bronskis have Leftist ideals, only Jimmy describes himself as a socialist.

"We always knew that Bronski Beat were going to be openly gay and that we'd be about politics too, but I was the one who was the stoker of the fire. I'm not the type of person to join a political party, but I can see where things are wrong, where the rich exploit the poor, and one of my main motives for being in Bronski Beat is to try to communicate a little.

"Anthony has been trying to persuade us to do a US tour supporting Madonna, every night of the week for eight weeks. I just don't want to do it, it's the promotion machine again. I'm not into trekking all over the world – that's what videos are for. Maybe you don't sell so many records that way, but that's okay. I'm not into making lots of money and I don't see why I should feel guilty about my decision stopping other people from making lots of money out of us. I'm not into millions, it's as simple as that.

"I feel bad about how I've gone about all this, but I was in a real state of crisis. Being busted by those two 'pretty policemen' in Hyde Park had an effect on me deep down, even though I pretended it didn't.

"It would have been a lot different if it had happened when I was on the dole, but given all the publicity it put a lot of pressure on me mentally. I was okay when I was with someone, but I went through a stage of being scared to go out the door, I felt really vulnerable. And I was worried about my mother – not her reaction, but if people would come up to her in the street and embarrass her.

"It was a really shitty period. I've come out of it feeling a lot better, and good things come out of it all. We'll see how the others feel about my plan when they come back from America."

Most young people who are so successful so fast, so publicly reach some kind of crisis point, though few do it as spectacularly as Bronski Beat. Their case is complicated by the politics of gay – and ordinary – life. Coming from the politicised gay scene that rejects the commercialised social life and self interest found elsewhere, Jimmy's crisis has been one of conscience. As for the group as a whole, the simple fact is that they never countenanced the pop star life.

They still complain privately that they have yet to sit down and decide what they want from the band. Yet they still believe in the quality of their music and are aware that if they represent something important to a lot of people, perhaps that will be enough to be getting on with. The best thing that could happen now is that "I feel love" is *not* the huge hit it deserves to be.

The Face, April 1985

Simply Divine

DIVINE

What a difference a frock makes. Compare the Divine that we all know and love with the man sitting in a room in the Marble Arch Holiday Inn: tasteful seersucker shirt and beige slacks, soft spoken, totally sedate. If it weren't for the large diamond in his earlobe you'd assume that Divine is what he once was, a vaguely camp hair stylist from Maryland called Glenn. But for those in the know, the diamond tells all: Divine will only wear his frock if he's getting well paid for it. "I'm a completely different person to the character Divine," drawls the recently slimmed-down one, now a relatively emaciated twenty stone, compared to the 400 lbs he once was. "I'm a bit shy, a bit Victorian in my real way of thinking. Just because I stand on stage using four letter curse words doesn't mean I'm like that in real life. I don't ever, unless I'm extremely angry, and it takes a lot to get me that sore. I don't walk around using a word like 'fuck', it's not necessary. The character does because she's a tough tart and a woman like that *would* talk like that. She's not Doris Day or Julie Andrews."

But doesn't he ever get fed up with being Divine? "Well, I'd be a liar if I said no, but I enjoy entertaining people and if it takes wearing that costume, it's alright by me. Besides I only have to wear it for an hour or so. Though I must say it was very nice recently to play a man in my latest film *Trouble in Mind*, in which I play a gangster: it was lovely not to have to totter around in stilettoes for hours on the film set. Also I think it will give me more credibility amongst the movie moguls and everybody else. People are under the impression that the only character I can play is a big bitchy tart, whereas that's not true at all."

But certainly the Divine character has done him proud. Things have certainly taken off in the last two or three years – a clutch of *huge* singles, three of which have gone gold, have made him into a major recording artist; he's in a prestigious big budget movie with Kris Kristofferson and Keith Carradine; he's broken all attendance records for the Hippodrome and Heaven...did hairdresser Glenn ever envisage such fame? "If you'd suggested it then, or even a few years ago, I have told you you were crazy. The whole thing started off by accident when I was a teenager in high school in Maryland. It was 1962 and there were no discos or anything, nothing to do. My friend John Waters was a movie buff and his parents gave him an 8mm Brownie camera and so at weekends a dozen or so of us would get together and make movies and then on Wednesday night we'd have a coke party – and I mean *Coca-Cola* – and eat potato chips and watch ourselves on screen and just *scream.*

"Divine was John's idea. He needed a fat lady – I hate the word obese – to play a sexy woman, very tarty and foul-mouthed. But he couldn't get a real woman to play the type he wanted, they fought him all along the line against wearing sleeveless dresses and low cut things. And then one day he said 'How could I be so stoo-pid! You'd be *perfect*'. Finally we did a movie called *Eat Your Make Up*, which was about some people who kidnapped high fashion models and made them eat their make up and *literally* model themselves to death. It got shown at the local university and became a cult thing and then came *Pink Flamingos* and the rest, and I guess I never looked back."

Any regrets? "Well obviously the thing of my eating doo-doo on camera is something I have to live up to – or down to. But I was young when I did it, I didn't care – I didn't think anything would happen afterwards. I just

145

thought it was John's sense of humour, very over the top. I'm not sure now if I should or shouldn't have done it, but it's too late now. Besides, I still get cheques from it... a movie that cost $12000 to make. You can't argue with ticket sales."

Not that everything has been rosy for the Big D: "When my parents realised what was going on they didn't speak to me for nine years. That was a sad time in my life, all of a sudden I was really on my own. I tried to convince them that I was doing what was right for me, but they're very conservative people and they didn't like to see their son in cocktail dresses and tight tubular numbers. Actually I suspect my mother was just jealous of my wardrobe. But about four years ago I heard from a couple of friends that my parents were worried about me, so I called them at Christmas. I suggested going over but my mother said 'Are your eyebrows still shaved? Did you get a toupee yet? You must come over *at night*.' They didn't want to see the real me, they wanted to see their idea of what I should be. But since then things have got better and I go to see them. My father is in a wheelchair now and the last time I went home we had the first real chat together that we'd had for years. He said to me 'Over the years many, many things have gone through my mind. I haven't seen your movies but your mother has, and she told me all about them and in the end I decided that if I could have made as much money from wearing a dress as you do, I'd have worn one myself'."

But frock wearing can be exhausting: "It's the touring and travelling that's exhausting, not the shows. I've recently been to Finland and Norway and though it would only take an hour's flight to get to the nearest airport to the club, I'd then have a two hour drive to the club itself. Maybe I'd have time to get a bite to eat, then it takes two or

146

three hours to get ready for the show. I still get nerves too, that's why I don't like people to come backstage before I go on because I'm not really myself. I'm a complete nervous wreck, any little thing makes me go AAAAGH!"

But at least you're seeing the world? "Listen, I remember when I first got a hit in Holland and they called me and said 'Divine honey, you've got to come here 'cos you've got a top ten hit' and I thought 'how lovely, I've always wanted to see Holland'... which I never did. My club dates were all at night so I only saw Holland by night. We'd be driving along and they'd say 'There's a windmill on your right, and there are fields and fields of too-lips on your left' and I'd say 'Oh yes' and I couldn't see a thing. Not that I'm complaining. This business has been very good to me. Though I just know by the time I get home I just won't be able to get through the door for four months of mail. I live alone in Woodstock – when I get back home my housekeeper moves back into her own place – and I like to be on my own after all the touring. I need to have some time to myself."

When I left Divine he was conducting a press conference with a load of foreign journalists, and answering some of the same questions that I had asked him almost word for word. At the risk of sounding patronising, I felt rather sorry for him. Though he seems happy enough with his money.

Mister, Autumn 1985

I'd Do Anything

DEAD OR ALIVE

"To put it bluntly, the pop charts is full of faggots – myself included to a degree. It's a real boot in the eye for the normal majority. Personally I don't think gay people have a hard time anymore – not the ones I know anyway who are at ease with their sexuality. But once music is involved with the gay thing, it'll bring an even wider acceptance and I look forward to this year being much more permissive. Everybody will be doing it – they'll all be dying to have a go."

Pete Burns, twenty five years old vocalist with Dead Or Alive, is giggling himself silly in the lounge of a Lancaster Gate hotel – hardly the "hard knock" I'd been led to expect by journalist friends and a generally hostile music press. Though the incessant arguments about whether it was he or Boy George who came first with the androgyny-with-dreadlocks image are now defunct, three or four years of being constantly described as a George clone have obviously left their mark: "The Boy George thing has crippled me to some extent, which is one of the reasons why I've been off the scene for a while," he says resignedly.

But much of the bitterness has evaporated and Burns puts most of the blame for the Liverpool band's recent low profile on the record company's myopia and conservatism. "It's only this year that Epic has given us free reign to do what we like. Before then they tried to get us to clean up our image, to follow in George's footsteps. They wanted me to go soap-scrubbed onto chat shows to tell them how long it takes me to do my hair, but I said 'no chance'. Rather than sell out like that, I was quite content to do nothing and sap their financial resources indefinitely."

Luckily, the release of Dead Or Alive's hottest, most-likely-to-succeed single yet – the spare, abrasive, slow burning electro-funk "I'd do anything" – has coincided with Frankie Goes To Hollywood's number one, "Relax", which Burns reckons has "totally changed things. Record companies are suddenly learning what to do with their "unwholesome" acts – to let them get on with it. I've always felt I'd rather go into what Epic thinks of as the more seedy side of the press, which is the gay mags. I'd prefer to see my face staring out of *HIM* than *Record Mirror*, and know that I'm appealing to people who've got more in common with me than ten year old girls with wet panties. Epic hated the idea, but now they're saying 'Do what you want...'"

Part of what Burns wants is "to get Dead Or Alive onto the Boystown chart which, though it's not a sales chart, is the most flattering chart to be on. Eighty five per cent of the national chart is an embarrassment musically, but a lot of the Boystown stuff is optimistic, powerful and very energetic. It's where the best music's being made. And I think the gay / Boystown following is a lot more loyal – it's because of them that people like Sylvester can keep going for years without a chart hit. The straight – or let's say average – punter is very fickle. One minute you're on their bedroom wall, the next minute you're off it."

Not that he approves of everything Boystown – Gloria Gaynor's "I am what I am" brings out the sharp tongue for which Burns is justly notorious: "It's a bloody tragedy of a record. Somebody should put a polythene bag over her head and knot it at the neck. It's for businessmen who live in bloody Penge and go home and put on their wives' nighties when they're out and mime to it in the mirror. That's the side of gay music that I hate – people stomping around the dancefloor to "I will survive", acting like

149

they're victimised. They're a small proportion, but I don't think they should be humoured."

And in what way is he "a faggot... to a degree"? "Well, I don't categorise myself as gay or straight. I'm almost exclusively one way, but I have a wife as well – though I wouldn't have another if this one wore out so to speak. Guys with handlebar moustaches don't do anything for me. I tend to nab the straight ones. I used to get a buzz out of nabbing straights when I was fourteen, but the thrill is gone! It's easy once you know how – with enough lipgloss you can do anything.

"But I'm in a completely different circle to most people. I've got a wife but I also live with my lover, Steve, as well. We all live together fine: I don't think I could stand it any other way. When I met my wife I was primarily the other way sexually. A leopard can't change his spots and I didn't want that part of me to go underboard and secret, so it's always been completely open. It's practically an ideal situation – we've got one huge bed and everything. Everyone around us accepts it totally, it's only when we go on tour that it freaks people out – hotel managers and tour managers. We have a triple hotel bedroom, but to make it fair we have three single beds. We can't ask for a triple bed at the moment – we'll have to wait until the budget's bigger."

But why bother to marry? "Because I wanted to. It wasn't a convenience thing. Lynne was the first person I'd met that I wanted to cement myself to, so to speak. Ships in the night may come and go, but you've got to have a good anchor." Under the mane of hair there's an arched eyebrow, waiting to see if I'll rise to the mock-chauvinism, but I just can't get over how he reminds me of the young Jane Russell. I tell him so. "Well that's a new one. Thank you." Later he explains why the band pulled out of its first

150

gig at Heaven. "We blew it out because we heard a rumour that they don't let women in, which is fucking grim. There's no need for that segregation. But then we found out that they *do* let tits and fannies in on Thursdays, so we did it a week later."

Burns, who "rose up in Liverpool when grey raincoats and crew cuts were obligatory" has been an outsider ever since he decided to try out his "Frankenstein Syndrome. I wanted to see what I could create from a boring male body. It's a bit sad in Liverpool that the gay clone element doesn't accept you if you look a bit peculiar. The bitching is very amateur – all they can manage to say is 'what was *that*'". And appearing on kiddiepop programmes like *Razamattaz* is "no place for me. I feel completely alienated amongst all those kids saying 'Are you a man or a lady?' – like a really upright straight would feel if they walked into a heavy leather night at Heaven. The place I belong in doesn't exist yet."

I'd disagree. Judging by the re-scheduled performance at Heaven, I'd say that Mr Burns belongs on stage in his rubber leotard, flashing the best legs in the business as well as the occasional glimpse of a bollock to the salivating mob. It's been a long time coming, but my guess is that stardom beckons in 1984.

Catch 'em while you can.

Him, March 1984

The Vinyl Closet

Though 1984 might be remembered as the year in which gay performers took over the music charts (again!), the question remains: Is it a help or a hindrance to be gay in the rock world?

"We used the gay front as a publicity ploy. It worked. But now it's over. Haven't you noticed the suit today?"
Holly Johnson, *Sounds*, January 1984

It's not so much the rampant hypocrisy displayed here which is so staggering – after all, Holly *might* have had his tongue firmly planted in his cheek, though the evidence of 1984 suggests otherwise. What is more astonishing is the assumption that overt homosexuality sells records – and related product – in the first place. It implies a remarkable turnaround in the music industry in the Eighties. After all, it has been one of life's eternal little ironies that though everybody in the business knew *MondoPop* was knee deep in faggots – both on-stage and behind the scenes – few people talked of it publicly, and no-one considered *selling* the fact. Until now.

"KAJAGOOGONE. Kajagoogoo and singer Limahl have parted company... Meanwhile, reports that DJ Paul Gambaccini's friendship with Limahl contributed to the split were strenuously denied by both the BBC and EMI Records."
NME news report, August 1983.

Well, they would, wouldn't they? Even though the public face of pop thrives on a combination of glamour, sex and rebellion, the industry itself is as conservative as any other. Corporate wisdom has always dictated that the mass market was primarily composed of little girls for pop and red-blooded het men for rock and that *naturally*, because neither group would relish the idea of their idol taking it up the bum, the merest whiff of homosexuality was considered commercial suicide.

"The biggest mistake I ever made was telling that Melody Maker writer that I was bisexual. Christ, I was so young then."
David Bowie, *Rolling Stone*, 1983

No doubt there was some sweat under the corporate collar during the early days of glamrock when a handful of mavericks began "admitting" they occasionally like a bit of the other. At the time it must have taken a certain amount of courage to bring the subject up at all, but to the record companies it was beside the point whether Mr Bowie's revelation was the result of a bout of sincerity or a greater commercial acumen than theirs. What they looked at were the sales figures, and they hadn't diminished one little bit.

The industry soon learned that AOR (Adult Orientated Rock) audiences at least were more broadminded than they'd thought and that a frisson of outrage/bit of camp never did an AOR act any harm. And Bisexual Chic was kosher because any artist putting one foot out of the closet could always pull it back in again sharpish. (Hi Elton! Bye Elton! Hi Ziggy! Bye Ziggy! Hi Lou...) Bi Chic soon became hypocrisy in shorthand, dealing true bisexuality a body blow from which it has never fully recovered.

Naturally fully fledged faggotry in the industry just wasn't on. The exception who proved this rule was Tom Robinson Phase 1 – out of the closet and into the dustbin in twelve months flat. Since that fall from grace he's been paraded as an object lesson to aspirant starines as to what they could expect if they hoped to be out-gay and get away with it. That Tom Robinson's decline was mainly due to duff discs was conveniently ignored. And barring one or two deviations from the norm – remember the Village People denying they were nellies once they hit number one? – that was how things stayed till the early Eighties.

"Everyone wants their token homo band now"
      Pete Burns on record companies in 1984, *Melody Maker*

So what changed, so that during 1984 there were weeks on end when it seemed you had to be gay, bi or trannie to get onto the chart? Well, the world outside for one thing, but we could argue the extent of that one till the cows come home. Nearer the centre of the industry, the strength of the punk shake-up in the late Seventies helped concentrate industrial minds wonderfully. One thing the major companies soon realised through punk was that "the kids" were a little more *perverse* than they'd thought; if they wanted their money they'd have to sign up pervert bands. Marc Almond might just have been one more camp little Northern boy with a hit record if he hadn't also been the genius of sleaze.

Marc Almond's New Year Resolution, when asked by teeny mag *Record Mirror*: *"To do as much of every vice as possible."*

Never actually one to say he was gay, Marc's first hit with Soft Cell was "Tainted love", and that's what he's sung of ever since – with the accent on tainted. Even his pet pythons are called Sodom and Gomorrah. Whether or not he was gay soon became academic; more to the point was whether there was any bag he *wasn't* into. For a while

Almond was huge, but instead of cutting his cloth and dropping songs about Sex Dwarves from his repertoire as he got bigger, he became even more wilful. By the time he was singing of "scum fucking sucks" (on *Torment and Toreros*) airplay was negligible. ("There's at least one line in every song that would stop it being played on the radio", he told the *NME*.) Almond's star shone bright whilst his admirers were an uneasy mix of teen fans and a more sophisticated crowd, but there came a time when only the staunch fans remained. Luckily his numerous loyal Gutterhearts (as they're called), plus a few people in the business who still admire Almond's integrity and compassion, continue to listen to his ever-improving work. His audience is smaller, but Almond continues to buck the system by singing of transsexual flamenco dancers whilst rotting the minds of the kiddies. But the first boy to make the system work *for* him was Georgie.

Fiona Russell Powell: "For once and for all are you gay?"

Boy George: "Well, to the local bricklayer I suppose I would be, but probably not to you if you think in that sort of terminology. I don't really know because I've never not done one or the other... I'm not a sexual person."

The Face, November 1982

It seems incredible that it's only two years since Musical Youth pulled out of supporting Culture Club on tour because of George's "dubious sexual image". Now that the tide is turning against him again, it's easy to underestimate George's effect on ordinary people. Whatever else, he has radically questioned stereotyped ideas of male and female, and ultimately that is probably the most important question there is. In a peculiar kind of way it does say something about the times that George is the first man ever to make the cover of *Cosmopolitan*. On the other hand – and despite wonderful quotes like telling *NME* that "the world dictates that heterosexuals make love whilst gays have sex" – George's description of himself as "an honest hypocrite" rings bells.

"Fuck credibility. Who needs credibility when you can end up like Jimi Hendrix?"

Boy George, *NME*, September 1984

The main thrust in George's interviews is that our sexuality is infinitely more complex and multi-layered than we presume it to be. It's a strong point to make, but the message doesn't reach out further than his interviews – mostly those in the more sophisticated end of the pop press. It seems strange that someone who obviously thinks hard about sexuality and gender chooses to completely ignore such topics in his lyrics, which is where most song-writers try to express their feelings. How much, I wonder, has he conceded to the showbiz assumption that you must never offend the ten year olds and grannies, because they're the people who turn you from a star into a megastar?

Because George's image, though androgynous, has *always* been totally unerotic and sexless; the friendly clown. Until recently, that is, when he has started to drag up like a very glamorous – and I'd say sexy – transvestite. Perhaps his popularity appears to be waning because he's looking more like a woman, or perhaps he's allowing himself to look more like a woman because he knows his popularity is waning. Maybe it's all just coincidental. Whichever way, it seems to be dawning on record buyers that recent Culture Club material is thin. George has settled for summery sounds on more than one level – but it looks like winter outside. Still, whether he sinks or swims, George will never be broke. And you can't tell me that he hasn't exhibited bravery and encouraged other people to test themselves. Which is, I guess, why the world chooses heroes.

"I love Kate and I want to have a baby by her... with my looks and Kate's I think we will be able to produce something sensational."
Marilyn (on Kate Garner, his manager's girlfriend) quoted in "The Girls In Marilyn's Life", a five-part series in *The Sun*.

Quite simply, some people will say anything to get into the papers. It's a sadness that Marilyn's music was beginning to improve by the time he had his first whopping flop single, but by then things had gone too far with the general public: cynical attitudes foster cynical responses. The most interesting aspect of the Big Mal phenomenon was that normally hetero punters admitted they wouldn't mind giving him a poke. One hears similar things about fellow-androgyne Pete Burns, but unlike Marilyn ("Nobody knows what I do in bed apart from me. I don't do anything in bed except sleep anyway."), Burns is *ferociously* bisexual. He's also a dirty-mouthed bitch.

'It should be mentioned that on tour Pete shares his hotel room with his wife AND one of the guys in the band. As at home there are lots of beds around. "So I can give it or take it depending on the mood I'm in. I don't know which way to turn sometimes. I mean, who needs masturbation?"'
Sandy Robertson, *Sounds*, March 1984.

Burns may not be in line for any Sensitive Young Man of

the Year awards, but at least he's not mealy mouthed. So why no fifteen minutes of fame? Until recently you could presume it was because Dead Or Alive was a musically uninteresting band. But that notion is stretched to the limit by the excellent "You spin me round (like a record)" which is atop the Boystown chart as I write. Quite simply it makes most Hi NRG records sound exactly what they are – the aural equivalent of watching paint dry. But it's not getting the airplay it needs. Maybe Burns has been around so long and was considered "dangerous" in the industry before Frankie made "danger" into big business. More to the point, Burn's record company has never given him the *real* hype.

"We really had to hit hard to get off the streets, child... we had to give it loads of sex because that was the easiest and quickest shocker to get attention."

Holly Johnson, NME, November 1983.

Note the word "easiest". At first Holly and Paul – let's face it, who can put a name to the three token hets? – seemed refreshing because unlike so many of their contemporaries they were outspokenly homo. The sob stories (doubtlessly true) about FGTH being considered too blatantly gay to sign up by record company execs who were themselves faggots, added fire. And a last minute BBC ban on "Relax" not only helped to push FGTH to number one but also gave them a name as Sexual Outlaws/ Everybody's Heroes. A year on, they're viewed with suspicion.

'"We're not a gay band, we're a band who just happened to be fronted by a couple of faggots," says Brian, revving up.'

Sounds, January 1983.

What "Relax" did was prove that, in a certain context anyway, the record buying public was again more easy-going about gayness than the industry had recognised and it took an independent-run label, ZTT (licensed, however, to a major company) to prove the point. What Frankie and ZTT sussed was that a bored public in the midst of a depression was ready for Bread and Circuses; the gay slant to "Relax" (plus the ads promising "twelve inches of pleasure") was the extra touch of shock/outrage that was the icing on the cake.

The Frankies prove there's nothing very liberating any more about admitting you're a gay man *per se* – if there ever was. What matters is what you do once you're out of the closet and – face it – integrity isn't a word you associate with Frankie or ZTT. Sex is incidental – what they are about is money. "Relax" might have been a stunning little record, but thirteen different remixes for public consumption is grasping even by music biz standards; it's no surprise that Holly's drunken message to Frankie fans on the B-side of the "The power of love" cassette-single was "If you're true fans you'll buy us all XJ-6s"! Maybe he's joking again. Who knows? You could believe anything of an organisation which pushes out FRANKIE SAY ARM THE UNEMPLOYED t-shirts while itself being the epitome of the capitalist money-making machine.

"I'm aiming at Mr and Mrs Bloggs, or that wee boy and lassie who live down the road."
Jimi Somerville, *NME*, November 1984.

The fascinating thing about Bronski Beat is that they're an openly gay band who, without pushing shock/outrage bombast have built up a devoted following on their music alone. And it's by no means only amongst gays. Sheryl

Garratt, in her astute and quite moving memoir of her days as a Bay City Roller fan (in her book *Signed, Sealed and Delivered*, co-written with Sue Steward) makes the point that everyone, including the record industry, always assumes that teenage girl fans are motivated by sex-obsession whereas in fact they're more likely to look on their male idols as chums. It goes some way towards explaining why three unpretentious homosexual men who have always been candid about their sexuality get mobbed by girls after an appearance on *The Tube*, and also get some of the heftier bags of fan-mail at *Smash Hits*. Indeed the only real reaction against them has been in the music press, particularly Biba Kopf's homophobic *NME* review of their album ("Nobody gives a toss what they get up to in the dark, and that's what troubles them.")

Bronski Beat have on the whole steered away from the agitprop stance of Tom Robinson while remaining idealists who sing openly about gay relationships and some of the every-day experiences of gay men. They seem aware of their present limitations ("I've yet to develop diversities in my singing," admits Jimi. "The sound gets a bit repetitive.") and though their message is secondary to the music they make, it's still very important to them. Whether they will suffer artistically because they have aligned themselves closely to the gay "movement" and being "ideologically sound" remains to be seen. The record industry is both hypocritical and tough, and the Bronskis still seem like three wee boys who have wandered into a business they haven't yet got the measure of. Whatever else, they're certainly not going to be forced into any vinyl closet.

"I don't recognise such terms as heterosexual, homosexual, bisexual and I think it's important that there's someone in pop

who's like that. These words do great damage, they confuse people and they make people unhappy so I want to do away with them."
Morrissey, *Smash Hits Annual 1985.*

My own particular candidate for sainthood is Morrissey, who artistically is streets ahead of most of the people we've been talking about. He's a man who monitors his emotions in public, who's not afraid of revealing himself as unable to play any of the games which men are expected to play. "That's what people use songs for, to look at their own mixed up feelings," says Pete Shelley, who Morrissey resembles and echoes. And, like Shelley, Morrissey is careful to leave his songs open to interpretation, to leave the lyrics to his love songs gender-free. In the end, part of the message is that "gay" and "straight" are just forms of shorthand to which the world pays too much attention and is thereby crippled by. It all makes complete sense. And yet...

The trouble is that in the real world pigeonholing still exists, and most of us have to live with it. Morrissey is celibate by choice and to an extent this frees him from being expected to comment on sex and sexuality in the way that most pop stars are going to have to deal with for a long while yet. The experience of recent years indicates what some of us have suspected for a long time – that a performer's "deviant sexuality" is considered more important or taboo by the music industry and press than by the public.

Whether attitudes appear to be changing because teen idols are becoming more open or whether pop is getting gayer because general attitudes are changing is impossible to answer. What will be interesting will be to see whether audience's attitudes become more illiberal in 1985 when we can expect questions about Aids and pornography/

censorship (re the Gay's The Word Trial) to loom large in all those pop star interviews. It will be a time which, to use a most sexist phrase, will sort the men from the boys. Speaking of which, the absence of women in this article will not have gone unnoticed. Quite simply: you show me an out lesbian mainstream singer, and I'll write about her. The added difficulties for women of being openly gay in the music business offer material rich enough for another article.

But meanwhile I leave you with pop manager Simon Napier-Bell, talking about his protegees, the rabidly "normal" Wham!

"But again, I saw something in Wham! that no-one else seemed to see, which is the Hollywood thing of the two buddies, the two cowboys. You know, during the film one falls in love, the other goes to a brothel, but at the end they always ride off together. It's never sexual but it's definitely homoerotic and it's never really been done in rock before."
Simon Napier-Bell, *NME*, October 29 1983.

Now you try telling me that the industry hasn't learned a few things over the last couple of decades.

Gay Times, February 1985

We've Only Just Begun

THE COMMUNARDS

What, "You are my world" *again*? Three singles off the album already, and now "You are my world" *again*? I know it should have been a hit the first time round and all that but are we not scraping barrel-bottom, boys?

"It's called London Records squeezing every last inch of spondulics they can out of the album," says the wee Scottish half of the double act.

"Wringing every single brass farthing out of it," leers the epicene other half.

So didn't you kick up?

"We couldnae really..."

"We both thought the song should have done better, so we were quite pleased really..."

"And it's just a few extra drumbeats added. We've done a whole new dance-mix that shows how far we've advanced since we first recorded it nearly two years ago. And, on the dub version my flat-mate Connie does a safe-sex rap; it's the first queen-rap ever!"

We three queens sit in a lugubrious TV studio canteen, overlooking the grey Father Thames and marvel at how wonderful Radio 1, who banned the single the first time round because it was a gay love song, have slapped it onto the A-list toot-sweet now the boys in the band are big stuff. An odd duo, these two. Jimmy is his well-scrubbed, rosy-cheeked Ovaltiney self, perky as ever. Richard, the chainsmoking aesthete who I always imagine sitting on a French boulevard in the 1890s drinking absinthe, tubercularly.

Cheese and chalk, these boys, which is probably what keeps them together; like Fred and Ginge, they just *love* to disagree.

"There was a point where Radio 1 could ignore us," says the lazy drawl. "But they don't dare to now."

"Och, but maybe it didn't get airplay first time round because the song itself was too advanced at the time. Now everybody's saying it's great whereas, before, they all said it wasnae right," says the pint-sized one.

The (triumphant) Eurotour is over. A few club dates in the US have nudged "Don't leave me" into the top sixty There are a couple of gigs to do in Spain. And then a month off to work at home, putting material together for the next album. I've never known everything be so calm on the Commie front. There's a danger we're all going to fall asleep. Except that – in that most disgusting phrase in the English language – I have a bone to pick with wee Jimmy.

That Mr Somerville has always been an openly gay pop star, and a loud one at that, is a marvellous thing. It is, however, something else when he and the NME between them begin dragging others out of the closet by the hair. We are talking Pet Shop Boys, of course; a story picked up by *The Sun* and trumpeted across the nation as "Say you're gay, Jimmy tells Pets". Does he regret invading Tennant and Lowe's privacy?

"The only thing I regret is that it made it sound like a bitching session, which it wasn't. I was asked about it at the time when there was anger there. Richard and I and Andy Bell of Erasure were trying to do something positive about Aids, get a benefit together, and no other gays on the pop scene would join in. It was a passionate emotional response on my part, but the whole context of the conversation was broken down into a couple of sentences. You know what it's like when you mention something to a journalist and it gets blown sky-high."

I'm sorry James, but surely it's a question of ethics. What, motives apart, is the difference between you dragging the Pets out of the closet and *The Sun*, as they did, dragging out three-quarters of The Housemartins?

"I'm sorry, I've no time for regrets when someone can be so influential, especially in the situation we're having to face now, with all the gay plague propaganda. It's any queen's duty, no matter how high a level they're at, or what business they're in, if they have the power where they can influence things, to be open about their gayness.

"It's different if you're working on the factory floor, but you're in a cushy position being a pop star, you've got so much more freedom and flexibility."

"I don't agree with that," says Richard. "I don't see why a gay pop star isn't entitled to the same sort of respect you give to someone else on the shop-floor. Obviously, I think gay people should come out, but of their own volition. And I think Jimmy should regret saying it. But I can understand his frustration as well. The indifference we came across trying to get the bill together for the benefit was really frustrating. We contacted lots of people, some of whom we knew to be gay and some were straight.

"But we got no response at all, other than people saying they'd phone back, which they never did. Paul Weller did the benefit and Daryll Pandy flew over especially to do it. But Andy Bell apart, none of the gay people responded to what we were doing."

But was it through indifference? Or fear of being associated with the "distasteful"?

"Who knows? All I know is that the situation required a better response than that, and I get fucked off with people being prissy and pathetic about it."

Jimmy: "They're shit-scared. But you cannae just sit back."

Richard: "More than anything, it makes you feel so isolated. It's ironic that gay people often feel isolated in

165

their work-places, we feel exactly the same thing in our work-place."

Jimmy: "Which is why, if Neil Tennant had seen what I'd said put into context, maybe he'd understand what I was saying. It's sad that it came out in the way that it did."

We sit like the three old codgers in *Last Of The Summer Wine*, chewing the cud. As a gay man, I share Jimmy's frustration. Yet, as someone who has worked in the gay press for years, I'm not about to give up my belief in the cardinal rule of gay journalism: that no one has the right to force other gays out into the open. If we're going to point fingers, the main fault lies with the journalist who reported Jimmy's remarks in the first instance, though, as Richard points out, "Journalists are providing copy to sell newspapers and, regardless of how good your intentions, if you give them a juicy piece of gossip it's going to get used."

But I still find something a little too near thought-police-time in Jimmy's attitude. Until now, the public scraps with Larry and Steve Bronski, Marc Almond et al have been good camp fun. But this is a bit different. Isn't he beginning to sound a bit self-righteous?

"I think you're treating these people a bit too sensitively. It's not like they've suddenly discovered something about themselves and they're traumatised by it. The reason they don't come out is for their own commercial safety."

But how can you be sure of that?

"Och, it's obvious."

"Funnily enough," says Richard, "on commercial terms I don't honestly think it makes that much difference. You could sleep with goats and people would still buy your records if they liked them. But if Jimmy does sound self-righteous in the press, it's been made to look that way. If *The Sun* can run what is supposed to be a two-page

166

'Exclusive interview' with him which is in fact a handful of old quotes of his taken out of context next to fake questions that have been cobbled together by Gary Bushell, it just shows we only have so much control over what's going on.

"You just have to take the risk. We feel we have a lot to say and it's important that our views get across, so we talk in the knowledge that there will inevitably be some amount of distortion."

"Either you don't do interviews," says Jimmy. "Or you do them and take the slap in the face that comes with it when you say something that's a bit out-of-hand."

Speaking of which, the final score of The Communards' Great Ethics Debate was one-all, with Richard seeing it as an "absolute moral value that you don't drag people out," and Jimmy sticking firmly to his guns. We agree to differ.

Two years on, after a shaky start, The Communards are now a well-established hit making band. They're not as popular as they were with some music critics, though, who are beginning to find them distinctly, well, *poppy*.

"Those people seem to think that we think of ourselves as being something different – arty, or something," says Jimmy. "But we're no'. We're just another pop band, that's coming from another angle maybe. There's nothing wrong with being a commercial band as long as you're putting out good stuff."

That wasn't quite the story in the early days.

"I think maybe back then we had the wrong interpretation of what the band was. In the beginning all a band has to rely on is the feedback from the music press. But the touring has changed us, now that we've seen the effect of the band on ordinary punters," reckons Richard. "Their reaction seems so much more important than what a journalist who's got particular views on music thinks about your record.

167

"Obviously the critics have gone distinctly lukewarm on us, but it doesn't bother me in the least. We never claimed to be representative of anything, we're not flogging any particular idea. We're just writing popular music to please ourselves and others, but, for some people, that's not sufficient. But it stands to reason that people who think The Jesus & Mary Chain are the best band in Britain aren't going to like us."

So who are *fave* bands, Ricardo?

"Abba and the London Symphony Orchestra."

Their new album may take some time yet, if it's left up to Jimmy.

"We've got loads of ideas that just need firming up," says Coles, pointedly staring at the Scottish one. "I'm the kind of person who likes to have three albums' worth of stuff up our sleeve before we go into the studio, but I have to do a great deal of whining and moral blackmail to persuade Jimmy to get an album's worth together."

Fred: "I think it's better if we take our own pace..."

Ginge, even more pointedly: "Yes, Jimmy, but of course the trouble is that our paces are very different."

There's no doubt The Communards are becoming increasingly aware that they're working in a market-place. Nowadays Richard doesn't blush at the word Presentation: "It's important that we represent ourselves and our ideas in a way we think is adequate. We've learned an awful lot very quickly about how those ideas we sit and talk about at home finally get presented as a product. We're much better at judging how things will be received and how to tailor what we want to put across in the form of messages and image."

"We don't really have an image," protests the wee one.

"Oh Jimmy, of course we do. Not one cooked up by a marketing manager. But everyone in this business has an image, including us. I think the live shows presented it very well, whereas the album-cover didn't. It was too po-faced, it didn't even hint that we have a sense of humour. But it'll be better now that Jimmy's beginning to take control of that art-work."

The Communards think of their careers as a series of year-long projects "for our own happiness" and are content enough to leave marketing decisions, reissues included, to London.

Jimmy: "It's quite important in a way that we do keep up momentum and keep visible, as at the moment we're the only two up-front gay men in the business, blah, blah. Okay, it's a reissue of an old song, but it's an 'up' gay love song and, at the moment, it's very important to make people realise that there is still reason to celebrate love between men. No matter how devastating the whole Aids thing is, love and gay love are going to go on forever. You have to show hope."

That's why they were delighted to do a public service ad on Aids for Scottish Television. "The whole message was 'We Can Beat Aids', except, for some reason, the IBA wouldn't let them use the word beat, and made STV change it to 'We Can Fight Aids'," says Jimmy. "We actually talked about condoms and safe sex – unlike the Government's ads where they have a bunch of lilies thudding on a coffin, which says absolutely nothing of any help to anybody."

Richard: "The message has to be that there's hope. I was watching TV with someone who actually has Aids when that advert came on, and it was so emotionally upsetting – all that chipping out of gravestones doesn't help anybody. What kind of service is the Government providing to people already in that situation?"

Jimmy: "Nothing at all's being done for people with the

illness which is why we're doing so much work for the Lighthouse Project, which is setting up hospices run on community lines where people can go and die with a bit of dignity."

We talked of Diamanda Galas, whose album *The Divine Punishment* Jimmy thinks is "brilliant, but so moving and depressing, I had to take it off after two minutes", and her conviction that we must also try to look on Aids as an opportunity given to us to find the humanity in ourselves.

"I often wonder what would happen if one of us developed it," muses Jimmy. "What the reaction would be. At least once a day I say to myself 'Would I just disappear and become a recluse? Or would I use it to my own advantage and other people's to talk directly about it as an Aids sufferer and try to give an insight to other people?'"

Richard: "Personally, I don't think you can blame anybody for choosing to fuck off and die in peace and quiet."

It's their readiness to talk about life and death and messy things like that which most irritates The Communards' critics, yet one wonders who else would be doing it if they weren't around. The Communards, too, are piss-bored with their Angry Gay Young Men media profile but, on the other hand, they're determined to keep talking about sexual politics if no-one else is prepared to do it.

"Everybody thinks that all being queer is is having a gay bar to go to on Saturday nights. But there's much more to work towards than that," says Jimmy. "There shouldn't even have to be those labels 'gay' and 'straight' but, until it's commonly accepted that it's perfectly natural for anybody to sleep with whoever they want you've got to define yourself."

We discuss the new album which Jimmy wants to be all-soul. Richard insists it'll be "diverse" like the last one. They agree it'll probably be a synthesis of the two, and that Jimmy will probably end up doing a solo soul set on his own, which he's desperate to tempt Norman Whitfield or Gamble & Huff into producing. They agree they miss Sarah Jane Morris – now off to pursue a solo career – though Richard points out that "we've never wanted to limit ourselves to working with any one person, and we'll probably be getting someone else in to sing." And they agree that over the years they've probably said everything they're ever going to say in an interview. Such unanimity is extraordinary.

Melody Maker, February 21, 1987

The Bell Boy

ERASURE

Andy Bell always knew he'd be a star. But now that he is one, he's shell-shocked. "I just can't imagine ninety three *thousand* people going into their record shops in one week and asking for our record. But that's what they did with "Sometimes" last week. It's just beginning to sink in..." Toasting his toes at the coal fire in the North London flat he shares with his American boyfriend Paul, the twenty two year old Peterborough born vocalist with Erasure appears shy and soft spoken. But there's a certain razzmatazz about his opinions that reminds you of his outrageous and wildly entertaining stage persona.

"I don't particularly go all out to be outrageous on stage, but I suppose I do inside. It's not for shock value, though – it's more personal, like seeing how far you can push people. It's like the first time you tell your mum or your best friend you're gay, you can always tell them more after that. I see it as an initiation thing. I'm not particularly in love with our songs really, and because I don't see them as serious I've had to put on this facade of being a comedian. It's interesting, because the new songs are more serious – we'll have to see how I'm going carry them off without laughing."

If a week is a long time in politics, you can image how long eighteen months is in pop. That's the amount of time it's taken Erasure to get a British hit single. It can't have been easy for Andy Bell – an unknown fronting a band formed by one of Eighties pop's most respected musicians, Vince Clark, who since 1981 has been forming bands, having huge hits and then immediately either leaving them (Depeche Mode) or breaking them up (Yazoo, The Assembly).

As well as having the unenviable task of stepping into the dead men's shoes of Alison Moyet and finding his voice constantly – and unflatteringly – compared to hers, Bell also watched a series of brilliant little pop singles bellyflop, apart from the occasional Australian number one. What kept Erasure going was their live shows, glued together by this ebullient young man with a bilious taste in stage drag, who soon proved himself a charismatic, aggressive, uncompromisingly camp stage performer. The critics hardly noticed, but Erasure were building up a huge and ever increasing devoted live following.

"I've always found I'm a show person and that's what I've got to give people. As to the camp, I really used to love Debbie Harry of Blondie and that whole glamorous thing of being just like another Monroe, which is what I used to trip into. So I suppose that's one of the reasons why I'm over the top on stage. Sometimes it was a bit disheartening, especially at the occasional university gig when the audience was very straight and they'd barrack you. I've been learning the hard way how to entertain a hall full of people and I'm still learning now. I don't honestly know if I'll ever be satisfied by a gig.

"What was nice was watching the number of diehard fans increase. A lot of them were heavily into Depeche Mode and Vince, and there were a few who were into Bronski Beat and The Communards and Marc Almond, and they put us in the same category. But we've never had much of a gay audience in straight venues, because not many gay men go out to gigs. I know I wouldn't go to a straight venue unless it was for someone I was really into: a lot of those venues are very hetero and macho."

Andy, who met Vince Clark by answering a 'Vocalist Wanted' ad in *Melody Maker*, has, of course, been out-gay from the beginning: "Right from the moment we started recording I used to say to myself 'You really have to come out in the press, 'cos that's who you are', but I didn't know how people did it. So I want to a seminar on *Gays & Rock* at the ICA to try to speak to Jimmy Somerville about it. He wasn't there so I got talking to Tom Robinson and asked him how to do it, because I thought maybe you had to put out a press release announcing it or something. He explained that he's just worn a badge and people asked what it meant at interviews. So I realised that it was no big deal, it's just something that develops – and it did."

The most remarkable feature about Mr Bell is his jaw dropping honesty. Personally I'll never forget my first interview with him and his then new partner Vince, when I asked them about any difficulties they faced as a gay man and a straight man working together and Andy admitted that he fancied Vince rotten. Had he actually told Vince this before the interview? "No. I find things like that in interviews. If I want to say something to him I'll wait for an interview and say it there. There have been times, and I'm sure there will be again, when I'm so into him that I get really hung up about it. It's sort of like a forbidden love, but I'd never try to intrude on him.

"After all, I don't think you need to affirm love by having sex. Vince isn't gay and it's enough for me that he can be so affectionate sometimes that I feel his love flooding out. That's really nice. There have been times in the past when I've heard him screwing with his girlfriend and it's freaked me out. I still get very jealous of her and she of me, but we've told each other that, and are agreed it's something that neither of us can help.

"I still feel a bit inhibited with Vince. I like talking about being gay a lot of the time and he's bound to get a bit fed up with it; he doesn't particularly want to make a big thing out of it. When he started Erasure he was just looking for another singer for a pop band, without any hassle. But he's really pleased with how it's turned out, because it's made the whole thing so much more interesting – we're not just doing it purely to make hits. We tend to talk about sex in a roundabout kind of way. Like at a photo session I'll say 'I really fancy sucking some dick tonight' and he'll go 'Urrgh, how can you say that...?' We're still sussing each other out, but we're getting to the point where we can say anything to each other. I just hope it'll be really good."

Not that Bell has always been so honest. Growing up in a working class family in Peterborough, he was "an awful child, I was really naughty when I was at junior school. If my mum sent me to bed early I'd threaten to leave home and she'd say 'Fuck off then' and throw my shoes at me. I'd escape out of my bedroom window and go round to my nan, who spoiled me rotten, and give her the whole biased story. I was jealous of my little brother and four sisters and I'd get crayons and write on the wallpaper left handed and sign their names so they'd get into trouble for it.

"I shared a bedroom with my little brother and when he was two years old I'd run across the landing on my tiptoes to make it sound like him so my parents would shout upstairs 'Gary, get back into bloody bed!' I'd nick whole packets of chocolate Penguins and eat them all at one go and hide the evidence, and nick money out of my mum's purse. But then one night I had a nightmare about how we were really poor and I stole from my mum's purse and threw the money in the garden so it was lost. I woke up crying and told my mum all about it and that changed things. By the time I went to senior school I'd started being really honest. Mum and I could talk together about anything – when I was thirteen or fourteen we used to talk about her sexual feelings and frustrations she'd feel about my dad, and I'd try to help her and advise her, because she could talk to me better than she could to my dad."

Although Andy didn't realise he was gay until after he'd left school and come down to London, there were early intimations. "I was quite lonely when I was nine or ten, and when I walked to my nan's there were always people on the street who shouted 'Quentin' at me, and I could never understand why because I didn't know about Quentin Crisp. And then when I was in the sixth form, all the other boys stopped talking to me. That was because I had a school friend stay at my home, and we'd talk all evening about how maybe we were bisexual, and he told me all these stories about how he'd stayed at his uncle's in London and had woken up in the morning to find himself being sucked off by his uncle.

"So when he was asleep I started playing with his cock and had a wank. When I woke up the next morning he wasn't there and for the rest of the week he slept on the sofa. By the time I got back to school all my friends were really stand offish and not speaking. A friend told me why and I felt really hurt that they didn't have the courage to tell me to my face, but after a while I thought 'Fuck you lot'. Because they'd always made out they were so open minded and could take anything, and of course they couldn't. After a while people started speaking again, but by then I couldn't have given a fuck."

Which has pretty much been his attitude ever since. Even when he was "thrown out of school" and spent three years on the dole ("I really enjoyed that because I'm dead lazy and I'd never had any money before and that was the first time I had money of my own to spend") Dinger, as he's known to his friends, "always said I'd go to London and be a pop singer and be as famous as David Bowie!" When he did move to London it was with a woman "who supported me for a year." Is he bisexual then? "I have slept with a woman though I didn't particularly enjoy it, and when I started sleeping with men I found I really loved it. But a girl started chatting me up a while ago and I found myself being interested on the level of 'just what is a fanny really like?' And I've had erotic dreams about it, but they only go so far. I can only really imagine maybe getting the woman turned on and putting my hand on her fanny, but that's about how far it goes."

Moving to London meant innumerable nights at The Bell "dancing all night and getting drunk and having a really good time" and his first band, a duo with his friend Pierre: "He was the kind of bloke who had gone round beating gay people up, so working with him was a challenge. We got to really respect each other and I still do so now – he's still struggling and doing his own thing and he'll never give up. He works on building sites and things, just to get the money to go and do recordings. He really believes in his music."

Now past that stage himself, Andy Bell is experiencing the record business's subtle pressures to conform. "My record company, Mute, know by now that if I want to do something I do it. Pauline, who looks after the press, didn't want me to do this interview at first, but then she made her mind up that I might as well do it because she reckoned that the papers would be writing about me anyway, whatever happens. That's the best attitude to take, though I'm not sure what it'll be like if the tabloids try turning the whole thing sordid. I don't know how I'd cope with that. Mute is very understanding, though when we went over to America, our US record company really tried to push us to keep quiet about the gay thing."

One area where Bell has had to compromise is over the question of clothes and image. "At the moment I haven't got enough patience or time to put together something as clever as Boy George did, but there is a bit of me that likes that sort of thing. But there have been pressures on me not to be too over the top; the person who gets us our TV spots persuaded me to wear jeans and a t-shirt because he reckons if I was too outrageous we wouldn't get on TV again, and I have to think of Vince and the other people who are involved. Our first video, which had me and Vince in drag doing a can-can, hardly got shown at all. For the second single I wanted to be like Jane in the cartoon strip, a kind of sexy space Judy Garland in cami-knickers, but the record company said no because they reckoned it wouldn't get shown on kids' telly, and when I thought it over I decided they were probably right.

"In the end we reached a compromise that I could be Judy Garland in *The Wizard of Oz*; that was acceptable to them because it was like panto. When the day came to shoot the video I was really disappointed with the costume – it was really tacky and stapled together, but I put it on anyway. We had all these little kids from a ballet school dressed up as little angels, and a really awful little eight year old girl came straight up to me, pulled a face and said 'Are you a pouf?' It really hurt me. I thought, 'You little bitch, how dare you?' But it made me so uncomfortable that I took it off in the end and wore a Captain Scarlet suit with ruby red slippers."

"If you don't care, they can't take it away from you" is a quote Andy Bell made early in his career, and he has lived up to it ever since. How much longer he'll be able to hang on in there and keep his principles intact remains to be seen.

Gay Times, January 1987.

Design for Living

PET SHOP BOYS

"I was a glass collector in 1980 at the Dixieland Showbar, a nightclub on Blackpool's Central Pier. It was the year "Ashes to ashes" came out, and The Gap Band's "Oops up side your head", not only did the customers get into formation lines of twenty and do the rowing dance with all the movements, but the bar staff stopped selling drinks to do the dance *and* the glass collectors joined in too. When that record came on it was like suddenly finding yourself in the middle of a huge musical. It was absolutely, positively one of *the* best and most *wonderful* experiences of my life!"

Chris Lowe speaking. Moody synth player with the moody Pet Shop Boys, ha! As he speaks he's banging an imaginary tambourine with abandon, and simultaneously demonstrating the Oops dance – a kind of manic Hustle – in the ultra-respectable bar/lounge of the swish Palace Hotel in Madrid. Lowe's cohort, the epigrammatic Neil Tennant, looks on in his avuncular way, blessing us with the occasional barbed comment. You'd never find Neil in a formation line.

Personality wise they're just as different, as they are physically: the lofty Tennant as stately as a galleon, the impish Lowe shuffling along in his wake. I thought these Pets were supposed to be humourless, uptight poseurs, but I've obviously been watching too many of their videos. In fact, they're an ace music hall double act, even to the extent of taking turns – like the twins in the Bernard Shaw play – at beginning and ending each other's sentences. One's a clown, the other's a wit and they've had me laughing like a drain all day.

179

Not that they don't have good reason for a chortle or three. With two monster hit singles this year and a third on its way (the divine "Rent"), a complete monopoly of the numero uno singles spots all over Europe, "It's a sin" screeching like the proverbial bat out of hell up the US chart, and – in its first week of release – their new album *Actually* only held off the UK album pole position by Michael Jackson's *Bad*, the boys are already at least this year's most successful Britpop band.

They've come a long way in a couple of years and made it look so easy that they're constantly accused of being cynical pop strategists. After four years as assistant editor on *Smash Hits*, the reasoning goes, Neil Tennant has learned all the ropes about how to present, package and flog the perfect pop combo.

"Actually, people tend to ignore the fact that I was an editor at MacDonald Educational Publishing for five years, and that's where my organisational ability really comes from," says Tennant, whose flat Geordie drawl is pure Alan Bennett-on-Tyne. "You had to do everything there, from commissioning and supervising the writer and designer and illustrator to pasting it up yourself – the lot. I've always said that after editing *The Dairy Book Of Home Management*, which had a huge budget and made millions, a lot of this pop stuff seems easy."

Certainly, the Pet Shop Boys exert a great deal of control over their careers. They are guarded with the media – granting this interview, for example, only on the understanding that I wouldn't pry into their private lives. They only do a very limited number of interviews per record. They carefully vet each photograph of themselves before it goes out. They spend an inordinate amount of time planning, helping design and supervising the packaging of their product. They won't do charity records.

They won't even nowadays appear on compilation albums.

Neil: "Are we stroppy? I hope so! People always think because I was a pop journalist all the Pet Shop Boys things come from me, but really the group's attitude is set much more by Chris, who has a completely different way of looking at things to me. Normally I spell out to him why they want us to do certain things, but Chris is the one who says 'I don't care, I won't do it'. Because he has no rock 'n' roll background at all he often has a refreshing way of looking at things."

For refreshing read annoying sometimes, no doubt, but they're agreed on the question of compilations.

"We've decided not to do them for both commercial and artistic reasons," explains Tennant. "Firstly, if we have an album out I don't want to be on some EMI *NOW* compilation and have our own record company competing against us with our own songs; we had a flaming row with EMI over it, but we just said that if people want 'It's a sin', they can either buy our single or our album."

But other bands would argue that it's worth it for the extra royalties.

"They're wrong. What the rock business does to you is that it weakens everything, it waters everything down. You become part of a big gang and that's a bad attitude. We just don't like to be thrown in with lots of other groups. We were going to do songs for a new Steven Spielberg film until they suddenly announced there'd be other groups involved. We pulled out immediately. Chris in particular hates all that."

Chris: "Ugh, I *hate* pop gangs! When we went to see Madonna, I loathed being surrounded by all those pop people in the special enclosure; I'd far rather have been out front with everyone else. It's really embarrassing – you've got this strange relationship with people you recognise, like Bob Geldof. You know them and they know you from the papers or the telly, but you don't really because you've never been introduced, and you don't know whether to nod or not. It makes me cringe. I hate the idea of us being part of the whole pop thing, even though we are."

But, of course, exclusivity can be a selling-point. Have they cultivated a mystique?

"If I was being really truthful I'd probably have to say yes," says the tall one. "We've kind of negatively cultivated one by not doing things, and you suddenly realise some people think you've got a bit of a mystique. But obviously we don't want to be over-exposed and it's a way of avoiding that. You know what Boy George said about Prince: it's good he doesn't do interviews because when you meet him you realise he's a boring normal person. He's a muso who can dance. We didn't necessarily set out to gain mystique, but what we definitely set out *not* to do from the beginning was to present ourselves as a jolly pop group on the back page of *Jackie*."

Tell me more. Is this why you never smile in photos or on the box?

"Look, being in a pop group isn't about being presented as two real people. It's about being The Pet Shop Boys, and you know what you want to look like so it's important to keep up with vetting all the photos. Not necessarily because you want to look cosmetically beautiful, but because you don't want some half witted shot of you grinning like a pop group. That's what it's all about. Yes, of course we have a strong idea of what image we want presented to the public."

But doesn't this rather run counter to the oft-told tale of the two young men who met by chance in a music store, whose sole ambition was to record a disco single that would only be available on import in Britain, who wangled being produced by legendary Hi NRG producer Bobby O, and were no sooner in the import rack at Record Shack than they were the hottest ticket in town?

Neil: "No, no, there's no dichotomy there. It's the same thing, we've just never watered it down. When we wanted to be only available on import, we got that..."

Chris: "We never had a long-term aim, we just had short term goals. The first step was wanting the record on import, but we didn't see past that. We did it, and then it was 'What are we going to do now?' And you just keep on..."

Neil: "People get watered down in this business, but when *we* do something we know exactly what we want – otherwise we wouldn't do it. Like the covers of our records: someone told our designers they were amazed how we got away with the cover of *Please*, because it was so uncompromising – a tiny little photo on a huge white sleeve. But EMI trust our instincts. We knew what we wanted for our tour as well, and we couldn't get it. So we didn't do it..."

Ah yes, touring. One reason why the Pets have time to lavish so much care and attention on product presentation (and recording) is that they aren't schlepping around Andalusian dancehalls playing rock 'n' roll to the punters. These boys' idea of a gruelling Spanish tour is a heady couple of days of radio and press interviews: "Really, the questions are so formularised and inevitable that by the end of the day the interpreter could do the interviews for you," says Neil, archly. This is true. The two inevitable Euro questions at the moment are "Why are you called the Pet Shop Boys?" and "Why did you record with Dusty Springfield?" Also very popular is: "Why do we never see The Pet Shop Boys live?"

It's a good question. The boys tell the Spanish radio DJ

they've been planning a tour for two years, that it would've been easy to get a band together but they didn't want to just do a normal rock 'n' roll tour, but to work in 2000 seaters with a director and designer from the English National Opera whose last production, volunteers Chris – licking his chops – was a *Macbeth* set in an abattoir. Though the projected dates sold out the production was such an epic they'd still have been out of pocket by half a million, explains Neil sensibly.

"We thought of sponsorship, but sometimes sponsors want you to appear in ads – like David Bowie having to do that awful Pepsi ad with Tina Turner. And we couldn't do *that*," Chris tells his Spanish listeners, stirring it further by adding: "Besides, neither of us likes going to concerts. Both of us would rather watch Sam Fox performing 'Touch me' at a PA in a disco than see U2 in some awful stadium."

Ah, have we not hit upon the lingering subtext here? I remember Pete Burns once asking me why the hell the Pets kept pretending they're going to tour when we all know they aren't. Hasn't pop changed so much that there's no reason why a band should pretend it wishes to perform when they don't? After all, the band are flogging plenty of vinyl without live work, which is normally its commercial rationale.

"Well, I think if you asked somebody at CBS Records, say, they'd argue that it was actually the other way round nowadays," says Tennant, who admits that a *Smash Hits* staffer recently told him the rest of the staff were scared of interviewing him because he knows the ropes so well.

"But yes, we do have suspicions about touring. Both of us feel that lots of concerts we see are boring. When I was at *Smash Hits*, if any rock journalist was put on the rack and you turned it a few ratchets, he'd admit that nearly every show he'd seen was boring. It's great when they come on and for the first few minutes you think 'Oh wow, this is fab'. And then a couple of minutes later you're bored to tears, the sound's awful and all the journalists are in the bar gossiping, which is far more fun...

"Besides, groups do change on the road, and the demands of a big live audience can change and vulgarise your music. Eurythmics would probably disagree with me but I personally think their music has changed for the worse. They started off as a pervy synth duo and I really liked their records. She was a good singer and they did their own videos, which they seem to have stopped now. But something seems to happen when you hit big in America. People feel they can't get away with being a pervy synth duo and they've got to have a proper rock drummer and backing singers, and suddenly they've got a different-sounding set of songs. And so the next album reflects that change.

"It's a great cliché of rock journalism when an artist tells you 'Our new album represents what the band sounds like live nowadays, which is a lot harder and tougher', ie they've become a rock 'n' roll cliché. Ironically of course – and I think this is where people lose the thread of the plot – the new Eurythmics album hasn't been that successful in America."

For all their pop strategy, however, the PSB wouldn't be where they are without their facility for crafting some splendidly catchy, intelligent pure pop records. Whether you loved or loathed "It's a sin", I bet you found yourself singing along to it; and although we may all have liked a touch more of La Springfield on "What have I done to deserve this?", it was a record most of us found compulsively hummable. The album contains quite a few more very special pop ditties; the most special to my mind, being the sinister-laden "Shopping", a surprisingly political – for the Pet Shop Boys – picture of a greed obsessed Britain.

"Like a lot of our songs, it began with the title," says Tennant. "It was towards the end of last year when all those bloody 'Tell Sid' ads were out for British Gas. That whole thing of this desire to involve everyone in this minor bourgeois capitalism drives me mad; I really don't approve of this 'Everyone's going to make £60 each from buying shares', you know. So given that I had to write the words, and I didn't want them to be 'Gucci, Pucci, Fiorucci...'"

Chris: "I would have quite liked that, but I'm just the moron in the corner here..."

Neil: "And given that I was so angry at seeing this whole situation of people not buying houses to live in but in order to make £50,000 in six months time, it struck me that peoples' approach was very much like shopping. The Government's approach to the nationalised industries is that they're there to be bought and sold. 'You bought that? Now you can buy this. Buy British Telecom and soon you'll be able to buy the water, and then the jewel in the crown, the NHS'..."

But I'd never considered the Pet Shop Boys as political creatures.

"Because we don't present ourselves as a political group. In many ways there's nothing more embarrassing than pop stars talking about politics. No matter how deep-rooted one's political feelings are – and a lot of people in pop groups are socialists, probably wet liberal socialists; you, me and Simon Le Bon all want to keep the NHS going – we're all basically saying the same thing, and after a bit it sounds banal. People don't realise they're just saying what everybody else is thinking anyway, and they're talking down to people as well. So in the past we've tended to avoid these sorts of issues, and people tend not to ask us

186

about them anyway because that's not what the Pet Shop Boys are about."

And what kind of things make Chris cross?

"The same types of things as Neil, I suppose," says Chris. "But I don't really express them very often. I've got rather a flippant attitude to lots of things, actually..."

If I were asked what the biggest difference between the two Pet Shop Boys was, I'd say that though they're both very intelligent, only Tennant presents himself as thinking. There's a five year gap between them; does it show very often?

Tennant: "I'm aware of a difference in attitude over quite a lot of things; the gap between us is almost like the gap between the Sixties and Seventies. I was taking my O levels in 1970 and he was just starting grammar school, which is quite a big difference. My formative years were the mid to late Sixties, those golden years of liberalism which I see going out the window..."

Lowe: "...whereas when I went to university, my generation voted in Margaret Thatcher, and what's happening in Britain now makes sense to me. But there's not much of a gap in attitude, because if I do think anything Neil corrects me and says 'Don't be stupid'. Sometimes I wind him up by saying how good Mrs Thatcher is..."

I'm told that Tennant is so neat and tidy that when he's on a promotion tour he won't leave his hotel room of a morning before making his bed; I bet Chris doesn't. Though it's probably the mainspring of their creativity, their personality differences obviously cause difficulties. We may dismiss as hype the "Pets To Split" stories in the tabloids that were published a few days after this interview took place, though we can also conclude that Lowe's not turning up for a video shoot would drive the conscientious

187

Tennant into apoplexy. I'm reminded of Roy Hay once saying that if the whole of Culture Club died tomorrow, when they reached the Gates of Heaven Boy George would be there to check that they'd brought the right clothes. Is Tennant the same?

Lowe: "He's not as bad with me as George was with Culture Club – like a headmaster with a cane – though he's a bit like that with the record company. But there again, we're both on our toes in that way; we're always at the airport first, it's usually us who think ahead to rebooking our cars at the other end if our flights are changed..."

Tennant: "It's exhausting, actually, and we're at the point where a lot of bands start to give up and weaken, but even when we're doing promotions like this we're always having artwork and stuff flown out to us. You've got to pay attention to everything because if you don't think of something, nobody else will necessarily think of it for you. So even when we're away we're checking to see that the flyposters have been put up and that the record artwork is okay, because the visual thing is such an important part of us. I thought the cover of our Dusty single was as good as – maybe even better than – the record itself. It had so many resonances to it..."

Haven't they strayed into more dangerous territory with the new single "Rent"?

"Why should we run into trouble with it? Because it's about rent boys?" asks Tennant, the band's lyricist. "Jon Savage said to me 'Oh no, it's going to be your "Numbers", which was the single that caused so much trouble for Soft Cell – but I don't see it. Really it's just a love song about the relationship between two young people with the refrain 'I love you, you pay my rent'.

"It could be about a prostitute – a kept man or a kept woman – and the person keeping them. It could be about a marriage where the woman has given up her life to bring up the children and give him his happy home. I always imagine it to be about a politician and his mistress or wife – that's what the video will portray – and when I'm singing it I'm the wife or the mistress of the kept man."

But is a pop single's audience mature enough to accept Tennant adopting a female persona? The only precedent I remember is Marc Almond's 'A woman's story' and that didn't exactly get saturation airplay.

"I said this to a guy from *Rolling Stone* and he found it a bit weird, but my favourite singers are nearly all women, from Billie Holiday to Miss Springfield, from Dionne Warwick to Nina Simone.

"And so consequently when we write songs I often hear their voices in my head and I'm possibly influenced by them. But the real answer is – does it matter? It's a pop song, it's really romantic, you could smooch to it at a disco if you wanted to. I don't see why we should have any trouble at all, but we'll see if we do when we do it on *Tarbuck At The London Palladium* or whatever it's called."

Melody Maker, October 3 1987

Birth Death Sex Dreams

MARC ALMOND

"I've always been more interested in looking at people who have a more ingrained life on their faces than the average Radio One-ised, *Sun* reading zombies who comprise the mass. I have a hatred of the mass and hatred for ninety per cent of the people in this country, but a real intense love for the other ten per cent. People think it's a ridiculous statement to make, but in general I always think the majority is wrong and the minority is right and that's probably because I don't think I've ever fitted in in any situation anywhere in my life."

Ever the rebel, it's typical that Marc Almond has brought out his most overtly sexual – as well as his finest – album at the height of the strongest moral backlash most of us have ever experienced. *Mother Fist and Her Five Daughters* – the title track an ode to the joy of masturbation, inspired by the Truman Capote short story of the same name – may well be a safe sex first but it's not going to get played on the radio.

That's okay by Marc.

"I've come to the conclusion recently that I just can't compete in the pop field any more anyway. I'm too arty, that's what people say to me – too left field and off the wall. And in a sense I like to think of myself as outside pop anyway, I aim for something more. The people I like listening to, like Jaques Brel and Juliette Greco, are legitimate singers whose work isn't subject to the foibles of fashion and I want to do work like theirs. I've just had some of Verlaine and Rimbaud's erotic poems translated and I'm putting them to music and that's more interesting to me than having another hit record.

"Besides, when I record something that I think is a pop song it seems to stand out like a sore thumb amongst everything that's around it; it's not what an '87 conception of a pop record is meant to be. When I did my version of Cher's 'A woman's story', where I didn't change the gender so it could be read on two or three levels – which was quite a dangerous thing to do in some ways – it got one of my best chart placings in a while and the radio actually seemed to like it, they played it quite a lot. But at the end of the day they wouldn't have me on TV promoting it."

Just as they wouldn't show the video for his single before that "Ruby red", because it showed men cavorting on a bed: "It's fine for them if there's a woman involved but not if it's men; there's so much hypocrisy it's not true. But it's me the media doesn't particularly like, not the material – it's me they feel threatened by. Maybe I represent some unacceptable face of homosexuality or something...I'd suspected a conspiracy at the BBC for a long time because they never play my records but I'd never had it confirmed until the record pluggers went in with the last couple of singles and were told that the BBC just had a policy of not playing Marc Almond records.

"And what it came down to, apart from my being too 'subversive' for young people and too 'arty' and a bad influence, was they were told that the Head of Radio One was very offended when walking out of the lift at the Prince party at the Gardens to be confronted by Marc Almond wearing a rubber miniskirt and rubber trousers, kissing a boy in front of his wife. He was offended! What the fuck is he going to a Prince party with his wife for then? Prince's whole set was peppered with obscene innuendos and 'fuck this' swearing, yet I notice that Prince hasn't been banned from the radio!"

191

It's no wonder the sexy little beast is upset at this censorship, particularly given the excellence of his new album which has drawn universally glowing reviews. Many of the songs revolve around beds ("All life's dramas are played out in bed – birth, death, sex, dreams"): most are sexually outspoken, a thing Marc feels is particularly important in an age of Aids. "People are trying to pretend now that sex doesn't exist anymore and I think it's wrong for people to turn round and say 'Well, we thought sex was bad in the first place.'

"I've had people accuse me of helping to fuel what's happening but my argument is that I hope that what I write about or sing about becomes subject matter for other people's fantasies and a release for their tensions, because heavy sex isn't going to take place in the future and masturbation is going to become more important. Instead of trying to ban pornographic magazines and videos they should be encouraging them – they're going to become very important for people soon because they can use them at home as a sexual outlet. Otherwise there's going to be a helluvalot of sexually frustrated people in this country, because sex is the basis of so many of our desires and motivations. But there again, I'm one of those people who think that masturbation should be taught in schools."

Ever since "Tainted love", his first number one with David Ball when they were Soft Cell, Marc Almond has been a provocative creature: does he look back to those early days of the controversial "Sex dwarf" video (did they really stuff maggots up a transsexual's fanny, or was it just raw mince?) or the Egyptian-eye-on-the-palm-of-his-hand phase and wince? "I just realise sometimes how very naive I was and how much of my growing up I did in public. I was a little boy lost in the world and to some extent I still am, but I think I've developed much more as a person.

192

People tell me I've become more cynical though I just think I've become more realistic.

"But I don't particularly regret any of those things. Maybe I feel a bit embarrassed when I see the 'Sex dwarf' video, but my regrets really are the more superficial things like what an awful outfit I was wearing or what a terrible hairstyle I had. I just think 'I must have had too much acid that day'. But though things like 'Sex dwarf' were naive, in a silly way they broke down barriers. Maybe the way we went about it wasn't always right or clever but at the end of the day we broke a lot of taboos and set the scene for a lot of groups that have come up since, who've just basically been Soft Cell with Fairlights – saying the same things in the same ways."

At the time – five or six years ago now – Almond was criticised for being a voyeur, slumming it in Soho and taking home movies of the whores and rentboys plying their trade. "People used to see shallowness in me because they thought I was writing about a life I wasn't involved in, but when I left Leeds and came down to London that's where I found myself and those were the people I mixed with. I wasn't just a voyeur, I was a participant too and the people I met were the people on the streets and they were the ones I found I had the greatest affinity with.

"I'm not saying this in a big headed way but in the past couple of years I've had a lot of imitators come up after me who aren't the genuine article. But I know myself to be the genuine article; I feel I try to put over my life and the way I see life with honesty, and I put my search for a meaning in life into my songs of love and experience. If that's not coming over and people don't see that as a genuine honesty in me then that's my fault and not theirs; it's always the communicator that's wrong, never the person receiving the communication. Because I feel a part of that life. I go off on my own for long periods and I travel and these are the sights and sounds I mix with. I'm not drawn to anything else."

While the little minx is making a cuppa, I ratch through his record collection. Amongst all the expected Yma Sumacs and Lola y Manuels and Billy Furys and Libby Holmans and Judy Garlands lies a surprise Joni Mitchell. It figures, particularly in the context of Almond's new album; a shared self astuteness, a mutual capacity to show emotion without embarrassment, a common propensity towards the confessional in their music. "When it comes to relationships I always say 'you'll disappoint me if you don't disappoint me' and I think I'm a very masochistic person in a lot of ways. I get these various troubles and I invite them back again and again.

"I often find in my songs that I'm retreading the same path, usually because I'm searching for meaning in my life. As much as I've tried to deny it, I've often thought there's an underlying guilt in what I do and I tend to write as a confessional, to be free of guilt and things. You see it's at times of emotional turmoil that I've been at my most creative. *Mother Fist* came out of one of my terrible periods when I was losing my footing on reality, one of my periods when I was having great difficulty in harmonising Marc Almond the person and Marc Almond the persona.

"The album's very reflective because when I was writing it last year, I went through that period when I was coming up to thirty. It's what's called your Saturn Return period, which is a crisis time most people go through in their lives when they're changing from being a young adult to an adult adult. It gives you a strong awareness of things, and I got very nostalgic. I had a yearning to retrace old steps in order to find out where I am now. Who I am."

Almond admits he's always worn his insecurities and

his failures on his sleeve, and the new album is the most intimate of autobiographies. "'The sea says' is about how when I was an asthmatic, bronchial child my grandfather used to take me down to the beach on his shoulders for the fresh air, and it turned out to be a really evocative song. 'The room below' is about the time I first left home and had my first proper affair with someone, an artist, and we lived in a small, squalid basement flat. It was a time I tend to look back on as a period of freedom and self discovery and happiness. When I look for happiness I mostly look at the past.

"Even 'Saint Judy' is less about Garland than about myself, put under every glaring cruel light. It's partly about how I do have this Judy Garland persona and it's partly looking at the people caught in that kind of fag syndrome of liking to see people martyred and destroyed. Certainly there's been a part of me that glorifies self destruction and believes that out of it comes something beautiful and pure, like a phoenix out of the ashes."

Though he's far more open than he's ever been about his sexuality – "Well obviously there's no doubt about it, I'm a raving fag" – Marc Almond has split feelings about gay militancy in the pop world. "I always tend to get quoted as knocking Jimmy Somerville, though in fact I respect him a great deal. He has a belief and he's sticking up for it and that's a noble thing to do, but sometimes it gets too much I think. Like when he made statements about the Pet Shop Boys being gay to the press, when they'd never talked about their sexuality. It bothers me that Jimmy's attitude is a mirror image of *The Sun* mentality – 'witchhunt 'em and string 'em up to make good examples for all to see'.

"What The Communards stand for is important, no doubt, but it upsets me to see people minding other people's business. And I tend to think anyway that there's a lot more potential for being subversive with the Pet Shop Boys because they bring a lot of messages across in things that they do, without cramming it down other people's throats and alienating them. They're easing people into acceptance in a gentler way, creeping up from behind to get people by the back of their throats, whereas Jimmy would lunge straight for the throat. Both of them are dealing with gay and sexual issues, and both should be allowed to do it their way."

You don't think the only reason things have improved over the years is because some people have been both brave and loud? "What's improved over the years? Maybe there were improvements in the Seventies or early Eighties, but I don't see them now. All I see are the danger signs of gay liberation being stamped under the jack booted heel. When you look at the gay witchhunts at the moment, I personally don't blame any gay person in 1987 if they stay in the closet because they want to survive in their jobs. Some boy in a factory in Wakefield has no chance of getting away from the place. It's alright for Jimmy, he's done it – he's got away. But there are a lot of trapped people who are very scared."

But isn't it a bit easier for performers? "In some ways, yes, but there are so many witchhunts going on, with gay artists and performers being strung up and being made examples of as filthy evil perverts who are destroying the fabric of our society. Sometimes the only way to get messages across is through art, through trying to be more subversive..."

Though he's gone farther than most in his lyrics – "I live the life that I write about, but though I often get called a hedonist I'm not entirely sure what that means" – Marc Almond refuses to sing only of one kind of loving: "The thing is that I don't feel ghettoised. I write about heterosexual experience and love for women as well. I can write from that experience and I can appreciate both types of love. But sometimes I can't be forgiven by certain people for daring to write about both and the appreciation of both. There's only love for dogs and horses I don't write about, because I haven't experienced that yet."

So no subject matter is taboo? "I don't think I'd draw any lines really, thinking about it. I did an ep of George Bataille's work which dwelt on themes of child murder." Do you feel you have any responsibilities as an artist? "Not in that condescending way of treating your audience with kid gloves and wrapping them up in cotton wool. My responsibility, I always feel, is to educate as well as to entertain – they go hand in hand with me. Some people come and see me and they only see the camp side of it, they don't want to see past that. It doesn't matter if that's all they see, but obviously I'd prefer to feel that they've learned something, that I've helped break down a barrier or two in their minds."

In this day and age that kind of thinking, refreshing as it is, sounds almost old fashioned. "I think I am in some ways like that, in some ways I'm a bit of a moralist. 'The hustler', on the album, is a bit of a moral cautionary tale about a male prostitute who's getting old. But at the same time I'd say that we never really learn those lessons ourselves, we're always guilty of the things we moralise about. It's the human trait of hypocrisy, which I am often very guilty of myself."

He's unique, this boy that many feel is the most talented artist of his generation, yet there's always the danger that his candour and lack of caution will prove too much for the industry he's working in and that he will one day be marginalised out of existence: he has, for example, just been dropped by his record company. "Obviously I don't

197

fit in with what's happening on the pop scene: everything is smothered with horrible blanket of AOR-style American pap, every group wants to sound like everybody else – they've all got the same drum sound, the same production sound, the same Fairlight horn sections pumping away in the background. It's as though no one *wants* to sound original and everybody's getting numbed with a marshmallow coating of complete bland nothingness.

"Lazy music makes people lazy and all we're getting is musical sedatives – nicely packaged, soft, safe, gooey and easy to digest. There's nothing to bring rebellion or colour or imagination out in anyone. It's turning into a mixture of 1975 meets Radio Two and groups like Five Star exactly sum up that horrible era of lycra flared stretch jumpsuits before punk. I don't fit in with all that, but there again I'm used to not fitting in – I never have. And I always seem to get by on a whisker. I'm quite tough in that way – I've always been a bit of a survivor."

Gay Times, June 1987

Notes on Camp and Pop

They say nothing grows in the shade and Jayne Mansfield sure was thin-waisted. Along with eight other voluptuous screen sirens of the Fifties, she co-stars in a delicious marshmallow confection from Rhino Records called *Va Va Voom*, in which Hollywood's chantoozy floozies croon and sizzle their way through four sides of pink vinyl. For those of us who appreciate such things, this double-disc is the quintessence of High Camp.

Naturally, it's the lesser luminaries who leave one most agog. Forget the over-rated Monroe whose languid "Heatwave" perspires but never sweats. Forget Sophia Loren and her "Bing bang bong" – a heavyweight Eurovision contender if ever I heard one – even if, as the LP's splendidly OTT booklet assures us, she *almost* sang with Duke Ellington. Forget even, if you can, Diana Dors (née Fluck) who sounds like she recorded "Come by sunday" while wearing her mink bikini. Tune in, turn on and drop dead instead to the glorious and desperately underrated Mamie Van Doren (aka Joan Olander) who sighs, squeals and struts her stuff through "Separate the men from the boys".

If the amply-proportioned Mansfield was a grotesque clone of Monroe, and Dors was Britain's imperfect answer to Mansfield, then poor Mamie was always fourth in line, a stunning blonde bombshell eternally relegated to second-feature teen high school exploitation flix like *High School Confidential*. Not one flick-knife-and-black-leather-jacket movie went off without Mamie squeezing herself back into her tight sweater and capri pants to perform her blatantly vulgar bad-girl routine in a series of numbers that Rhino has collected together called, appropriately enough, *The Girl Who Invented Rock & Roll.*

The other gobsmacker, of course, is poor dead Jayne, decapitated – along with her doggie – in her pink Cadillac in a 1967 car smash. It appears that La Mansfield – whose version here of "Little things mean a lot" is *some* kind of classic – pouted and gushed her way through over a dozen albums. The most mind-boggling has to be a creation called "Shakespeare, Tchaikovsky and me", on which she recites Elizabethan verse to the strains of a large orchestra playing symphonies behind her.

It beggars belief that Mansfield didn't have her tongue in her cheek when she cut these albums, or knew that what she was producing was High Camp. Yet the concept of Camp, even by the early Sixties, was still a little-known private joke, a secret code confined primarily to a relatively small circle of hip faggots. It wasn't until intellectuals like author Susan Sontag started talking about it in the mid-Sixties that Camp sensibility began to float into the general consciousness, where it's lodged today.

Perhaps Mansfield and Van Doren just had an instinctive feel for the hidden joke in themselves; maybe they were surrounded by queens who spelled out to them how they could make Great Art. Either way they were ladies ahead of their time – not least in their easy transition from celluloid to vinyl. Because now that the biggest jugs in Hollywood belong to Sylvester Stallone, Camp's major stomping-ground has shifted to Pop.

"The essence of Camp is its love of the unnatural: of artifice and exaggeration. And Camp is esoteric – something of a private code." (Susan Sontag, "Notes On Camp", 1964)

Camp began as a mutual appreciation by faggots that the "normal" world they were supposed not to be a part wasn't "normal" at all, but a fantasy-reality of stereotypes and conventions which everyone aspired to but no-one ever achieved. It was the Emperor's New Clothes all over, and by the Sixties most post-War babes, gay or straight, were feeling trammelled by the 100 per cent butch or femme roles they were expected to play out for the rest of their lives. It's only when the stereotypes presented to us are pushed to their furthest extremes that people en masse begin to realise how ludicrous they are. The statuesque showgirls gave us all a break by caricaturing the "ideal" woman and letting it be known they were sharing a mutual joke. Mix sex with humour and facades crumble. Of course Camp isn't just about over-the-top glamazons sending themselves up; it's often a great deal more subtle than that. More than anything, Camp is about relishing the incongruous. Once we notice it, we can all appreciate, for its own sake, the gap between image and reality, the chasm between the fantasy presented to us and our knowledge of what's going on behind the scenes. A perfect example of this is the godlike-duo Dollar who, praise the Lord, have just made a more than welcome return to the Hollywood Babble-On of Pop and who, whether they know it or not, are High Camp par excellence.

"Camp is a vision of the world in terms of style – but a particular kind of style. It is the love of the exaggerated, the off, of things-being-what-they-are-not." (Sontag, ibid).

When the glamorously-monickered David Van Day and Thereza Bazaar were fired from chicken-in-a-basket MOR pop sextet Guys & Dolls they were obviously still madly in love, true believers in the hearts-and-flowers myth they were soon peddling for mass consumption with Dollar. Holding hands on telly they "oohed" and "aahed" their way up the chart with "Love's got a hold on me", they probably still looked into each other's eyes and saw twinkling stars while congratulating themselves on having found the perfect concocted pop image. To the observant, their early singles and telly appearances were Camp, but not High Camp. That was to come later.

Ideally, Camp mixes naivety with guile. On a pop level David and Thereza had come a long way since their Guys & Dolls days when David (fresh from playing a Womble on stage in Manchester) sang "The Wombles of Wimbledon" for his G&D audition and Thereza chose what she thought was a highly contemporary pop number, namely "Somewhere" from *West Side Story*. But real pop maturity only came when the ever-astute Thereza bludgeoned a then-unknown Trevor Horn into producing a seamless series of stunning singles, highly dramatic dreamy love songs like "Give me back my heart" performed with perfect breathless harmonies by Pop's Dream Couple.

From a Camp point of view, the fact that David and Thereza had begun to loathe each other seemed like gilding the lily. Despite their highly-publicised public arguments, with Thereza setting fire to restaurant tablecloths and throwing food over David, the love songs continued, the young lovers still emoted for the cameras. It was Fred and Ginge all over again.

Something had to give and a professional split occurred three years ago when they went solo. They soon proved that half a dollar buys nowt nowadays and are now back together again, professionally if not romantically: older, wiser and with their sense of humour intact, they compare their private life melodrama with *Dallas* and *Dynasty*. Sighing with relief, we can all play the game again – for, make no mistake, Dollar know exactly what they're doing.

Camp is all about not being sure whether art imitates life

or vice-versa. Soon after screen goddess Lana Turner's daughter was tried for the murder of Lana's gangster lover, Turner made two films in which she played sexy mums involved in murder cases and one in which she starred as an ambitious actress whose career is destroyed by her daughter. That movie was called *Imitation Of Life*. It would make a good title for the next album by David and Thereza, whose new single, full of yearning and regret, has, as its refrain: "We walked in love/ At least we tried". No doubt we'll get a reconciliation single next...

The difference between Low Camp is that Low Camp is out-and-out tat while High Camp, at its best, moves you while making you laugh. Dollar, whatever else, are never tat – they'll always be able to hold their heads up because they made great pop records. Ditto The Shangri-Las, whose wonderful teen angst melodramas of the Sixties (*Peyton Place* vignettes of girls thrown on to the streets by their mothers, falling in love with suicidal leather boys, and coping with being frigid), all delivered in the pain-hardened, deadpan Bro whine of Betty Weiss, are so splendidly artificial yet so sincere.

Ditto Phil Spector's girl groups. There's no-one camper than The Ronettes with their bird's-nest hair-dos and their slit-leg Chinese shantung frocks, but their Wall Of Sound singles like "Be my baby" (which Spector used to contemptuously describe as "little symphonies for the kids") are Mega-Art, if any pop record can be so described. Perhaps Pete Burns, who knows a thing or two about Camp, sums it up best when talking of the link between Ronnie Ronnette, Chaka Khan and himself, and admits: "Behind everything glamorous there's a joke too."

Which is not to say there aren't any borderline cases. Sinitta, with her current chart single "So macho", lies somewhere between Kitsch (so bad it's good) and High-

Tack (so bad it's unspeakable). "So macho" is a Hi-NRG single targeted especially at the male gay market that has crossed over, dragging with it so many ironies that one feels trapped in a Hall of Mirrors. Sinitta herself is a Disco Diva, one of that breed of painted ladies in little clothing who schlep around gay clubs miming vigorously to their latest three-minute-wonder while acting deeply sexy to a wildly enthusiastic all-male audience who would run a mile if approached by a "real" woman.

The daughter of Miquel Brown, who recorded "So many men, so little time" – vulgarity obviously runs in the family – Sinitta sings some frightfully liberated lyrics like "I don't want no seven stone weakling/ Or a boy who thinks he's a girl", thus proving either that there's a strong streak of self-hate among some gay men or that some people's sense of humour is even more perverse than mine.

That the record is top ten with a bullet as I write must be put down to the brilliance of the video, in which Sinitta, not even pretending to lip-synch, seduces a psychiatrist who looks like a Smurf. A dead ringer for a Woolworth's ad, the video is bright, tacky and appears to have been made for twopence-ha'penny. This is a trick.

Woolie's ads are cheap, vulgar and lengthy not because they can't afford to employ Saatchi & Saatchi to film swish footage, but because they know exactly the audience they're pitching their ad at. Ditto Sinitta, who has cornered the *Sun*-reading, Pot Noodle-eating, Woolies market and must be crying all the way to the bank. And that, given the record's poppers-soaked beginnings, I guess is called Camp too.

IRONY: 1) A figure of speech in which the extended meaning is the opposite of that expressed in the words used. 2) a contradictory outcome of events as if in mockery of the promise and fitness of things. (OED)

Of course Camp is in the eye of the beholder and nowhere does it become more confusing than when we look at pop's men. Glamour and froth are normally required elements in Camp and you'd expect gay men who, after all, started the whole idea, to be good providers of it. The truth is that faggots, or men who spend their time with faggots, are often too educated in that concept to provide that naivety that is so essential in High Camp; paradoxically they're good at recognising it, but are often far behind the unwitting heterosexual in giving us the best of Camp.

Take drag. Camp is subversive of commonly received standards and, by pointing out the gap between reality and appearance, shows life as theatre. Camp is about confusion and so, initially, is drag; yet cross-dressing, once a novelty in pop, has become subject to the law of diminishing returns on a Camp level. A private joke cannot go public without being adulterated and eventually destroyed: from David "The one thing I regret in life is telling *Melody Maker* I was bisexual" Bowie to the teeth-grindingly-named Gender Benders and on to the not-very-Divine, the cross-dressers are simply not very interesting any longer from a Camp point of view because their incongruity is too calculated for the connoisseur. Somewhere along the line the joke has been lost and the only remnant of Camp lies in those who try but fail, like The Sweet and the tubby-in-tinfoil Gladys Glitter.

Male drag is a more fruitful area, though again it cannot be too calculated as the cartoon caricatures of the Village People proved; they were funny for about one minute but the only vestige of humour left now is their determined attempt to deny that they're gay. More to the point are the

205

butch images of Freddie "Clone" Mercury and Rob "Leather Boy" Halford because one isn't quite sure whether they're *trying* to look mucho-macho or in fact sharing a joke.

Indeed it we take the Jayne-Mansfield-as-ideal-woman joke to its natural conclusion, Heavy Metal, Pomp Rock and their associated genres should be High Camp, given the gap between the Big Boy image and the Little Boy mentality that was so gloriously lampooned in the *Spinal Tap* movie.

Unhappily, Camp should also be amusing and HM narrowly avoids being Camp because the essential component of wit – even a shred of it – is rarely in evidence.

"We provide a distraction, an entertainment, a fantasy." Holly Johnson, Melody Maker.

When Frankie Goes To Hollywood first met Trevor Horn (the producer who Dollar had taught so much to) and began their early "Pleasure Dome" fantasies by simulating sex on stage with trannies and on record with each other, there was about them the whiff of poppers, a sense of real danger and backroom sex.

By presenting the Hollywood Babylon myth as real, they appeared both subversive and dangerous at the same time, and so – despite the gay background of Holly and Paul – avoided altogether even a frisson of Camp. But now that they've shown they can record a song for grannies ("The power of lurve"). dropped the gay angle and thrown the spotlight on the three drongo belchers, we're reminded that the after-smell of amyl nitrate is always one of sweaty socks.

Ironically, it was only when Frankie showed that the

only place they were going was Wallyhood that they proved that they're quite Camp, really. Which is more than can be said for Sigue Sigue Sputnik, poor lambs, who wouldn't know Camp if they stepped into it. Perhaps if, as looks increasingly likely, they end up on the provincial drag circuit, they'll learn something about it there.

For there's no doubt that among pop men, Camp has had its greatest effect not on those who like Camp or act Camp but those who genuinely love Camp. Marc Almond – Garland disinterred – is drenched in it; he exudes Camp by being Camp. But he's an exception. In fact it is the Sensitive Young Thugs who, on the whole, are the greatest proponents of Camp sensibility nowadays. Paul Weller – not a gay, bisexual or celibate man as far as one knows – plays with it like a kitten with a mouse. The man who told *Smash Hits* that his Most Fanciable Person Of The Year was Rupert Everett has been responsible for some of the great camp artifacts of our time, from his homo-erotic Brideshead Revisited pastiche video for "Long hot summer" to the contents of his *Favourite Shop* cluttered with Fifties gay porno books and bios of Kenneth Williams and Joe Orton.

Love of ambiguity and the incongruous is the name of the game, an appreciation of that private joke which is the gap between our fantasies and reality. And the arch exponent, of course, is Mr Morrissey.

Morrissey knows all about artifice and the private joke. He should do. After all, he has been weaned on Camp. From the New York Dolls through Oscar Wilde via weeping Johnnie Ray and his hearing-aid, Hollywood's human ashtray Jimmy Dean and his long-forgotten Sixties girl singers like Italian midget foghorn Rita Pavone, all his influences are the highest of HC.

From his record covers to his interviews, Morrissey

attracts our attention with Camp and then serves us, in his songs, with a grisly picture of what most people's real lives are like.

Like his socialist fop of a mentor, Oscar Wilde, Morrissey is a moralist who uses Camp to show that impoverished lives need not beget impoverished imagination, but that we must never confuse our dreams with reality. In an age like the present one, whose political climate encourages us to retreat into our private fantasies because there seems nowhere else to go, it is not a bad lesson to teach.

Melody Maker, August 16th, 1986

Tears of a Clone

KENNY EVERETT

He's an absolute enigma, this pint-sized, wise-cracking forty-one-year-old Scouse tugboat captain's son. In all my dealings with Kenny Everett he's been generous to a fault – warm, kind, considerate. Yet when I ask him whether, now that he's as out as you can get, he'd consider appearing in the next *Pretty Policeman's Ball,* he says "I'm just not a charity person. Cos it all gets lost, it goes the wrong way. Obviously something like Band Aid does more good than bad, but I think it's typical that they've discovered a lot of the Band Aid money is going to the IRA.

"Personally, I only feel good about being charitable to people I know; anything beyond that is hypocritical to me. Why should I give to people when I don't even know if they exist? I'm good to my family, good to my friends – is there anything over and above that worthy of consideration?... Oh, God, you're giving me that old-fashioned look. Am I being provocative? Am I going to get into more trouble now?"

Trouble is something Mr E has become well used to this year after the thorough roasting given him by a virulent, homophobic tabloid press who, having got him to publicly admit his gayness through a mixture of trickery and guile, gave their once-favoured son the old screaming-banner-headline, fake-Aids-related-story treatment. And just as the interminable "revelations" of his "amazing three-way menage" were dying down and the gangs of clamouring hacks were beginning to squat on somebody else's doorstep, it started all over again with a "Gay Murder Cops Quiz Kenny" *Sun* front-pager, a concoction based on the fact that Everett's name along with 700 others, including Princess Di's – was found in the diary of a man accused of murder.

Months after his admission that he'd been so depressed that he'd contemplated suicide, Everett is still well pissed off. "It's strange, you know, it still really hurts when scaffold-workers shout out 'I hope you get Aids, pouf' and the ugly, sweaty shit-heads pull out their dicks and say 'Cop this, Ken'... I can tell myself that blacks and women have to deal with similar things every day of the week, but I still walk away needing a drink, or someone to scoop me up and make me feel good. Maybe it's a sign of a weak character, maybe I should just shrug it off. But it still gets to me."

He must then, I suggest, have had every sympathy with Boy George in his recent battle with Fleet Street? "I would have felt sorry for him if he hadn't taken advantage of the press in the past. Contrary to what *Gay Times* recently insinuated, I've never said to the press 'I've got this amazing life-style and amazing sex-life' – it was the papers themselves who put that interpretation on what I consider to be something that's fairly average. But with George I thought 'You've used Fleet Street for so many years, it's about time they had a go at you.' Anyway, it was so cartoon – all that kicking down doors at midnight! I think it could all be a chapter for his forthcoming autobiography – he's priming us for a big sell on his book, and then he'll retire. I think it's all cobblers about the heroin, I don't think he's even touched the stuff."

Cynicism? "I was watching the telly last night and somebody said that cynicism was just an ugly way, a more brutal way, of telling the truth. That sounds about right to me." A comment like that makes Everett sound like a hard knock, when he isn't. Unthinking, perhaps. And he certainly isn't the most joyous of men, corresponding very

210

closely to the stock Pagliaccan image of the privately unhappy funny-man: "There's lots to be depressed about, isn't there? I don't love myself and I don't hate myself, I'm totally 50-50 about it. But I don't think any gay people are happy about being different, are they? Is any minority happy about being in a minority? People who do Gay Pride – it's just a backlash against being got at, isn't it? A kick-back unit. But I don't know if it's that good an idea because then you usually get kicked twice."

Everett constantly accuses himself of timidity and yet is braver than most in talking frankly about his private life ("I'm still in love with me ex-husband Nikky, who's in love with Pepe who lives with us and does cleaning for me who's in love with Nikky, who's in love with champagne. It's one of those *Dynasty* situations.") Does he have *any* qualms about revealing intimate details, any concept of privacy? "I don't mind at all the size of my knob being printed, what I do in bed, various sexual kinks I have. What I do mind is people on the street who can't cope with anything other than swilling beer, Queen's Park Rangers and fucking chicks, passing judgement on me."

Is he happy at the moment? "No, I'm still waiting for my knight on a white charger. Or grey charger – any colour will do." He's lonely, then? "Oh God, yeah. Everybody in a gay club is, they all seem to be out to meet somebody and pretend not to be desperate. Every gay club is a huge room for games-playing lonely people.

"That's the thing about faggots – we're just after the ultimate dream. You look at somebody and think 'Fab legs, cute moustache, eyes could be better'... and you go back with them 'cos you're desperate for affection. Then next time it's 'Cute mouth, fab eyes, legs could be better'... it's like shopping round in a supermarket. So I've developed this philosophy where I keep doing it and maybe if I ever meet that magic person who strikes all the bells in me, and there have only been two of those so far, we'll have to say 'Right, let's stop all this and run away together on our own'."

A romantic cynic, a generous Scrooge, a brave coward; I suggest to Mr E that he's a mass of contradictions. One part of him is naturally rebellious; the iconoclast who got sacked from the BBC for suggesting on the radio that the Minister of Transport's wife bribed her driving-test examiner, the sparky David who took on the Goliath Whitehouse and won ("Fuck her, she's a monster. I have fantasies that she's at the end of my bed with needle-sharp teeth eating her way up my legs. She looks just like a flesh-eater, with that hypocritical smile and her heinous glasses."). The other half is deeply Establishment and reactionary: his grossly unfunny "joke" about nuking the Russians might have been dismissed as just a silly gag that backfired, had he not hollered it at the Tory Party Conference. Is he *really* a Thatcherite? I ask him.

"I supported the fact that she smashed Scargill to bits because he to me was an evil man – I just felt instinctively. He's a power-crazed loon who twisted the rabble for his own ends and he would have got away with it if someone hadn't stood firm and said 'You bastard, you're a fucker and I'll get you.' And she did. But I think she's going crazy now, what she's doing to the country. I punch my cat when it shits in the palm tree, but I don't punch her every minute of the day. I just punch her to show her she's done wrong and then I give her a cuddle and a hug and it's all over. But Thatcher doesn't know when to stop punching.

"Not that I can stand the Labour lot – they just say 'Hey, rabble, what would you like next? Free money, alcohol till midnight, free balloons? Right you are...' and they give them away till there's no money left and the Tories get

212

back in saying 'Now let's be sensible and pull together' and on and on it goes. I'm sure they're in complicity together, I don't like either of 'em. I think the SDP sounds cosy, don't you?" No, actually, but if you now want to be an embarrassment to David Owen, Kenny, that's all right by moi.

None of this, however, appears to have affected his work. There's a new Kenny Everett telly series beginning in the Autumn and a science quiz series starts shooting in January, plus the beginnings of an idea for a sitcom starring God. "So I'll be famous for another few years. This time after the telly series I decided to take three months off and go to some smelly dago bars in Spain to decide what to do next and what to do it with. During the worst of the 'scandal' I thought maybe I'd sell this flat – I'd get about £200,000 for it – and go round the world being cheap, not washing a lot and not staying in 4-star hotels. Then I thought 'No Ken, don't be silly – you'd miss the Badedas'."

On a 'success' level, Kenny Everett has come a long way. He went away to a seminary to be a priest when he was an adolescent in order to escape a Liverpool he loathed ("They sent me back because they said I wasn't suitable priest material. I still can't see why – after all, I was a faggot and I loved dressing up") but in the end it was Liverpool that made him. The Scouse boffin who spliced together his own radio programmes on a home tape-recorder managed to "sneak in between the Petula Clarks and the Frankie Vaughans. I was just a cheeky, devil-may-care chap from Liverpool, happy to go to London at the same time as the Beatles. In '67 the pirate stations, Carnaby Street, Beatlemania all came together and anything that was around with a Liverpool accent was acceptable and somehow I was getting breaks."

That run of professional luck never stopped – deejaying

gave way to Light Ent telly shows, hit records, advert voice-overs and a life that many would envy. Yet I don't think anyone would describe him as a happy man.

I abhor Kenny Everett's politics, am embarrassed by his tendencies towards maudlin self-pity and misanthropy, find his story-book romanticism risible and don't even like his telly programmes. But I'd insist on a personal level he's an extremely sweet and kind man – the type of person who, if he was your next door neighbour, you'd never be afraid of asking for a cup of sugar.

And maybe he's learning a little. His ex-wife Lee has written a book that tells of their marriage, warts and all. "She sent me the proofs saying if there were anything I wanted changing or throwing away, to do so. It really was quite distressing to read it, because it was the absolute truth and I realised I've made more mistakes on this planet than Soft Joe. But I've got a funny feeling that's what we're here for, and so I told her to print it exactly as it was. Because that might help someone else who finds themselves in the same situation that I was in – thinking I was the only one in the world, marrying in the hope that it would change me, screwing up other people because of it. The mistakes I've made are legion, obvious and embarrassing. But if that helps somebody else not to make similar mistakes, then I feel I must be completely honest."

Gay Times, September 1986

Jesus Christ!

STRYPER

It sounds like a script for *Spinal Tap II*. Pretty-boy heavy metal band Roxx Regime are just one of the Los Angeles HM horde, no-hopers without a record deal. Brothers Robert and Michael Sweet get Born Again, squeeze out the band's agnostics, draft in two more zealots and change their name to Stryper. In tight black and yellow striped Spandex, the boys begin chucking Bibles at the audience while performing Queen-meets-Van Halen paeans to Jesus. They start flogging records...

Nearly half a million of their last album, *Soldiers Under Command,* according to Stryper drummer Robert Sweet whose true story, of course, this is. Except that Bob would quarrel with my emphasis. The decision to glorify God came first, he maintains; the success just followed on. "I've heard the argument so many times, that we used Christianity as a gimmick to sell records. All I can say is that, in late 83, what we were doing was very unacceptable, and we had investors saying they'd put money into the band if only we'd drop the Jesus line. So if I was into money, why didn't I do that?

"We have a friend in a high place who wants us to be like this and I think we'll make money. We'll make a lot of money. But it'll just be that much more money to do good things with."

So you pay tithes?

"Yes, we do. Not that we're wealthy: we do make a lot of money, but the bills from overheads can kill you. What we mainly try to do with our money is, for example, pay for the Bibles we give out, 'cos we don't get them free. You go and buy a case of Bibles and see what it costs you!"

215

As ever, I'm mesmerised by the literal mind of an evangelical Christian, particularly when it's that of a demure bleached blond who's tricked out in hair lacquer, a little mascara and a pair of skin-tight jeans that leave absolutely no doubt as to which side he dresses. (The right.)

A typically fly-blown HM tart, right? Except this one has vowed chastity till he's married. So is he a virgin?

"I look at it this way. Since Stryper began, yes. Before then, no."

And do you miss it?

"It's not just that I don't miss it. Sex feels great, but just because it feels great doesn't mean it's right. There are certain things a Christian must hold, and when it comes to sexual sin the Bible is explicit."

Is that *all* sex?

"Yes."

You don't even masturbate?

"No."

And you don't miss it?

"Seriously, no. Though I have to say you're the first person who's gone into detail that far. It surprises me."

Sweet by name and sweet by nature, Mr S has that wide-eyed unflappability that appears to go hand-in-hand with Christian sincerity. And if Bobby isn't sincere, he's a wonderful actor.

"It doesn't mean I'm not tempted. It seems like as every day goes by I meet more and more beautiful women. I have desires like everybody else, but I think it's important if you have made a promise to God to keep it. Why is there Aids and herpes today? I feel, because of sexual sin."

Do you believe in Divine Retribution?

"Do you know where syphilis came from? From men having sex with animals. It's not like I'm saying 'You're bad and God's going to punish you.' But certain things form a chain reaction. Sin is like throwing a boomerang into the darkness. If you sin you pay the penalty at one time or another."

Stryper, it must be said, have been shot at from both sides – from metallurgists, for being the very antithesis of rock 'n' roll rebellion, to fellow-zealots: "Some say we aren't Christian because of the type of music we play and the way we look. Some people take what they don't like and call it a sin. And what I say is the exact words of Christ – that with God all things are possible. The Christian shouldn't walk round and point the finger. Many do and it hurts the purpose of Christianity, which is to reach people. Have you noticed God doesn't do that?"

It's the assumption that we all believe in God *really* that sticks in the craw. If I did, what I'd object to most is the music they're offering to Jesus. As you might expect, Stryper music is unadventurous and derivative – HM clichés with vocals delivered through clenched teeth, though topped off with unspeakably kitsch ("I will follow you because you died for me") lyrics. Not that a bit of kitsch has ever been known to put of a HM enthusiast.

Kitsch is a word that might have been invented for Stryper. Take the genesis of their name: "We chose it first because we wore yellow and black stripes, but we spelt it with a Y so no-one could mistake it for Stripper. After that, in Bible study, I came across Isaiah 53:5, 'By his stripes are we healed' – the stripes, of course, referring to the lashes on Jesus's back. Then, one day, we were out rehearsing and just after we'd said our prayers I saw one of our bumper stickers on the wall and it just came to me: Stryper stands for Salvation Through Redemption Yielding Peace, Encouragement and Righteousness".

Hmph. HM's a funny world for a Christian, isn't it, with all that Satanism and chicken-neckwringing?

"I think people who do Satanic lyrics are sincerely looking for something. One definition of Satan is Little God and I feel sorry for those people 'cos they're finding the answer in the Little God instead of the Big One."

When Vince Neil of Motley Crue was involved recently in a gruesome car accident, Sweet was quoted as saying "When you're outside (God's) protection you're gonna get nailed."

Divine retribution or what?

"That was a long interview and my quote was truncated. I wasn't saying he deserved that. But, if you get in a car while you're drunk, you might expect something like that to happen. It was too bad it had to happen. Who knows if it was Divine Retribution? Do you know? Do know if it wasn't? I'm not the type of person to say 'Hey, you're an evil person and God's going to get you.' But I think everybody, for example, knows that crime doesn't pay. I wish no bad on anybody, but does the Bible say the wages of sin is death? The answer is yes."

Glad we've got that straight. So Robert, being a good Christian I'm sure you're expending a lot of your righteousness on the South African situation, denouncing the Ungodly there.

"It's a terrible thing, but I feel I have to devote all my time and energy to Christ. If people in Africa knew Jesus Christ, the type of stuff going on there wouldn't be going on. There are always going to be political things in the world to spend our time talking about but, if we covered things like that, we'd never get to the main thing. There's so much coverage anyway – and that's good. But for us the best thing to be singing about is Christ."

Stryper's new album is called *To Hell With The Devil!* It left this personable young man thinking that if there is a Hell, may Stryper rot in it.

Melody Maker, October 4, 1986

The Voice of the Plague

DIAMANDA GALAS

"Living in San Francisco I become so irritated with a lot of people in the art world who were so terrified of this whole Aids thing. I'd hear people say 'isn't it *disgusting*, all those gay men getting together for sensitivity sessions on Aids – who cares about those fuckers?' I'd get so angry I'd shout at them for wilfully using homophobic terrorism."

Diamanda Galas has been practising heterophobic terrorism on these shores for the last year, in the shape of *The Divine Punishment* and *Saint of the Pit*, the first two excellent albums in a trilogy named *The Masque of the Red Death*. Her subject is Aids/the plague/mortality (delete as you wish). In America Galas lived on the very margin of pop – where her subject matter has hardly charmed the socks off her fellow artists and labelmates.

"People keep saying 'Why use a subject like Aids? You should keep to more general things.' And I think 'Oh, you mean like lovers and drug addiction and all that old shit?' I'm so bored with these little boys whose girlfriends have left them. So many of them use expressions like "Death and Destruction" as some sort of trendy fashion statement, but as soon as you start discussing death with them, they say 'Oh, I really can't handle that right now. I really have to go...'"

The truth is that none of us can run away from the subject of Aids, however much we may like to. *The Divine Punishment* confronts the fear head on. Galas, an American Greek who creates soundscapes with her electronically treated operatic voice, uses texts from the Old Testament to "express the nuances of what someone going through a really slow death feels, to get across the kinds of situations and emotional states they get into."

Listening to these pieces can be a harrowing experience but, in an extraordinary way, the music is also strangely comforting. It reminds us that we will all share the same thoughts as we are dying: one of the most moving pieces uses *Psalm 22*, supposedly uttered by Jesus on the cross, *Lord Why Hast Thou Forsaken Me?* "The Divine Punishment is the Italian phrase for the Plague, but obviously I've used the title ironically. I might have been an agnostic once, but now I'm definitely an atheist. You don't watch a thirty year old boy die of Aids and still believe in God, it's impossible."

That boy was a "very close" friend of Galas, who she saw waste away. "Two weeks before he died he begged me to play *The Divine Punishment*. He was sitting there with white hair, like a skeleton, with all his friends around him. And while it was playing I felt like a real criminal, like someone sticking a machete through everyone. I was crying throughout it, because it was too close. After it was played there was silence, and then everyone started talking about it. And my friend really loved it, and related very strongly to it. It was an immense relief to me, because obviously I've had horrors of conscience with these records; nightmares about not doing them properly and thereby defaming his grave. But basically all I know is what's in my heart, and I'm very glad I've done them."

When a society is gripped in panic, it is at its most dangerous and most intolerant. It's called plague mentality. From its beginnings, Galas has seen Aids as a "contemporary plague, especially sociologically speaking, with all the societal symptoms being the same as they always have been. So little changed since the Old Testament was written: people are still lemmings, they're

220

still voting for quarantines and looking for scapegoats..."

Galas conveys this atmospherically with her use of Leviticus ('This is the law of the plague') amidst *The Divine Punishment*'s lamentations. "The trilogy now has the concept of a Plague Mass, but it didn't at the beginning. I've always seen the plague as a metaphor for all the other interests I've had like insanity. Things that were more intimate to my experience and, I guess, many other people's. And I was using the plague as a metaphor for the flesh incarnation of a nightmare on the inescapability of pain and the fact that death can't be put off.

"But when I was living in San Francisco it became more apparent to me that I couldn't escape the analogy with the Aids issue. The metaphors became too arty and real life beckoned. The more I became aware that other people were being so cowardly in the face of something hitting them over the head, the more I said it was obvious that society hadn't learned anything, the more irritation I'd get from other artists. That's why in the face of a lot of opposition from a large part of the art world and the music world I've made it very clear that the Aids thing is very strongly related to the record. So I'm seen as the one who takes the side of the Sodomists. Well, not only do I take their side – I am the voice of the plague."

So what attitude *can* one take? "The only thing that a contagion really allows people to do is decide between being men or cowards. They have the opportunity to understand what fraternity means, in Camus' sense, where he used Dr Rieux as the symbol of a man who works in an impossible situation to help people. It's the only opportunity. We have a choice, we have a chance to face up to things. It's a great opportunity."

In the knowledge that one may get it oneself? "Yes."

This extraordinary woman is also a very witty one – far

221

less intimidating than her demented witch image would suggest, though she's quick to point out that "I'm not some piece of Hollywood camp shit who's not really serious, as some people would think of me." The new album, another electro-acoustic set that this time uses texts by the nineteenth century French poets Baudelaire, Nerval and Corbiere, shows again that Galas is more than just an extraordinary voice: as well as performing all soprano and bass voices, she wrote the music and plays organ, digital synthesizers and piano. "People come up to me after a live show and say 'Who did all the tapes?' They think I'm just some bitch who comes out in a sequined dress with a microphone and poses. That might be Grace Jones, but it's not Diamanda."

Gay Times, February 1987

Against Nature

MOMUS

"I myself am heterosexual, but I have a fascination with the homosexual view of the world, the deep seated bitterness against the predominant culture. I've always been stigmatised as a homosexual, and if that happens to you, you tend to hold up the stigmata."

There is the pop mainstream. And then there are those on the outskirts of the industry who may be offering something a little more challenging, a little bit more difficult. Often their voices are hardly more than a murmur behind the babble, challenging the banality or the misconceptions. Perhaps occasionally making you think.

Thirty year old Scot Nick Currie is Momus – named after the Greek God of satire, chucked off Mount Olympus for being too cheeky and bold – and over the last decade Momus has released a handful of albums with titles like *The Tender Pervert*, *The Poison Boyfriend* and *Circus Maximus* whose extraordinary content and quality make me think him the most interesting singer/songwriter/lyricist in Britain today. Currie has always been personally fascinated by sex, and the pain and pleasure of the erotic urge pervade his material; nothing is taboo, from necrophilia ("The cabriolet") to paedophilia ("The guitar lesson") when it comes to his special brand of voyeurism. Needless to say, homosex features very strongly in his work. For Currie is that fascinating thing, a Straight Queen.

"I suppose my attraction to that outsiderdom has a pretty banal explanation," says Currie, a beautiful languid beanpole of a boy with a blond cow-lick and a big mouth full of teeth like Jaques Brel, one of his many heroes. "I went to boarding school and we were all into Glamrock and at twelve everybody at school was in bed with somebody else in the dorm; it was that big latency period. We were all listening to David Bowie and Lou Reed and Marc Bolan, and convinced we were gay ourselves and that that was a good thing to be."

But there's an intellectual fascination with homosexuality too, as in the duplicity of the homosexual in his song of the same name. "The homosexual" isn't gay, though everyone presumes he is, and he continually takes advantage of the fact by screwing other people's wives. "People always assume I'm gay, and I'll always remember my first girlfriend turning round to me and saying 'I feel so privileged you chose me to go straight with'. But there's far more to it than just the personal angle...

"It's like with Jewish people, who've always been persecuted. There must be a bitterness about being persecuted, but at the same time there's a refusal to be alienated, so an internal exile must come as a result of that. You can't really generalise, but I'm fascinated by how people come in and infiltrate when they know privately that they are not like other people, and rise to the top. Jewish people have done that with Hollywood, publishing, the art world – they're all pretty well Jewish-run. And it's similar with gays, especially in entertainment and pop. The best pop musicians have always been gay; they turn their stigma into kudos somehow by this magical alchemical process. So what people in the street and in normal life normally look at askance or persecute, when it's up on stage they enjoy it and celebrate it and applaud it. And that fascinates me."

Born in Paisley in 1960 into an academic family (his brother is a deconstructionist critic and lecturer), Currie went to Aberdeen University where – ever the gauche and shy outsider at parties – he gained a first in English. A serious minded intellectual saved by a dry, ironic sense of humour and sense of fun, he is by nature an iconoclast, a kicker against the norms. "I feel that in public life, gays who "come out" and constitute themselves as a public body defined by sexuality make the most interesting public form of debate. There are few things that move or touch me, but I'm always moved by watching public issues about gay life. Like a recent documentary on gay clergy really touched me, and I don't know why that is. I always think 'This is something I'm part of, though I'm not sexually part of it.' I'm like a fellow traveller. I relate to the stereotypes. Not the macho clone stereotype, but all that refined, delicate aesthetic 1890s Alfred Douglas side of things."

But those were secretive days; are gay men the inner rebels they were? Aren't they mostly trying to legitimise themselves nowadays, saying "We're just the same as everybody else"?

"Gay people won't ever feel themselves sufficiently legitimised not to be in some way bitter. The transparency of normality disappears when you haven't internalised the values of the dominant culture. That's when things get interesting, when you realise everything is arbitrary and to do with power structures. Like the concept of the family, which most people think is natural and God-given, but gay people know in their bones it's a totally arbitrary politically motivated structure. With a different pair of eyes you automatically see all the hypocrisy of that stuff, that none of it is 'natural'."

Gay themes have continually been grist to Momus' artistic mill, from his first solo album *Circus Maximus* (set in Ancient Rome and about "characters in *The Bible* or from Ancient Rome whose high intentions were undermined by their sexuality. My theme has always been seduction") via *The Tender Pervert* ("I wanted to call the album *The*

Homosexual but my record company dissuaded me in the end") to his more recent material about pantomime hairdressers and sapphic masturbators. "Gay themes are like the world turned upside down. Like the ice skaters who are meant to be the perfect couple and yet they're gay, they're not attracted to each other at all. I love looking at that gap between appearance and reality. And the gay thing really annoys people. I love to tease with gay themes, because the whole subject of homosexuality still really sorts out the sheep from the goats. You can meet somebody who seems like a really liberal, open minded guy and you say 'gay' and instantly the gates of prejudice are slammed down. I'm always drawn to taboos. I've always felt that writing is just verbal waffle unless you stand on people's corns."

It's like I'm talking to somebody who's more gay than I am.

"People have always assumed I'm gay. Or maybe I'm paranoid and just assuming they were assuming and projecting my own gay element onto them. But at school they always called me poof, and I always gravitated to gay people, especially if they were literary because they often had the best libraries! I'd hear people assuming that I was gay and my attitude always was 'I don't mind your saying that – what's the big deal about it?' Women especially always assumed that I was gay, until I started making moves on them. Funnily enough, I've often thought I'd probably have much better relationships if I *were* gay. But it so happens that what I'm sexually turned on by is women. Preferably small women with black hair. Preferably Japanese. And – I don't know what this says about me – preferably unable to speak the language!"

With Momus the lyrics take care of themselves. But then there is the music. Currie – like some of his critics – tends to put the music down. Of course he's not completely original – Momus admits "Everything I write is parody or pastiche. I don't have a musical style which is me expressing myself. There again, you can make a case for all pop music being self aware parody. The Rolling Stones have to be very aware what they're doing is a complete parody of black music and rock & roll."

Pastiche perhaps, but there's something more to Momus' music than that. Not just the insidious melodies he keeps finding which put him up there with the Pet Shop Boys in the cheap, evocative, moving pop bubblegum stakes. (It's no surprise when Currie mentions "You know Neil Tennant and I run a mutual appreciation society?") There's something about the way he fuses all sorts of influences – Brel with Weill, Kafka with Mishima, Bowie with Gainsbourg and chanson with Europop – with his own tongue-in-cheek immense seriousness that sets him apart as a completely original talent on today's constipated pop scene. "They say East Coast Scots look to Europe and West Coast Scots look to the US, and it's true of me. I look to Europe and even further East, and I always have. I have real problems with US culture – all that wearing baseball caps and putting their boots on the table. This awful compulsively conformist, macho, laid-back kind of attitude."

Far more to his taste are those Europeans who fit yet don't fit into Twentieth Century pop culture, like Jaques Brel. Because of his extraordinary 1986 translation/ complete re-work of Brel's "Jackie" which he renamed "Nicky", Momus has been linked too closely perhaps with the Belgian chansonnier. ("Because I got lots of press on that record I somehow became the archivist for Jaques Brel's reputation for a couple of years, doing radio interviews on him and stuff. But I got really sick of that

227

academic thing.") Nevertheless, Brel's sheer dynamism and emotionalism still have their influence on Momus. "As an artist, part of me still loves the pure dynamics and tension and stress which force Brel into that level of intensity where he climbs through notes and through keys and gets up there and shouts at the end of each song so it's like watching a circus act. But recently I've been much more influenced by Serge Gainsbourg, who in French culture represents the other end of things. His music is static, it murmurs. Sex is almost like a physical expression of formalism and in that way it's very Japanese. Gainsbourg deals with sexual taboo by dry dissection – it's almost like scientific exploration. He's analytical and rational rather than passionate, and I guess that's the other side of me."

Trouble is, you may find Momus' recordings a bit difficult to come by soon. For Currie – whose record sales have increased with each release, but who admits that his "constituency" numbers 15,000 "and that's a generous estimate" – has just walked out of his contract with Creation Records. "In one sense I suppose it is crazy, because I was doing well financially and Creation were beginning to give me decent amounts of money for my recordings, and sending me out touring. But I suppose I'm even more of a megalomaniac than somebody like Morrissey, and to me the last album showed signs of my beginning to get desperate. Because my single 'Hairstyle of the Devil' got a lot of airplay, especially from Steve Wright, there was pressure to go for 'the big hit single' on the last album; there was too much of the disco work-out. It was like being taken to the top of the mountain by Satan, and being offered the 'One day all this could be yours' line. And I did try. But I know anyway that doing crass Stock, Aiken and Waterman stuff in a pastichey way isn't going to get me anywhere, because it's with the stuff that has more integrity than I was demonstrating at that period that I've had my most commercial success."

Though he should be up there with Morrissey and co., perhaps it's the lack of attention which keeps him working. "I think that's true. I've always had this thing about unrequited love, about being fascinated by someone who thinks I'm a little shit. At the moment the great music audience out there thinks I'm a little shit, so I love them. The moment they start coming to my gigs, I just think 'What creeps'. Maybe I like to keep knocking and be turned away from the gates!"

Sadly for Momus, he is presently being pursued by one of Britain's best respected and largest indie labels, with whom he will probably sign. Fame beckons, and he will not be able to avoid if for much longer. And after that? "Well yes, I'd love to be on EMI – amongst that great pantheon of gay writers and artists. Ha!"

Gay Times, November 1990

Erotophobia

TONGUE MAN

"Taste the whip, you bastard", "The blond boy buggered me/ sober-ly and seriously"... with lyrics like these on their new mini-album, gay pop electroduo Spud Jones and Andy Fenby aka Tongue Man are working in dangerous territory. It's unlikely these indie musos will ever be commercial enough for the mullahs from *The Sun* to launch one of their hypothetical 'These Men Are Dangerous' features against the boys.

But won't even some of the more liberal amongst us question whether the music's graphic rough-trade content – most of their scenarios are S&M-based, I'd say, though Tongue Man disagree – isn't a little out-of-place in the present safe-sex climate? Mainman, Spud – lyrics, voice and sample – isn't about to be defensive.

"I don't want to write songs about Aids; if I did that would be the end of my career! There's a down sort of attitude towards sex at the moment and it would show a real negative attitude if the music talked about Aids. Of course I'm scared about it; everybody is in this day and age. But I can't go through the rest of my life with my dick between my legs. I'm not here to preach or moralise about Aids. I trust the public to distinguish between safe and non-safe sex. I don't know if I agree with you that ours is porno music, but given that masturbation is the safest form of sex there is, maybe we're making the world safer by providing stuff for people to fantasise to."

It's fairly bleak music, I'd suggest. "Not really – it's not particularly black. Dramatic, yes. And angry. But it isn't melancholy. Okay, we sing about a seamy side of life – which happens to be based on my own sex experiences.

But let's face it, there are enough Kylie Minogues and Jason Donovans around singing about all the pleasant bits, so why shouldn't we be singing about some of the unsavoury bits of life? Actually most gays are quite aloof about the whole thing too, they don't want to know. They don't want you pushing your opinion forward. The English have always been scared of sex. There's nothing new in what I'm saying; it's just that I'm upfront and confronting fears. And other people are going in the opposite direction."

But aren't you taking your audience into a sexual world they've never before seen into? Surely heavy S&M isn't universal?

"Well, for a start these are my experiences and it doesn't matter to me whether they're universal, even in the gay world – after all, we're unlikely ever to have mass appeal and I wouldn't particularly want it. But I don't think the scenarios are particularly S&M anyway; 'Taste the whip' is actually about my own sister's murder. It's about a man who's a serial killer, it's meant to be nasty. My sister was murdered two years ago; that inspired me to create even more. You need something like that to rock your life."

Spud Jones certainly seems serious about his art and his band ("It's a full-time thing for me. I'm twenty-nine now, I've spent the last three years on Tongue Man. It matters a lot") and he almost seems to thrive on confrontation. Like the first (pre-Alan) incarnations of Tongue Man; "There were straights in the first band, and though I was using the same kind of themes they said at first it didn't matter. But then it got that people didn't phone back." Or like with the hecklers in their audience; "We've had one or two gigs where people have done silly-bugger things. I was a bit shocked to see someone pointing a finger-gun at us, you could tell he really wanted us to be shot dead." Or even indie distributors Rough Trade, who weren't interested in distributing Tongue Man; "They're supposed to have a liberal attitude, but they're just as homophobic as everybody else in the music business." Even Aids-activists Act-Up come in for Spud's criticism; "We were going to do our first benefit for them, but they were extremely disorganised, and they didn't want to bill us for some reason. It was like they were doing *us* a favour. I don't know whether they were embarrassed by us or not, but there was no way we were going to waste our time if they weren't going to give us publicity."

A man with a mission, but does the till-now silent Andy feel as strongly paranoid?

"I worked for *The Pink Paper* doing record reviews at one time and generally we found the record companies very supportive and good to their gay artists, and not apparently homophobic at all. But of course they wanted publicity so they *would* be nice. But certainly I've come across a lot of homophobia in the music business since Tongue Man. And no doubt there will be flak to come. You can't please everybody and there's clearly a lot of material there which, because of the homosexual content, will be slagged off by all those people who love to slag off homosexuality. But we're not pushing anything; we're certainly not pushing promiscuity. After all, what evil is Kylie Minogue pushing when she's singing 'I should be so lucky'?"

Can you ever imagine writing a lyric that wasn't sexual, Spud? Do you ever think of anything but sex?

"I can't say, really. I can't write enough about sex. It's the easiest thing to talk about to me."

And does your mum like the music, Mr Jones?

"Actually, I haven't sent her a copy. I think she might not approve of it."

Gay Times, July 1990

Idol on Parade

MORRISSEY

And if the people stare,
then the people stare
I really don't know
and I really don't care

"Hand in glove"

Was I or was I not a *fan* of Mr Morrissey? Well...I did fall
for him. Not in the way of his young zealot followers,
copying his quiff and his brooches and his ugly black specs
and his outsize shirts. He was never a guru to me as he
was to them, and I never felt proprietorial towards him like
they did. But I do distinctly remember being driven up
some black m-way in the middle of the night in May 1983
and hearing The Smiths' incandescent first single "Hand in
glove" on the radio for the first time and feeling like I
wanted to pirouette madly and burst into tears at the same
time. And I do remember going to what I believe was the
band's first London gig at the now-defunct Venue in
Victoria, to be tenderly trapped amongst a seething mass of
mostly young men swooning over the charismatic, callow
lump-of-a-lad on stage who was pelting us with gladioli.
And perhaps most of all I remember for a long time
thinking that here was a young shaver whose oxters I'd
dearly love to sniff close up.

"I want an endless stream of priceless singles"

Morrissey

In 1984 the ball began rolling for real for Morrissey – the
christian name (Steven) had been long dropped – and his

233

three then faceless fellow Mancunians. The Smiths hit the mid-Eighties Britpop scene like a breath of fresh air – or, perhaps more accurately, a fresh breath of fetid air. For this was the tail end of the squeaky clean post punk era of the New Pop, begun by ABC and the Human League and perpetuated by Culture Club and co, i.e. lots of style but little or no substance. Punk, at least, had set itself against the status quo; New Pop colluded with it in flogging the idea of *disposability* as virtue. In a pop world whose values centred round careerism, business acumen and material wealth, Morrissey insisted that pop wasn't (or shouldn't be) trivial and that music should speak to and reflect the lives and concerns of ordinary people. It was a refreshing – if not original – notion and many disenfranchised music lovers responded with a passion that was glorious to behold.

"Manchester – so much to answer for"
"Suffer little children"

Not since punk had opinions been so polarised. Where New Pop had dealt in primary colours, Smithmusic appeared to its detractors at least to be dealing only in various shades of grey. Here was a music whose roots were Northern – specifically Mancunian – and working class; a musical throwback to the grainy Sixties black and white kitchen sink movies like *Saturday Night and Sunday Morning* and *A Taste of Honey* which meant so much to an earnest young man who, it transpired, had been scribbling away at lyrics for years in a rented room in Whalley Range. A large body of people – most vocally led by a posse of Radio One deejays – could have cheerfully strangled the band, and they called The Smiths' music "morbid", "glum", "miserable". As indeed it often was.

"My motivation to write came through my own general depression, my disgust, my horror"

Morrissey

Morrisey broke many boundaries as a lyricist and some of his subject matter was morbid ("Suffer little children" was a comment on the Myra Hindley/Moors Murders case) and dangerous ("Handsome devil" was foolishly misinterpreted by the gutter press as an endorsement of paedophilia). On the other hand, with his evocation of drizzly afternoons, deserted parks and viaducts and romance behind rusty bike sheds, he was a wordsmith who made all other contemporary pop song writers appear unbearably prosaic. Outsiders themselves, Morrissey's audience (made up in the main of the young unemployed, penniless students and, often, the bedsit-based lonely) saw him as the poet of outsiders. Their loyalty was legendary; for many, he was literally a lifeline. And if he sometimes lapsed into self pity then, very well, so did they themselves.

"I regard modern architecture as more dangerous than nuclear war"

Morrissey

There are very few literate, amusing, quotable people in pop; so when The Smiths started breaking big, *everyone* wanted to interview the eloquent Mr M. And Morrissey was prepared – to tell anyone who'd listen *exactly* what it was like to be pop's first agnostic celibate vegetarian. A motormouth who blithely admitted "I always had a religious obsession with fame". Morrissey took the spotlight with a long running series of audacious vaudevillian performances wherein he revealed just so much and no more of himself. He was arrogant ("Our reception hasn't surprised me at all"). He was florid and depressive ("Yes, I have a dramatic, unswayable, unavoidable obsession with death"). He was inclined to be vindictive ("I wanted to kick the whole Manchester scene in the teeth, and now I have my chance"). He knew a good joke when he saw one ("The Band Aid single? It's one thing to want to save lives in Ethiopia but it's another thing to inflict so much torture on the British public"). And with it all came a stance on sex which was, at first, new, interesting and faintly shocking.

"I find it ultimately dull, the absolute emphasis on sexuality in society. I consider the whole idea of sexuality totally redundant...I couldn't recognise those terms heterosexuality, bisexuality or homosexuality, because they were all just words in front of sexuality and they imply that there is an extreme difference between people and there isn't; people require exactly the same thing. I don't recognise heterosexuality in any degree, it doesn't exist and I'm quite convinced that homosexuality doesn't really exist either."

Morrissey, *Square Peg* magazine 1983

Amongst the groups of people desperate for an outsider-hero who latched onto Morrissey were a large number of gay/bi/ambisexual young men who noted the bare bum Fifties locker room cover of "Hand in glove" and the male love affair theme of 'This charming man' and various other lyrics. They also noted the camp influences and camp taste of their idol who, refreshingly, was himself a fan of others. Encouraged as a child by his formidable librarian mother, Morrissey was weaned on Oscar Wilde, whose epigrammatic style he often emulated, and his fan worship continued in his idolising of the New York Dolls, Jimmy Dean, *Coronation Street* and camp girl singers of the Sixties.

236

From Joe Dallesandro to Jean Marais and Truman Capote, his sexually ambiguous faves continually popped up on Smiths' record sleeves. So when Morrissey confessed that he wasn't interested in *having* sex there were many who, quite frankly, didn't believe him.

"Celibacy? I can't even recommend it. It's just right for me and wrong for the rest of the population."

Morrissey

The shock was to hear such a divinely sexy man being so anti-sexual. Back in those carefreeish mid-Eighties you could hardly move for gay groups and imagery in pop, from the leather and chains of Frankie Goes to the frock wearing of Boy George. But to say, as Morrissey did, "I find it ultimately dull, the absolute emphasis on sexuality in society. I consider the whole idea of sexuality totally redundant" was, ironically, threatening to many people. Personally as a committed androgynist/ bisexualist, I found it refreshing to hear a pop star railing against sexual objectification in pop, a vulnerable sounding male voice propounding non-divisive feminist ideals ("I have a very non-sexual stance, seeing people as humanist. There's so much segregation in modern life the last thing we need is a massive chasm between the sexes, which gets wider as the year passes") but the common reaction of journalists was to assume he was a fake and get on the next train to Manchester to dig the dirt about his past.

Sadly, there did turn out to be something of the prick tease in Morrissey. The first thing that made me think "here's one fucked up guy" was seeing the cover of a February 1985 *NME* where a pouting Mr M is pulling a t-shirt above his nipples to reveal a lipstick "Initiate me" slogan plastered over his midriff. It's cute and sexy, but it's hypocrisy too. Say what you like about creepy Cliff, at least he doesn't peddle sex whilst vilifying it. With Morrissey there really was something that doesn't quite add up.

"Morrissey doesn't need to have sex in private because he does it all on stage"

Frank Owen, *Melody Maker*

Trouble was that Morrissey was very quickly seeming to become a parody of himself. Over exposed even in 1984, Morrissey's self-mythologising went into overkill soon after. He had a – usually vituperative – opinion on everything and the more serious he got the more of a pain in the arse he became. It's significant that he titled his first solo album *Viva Hate*, because over the years Morrissey really seemed to become a hater. He hated the Royals (fine), he hated Thatcher (fine), he hated meat eaters, he hated "brontosauri" like Bob Geldof, he hated the press, he hated the music biz... why, he hated *everybody*. ("I find most people totally repugnant...I don't trust a single human being".) When it was funny, it was funny ("The writers and designers of *Spitting Image* should be unmercifully sued for making the Royal Family seem more attractive and intelligent than they are") but sometimes when it was serious, it was frightening. You'll find no one more anti-Thatcherite than me, but Morrissey's saying that he'd wished Mrs T had perished in the Brighton bombing seems to me like plain daft talk from a man who's supposed to place so much faith in compassion and the value of life. One by one you could feel his careless remarks about black music, his endorsement/romanticising of suicide, his praise for the Animal Liberation Front and his sheer spite ("That's another function of song writing. If people double cross me, I'll just sit down and write a nasty song about

238

them") positively driving people away.

"I know Morrissey did control what was said by The Smiths. I think Mike once did an interview and Morrissey didn't like the sound of it; after that Mike didn't do any more interviews."

Stephen Street, producer of *Viva Hate*

Ever the poet of alienation, by the end of the decade Morrissey was alienated like never before. Throughout his young life, Morrissey had fallen out with people – their first manager Joe Moss, Geoff Travis of Rough Trade records, new manager Ken Friedman, a lot of old friends like James Maker, you count 'em... but now he also began falling out with his band including, sadly, the (heterosexual) young guitarist and songwriter Johnny Marr who many thought to be the real talent in the band and whose romantic friendship had sustained Morrissey's emotional needs. Worse, the fans too were beginning to drift, not least because many of them felt Morrissey had let them down all along the line, from boasting that he'd never make videos and then proceeding to make them, to betraying the band's much trumpeted indie status by signing with that most monolithic of record company majors EMI. And for an artist whose usually penniless fans identified with him so strongly, whingeing constantly about his tax returns wasn't exactly the brightest of moves.

"Fame, fame, fatal fame
it can play hideous tricks on the brain"

"Frankly Mr Shankly"

Pop music takes a perfectly ordinary person off the street and sticks him under a spotlight and tells him he's God, and he believes it. Morrissey knew all about pop, except he forgot the sheer fickleness of the beast he was riding. "We're not a group, we're a crusade" he was fond of saying, and he probably believed *his* band would last forever, unlike all the others. In fact when the band split it came quickly ("The thing that used to make me happy was making me miserable" said a departing Johnny) and Morrissey was left on his tod, a solo artist.

The career has been, to put it mildly, a bit of a struggle. Very special music in the beginning, by the end the Smiths' music was sounding tired; Morrissey solo has been little better. The poor boy, now that he's lost Johnny, just doesn't have the tunes anymore. Though we've had glimpses of him (a triumphal one off gig, the occasional interview, cavorting around James Dean's grave for the "Suedehead" video) the normally-paranoid Mr M ("Some days I feel I can't answer the door") is presently very reclusive indeed. According to other journalists his phone is always either engaged or unobtainable; he's a PR's nightmare. Work on his latest solo album – tentatively titled *Bona Drag* – has been postponed. I actually feel very sorry for him.

Morrissey always mistakenly attributed a saying of Teresa of Avila's – "When the gods wish to punish us, they answer our prayers" – to Oscar Wilde; no doubt that adage is presently very much on his mind. Pop is a very difficult world to make a comeback in. A lot of his fans have moved on, and he's not really picking up any new ones. He's becoming a bit of a brontosaurus himself on pop terms. It's a shame because he has a talent. Perhaps he should take a couple of years off from the whole thing and go write a book. Myself, I'd still like to meet the young bluffer. And sniff his oxters too.

Gay Times, August 1990

Coming Clean

BOY GEORGE

"Of course I still want to be famous. What other reason could there be for doing what I'm doing, except for love of being famous? Sure, I go through periods of wishing I weren't – almost constantly! But I am. And I worked so hard at wanting to be famous and at being famous that even now if I have a bad day I say to myself 'You asked for this, bitch'."

The last time I interviewed George O'Dowd, he played me a song he'd just recorded with Culture Club the previous day. It was called "Do you really want to hurt me?" The rest is history. Over the intervening five years the Boy has been, as the tabloids would have it, To Hell and Back. At the time of the "depraved junkie" headlines, many predicted George would never work again. But here he is, sitting in Rome's Sheraton Hotel midway through a Eurotour – his first live concerts for three years – and with a classic hit single on his hands. Appropriately, it's called "To be reborn".

Much has changed since the last time we chewed cud. The one time no-smoking teetotaller, who never admitted to anything more than sexual ambiguity, is sitting chainsmoking Silk Cuts, quaffing champagne like there's no tomorrow and gossiping about his early gay days, and a few present day ones too. George may have lost both his virginity and his reputation at an early age, but he's never lost his sense of humour.

"Okay, so in the past I didn't go round saying 'I'm homosexual', but surely I made it quite clear through all the visual statements. What else did I have to do for people to actually say 'There's a queen'? Hop, skip and jump across Red Square in a fucking tutu? But I suppose since then I've realised I was mentally closeted in a way, even though it was blatantly obvious. And I've decided that I can't live like that any more. I was never lying when I said that I had affairs with women, but the main thing is that it's men I fall in love with and men I have serious relationships with.

"Maybe realising that it's important to say that is part of growing up. When you're young, you're queeny and camp and frivolous. But as you grow up, these relationship things become more important. And one of the things was that my boyfriend Michael was so strong throughout my heroin addiction. He's been such a major force in my life. I remember Paul, my friend and make up artist, saying to Michael after he'd finished doing my face, 'Do you like how he looks?' And Michael said 'I *always* like the way he looks'. What was so lovely about that wasn't that he said it, but that he meant it. I was always very conscious of being a blimp in the past and I still am one to some degree. But I honestly don't think that matters to him."

A blimp? "I used to think I was everybody's fat friend – especially when I got friendly with Marilyn, and Marilyn was so beautiful. I was good at make up and the frocks were a way of hiding myself, but they're not that now. Now I know I'm attractive on my own terms, because Michael's so beautiful and he makes me so proud. You need somebody beautiful in your own life to make yourself feel beautiful."

The last big boyfriend was, of course, Culture Club drummer Jon Moss. "Maybe I should say people were right when they called me closeted back in those days, but part of the reason for that was because I was having a sexual relationship with a so called straight man called Jon Moss. I was very much in love with him and I didn't want to lose

242

that, and it was much more sacred to me than announcing my homosexuality. I suppose I thought if I announced 'Hey everybody, I'm having an affair with the drummer – isn't he lovely?' everybody would go off me.

"Whereas now it's different. Everyone knows I have a boyfriend called Michael, it's been in all the papers. And he's the first boyfriend I've had who says, 'Yes, I'm homosexual, I don't fancy women'. And there isn't that much you can say about me that hasn't been said already, so I figure I've got to the stage where honesty is the best policy. It's so much easier just sticking the tape recorder on and telling the truth. Then there's nothing really they can ask you that's going to embarrass you or make you feel humiliated. They can't contradict you and you can't contradict yourself."

At one time George had a lot of people around him whom he considered friends. Many aren't around now. Either they're dead – "I've lost the most beautiful people in my life – they're gone and I'll never see them again" – or they proved to be of the fair weathered variety. "Jon Moss? Actually, we're quite friendly again now. It's funny, a while ago at a press conference in Italy they asked me what my relationship was with Jon and I said 'He was a great fuck'. And I spoke to him a couple of weeks later and coincidentally he'd been asked the same question and he'd said 'George was a great fuck!'

"It's okay between us now, even though when I was a heroin addict he didn't do anything to help me. He just walked away. But then looking back, he couldn't have helped me because I was completely helpless. When you get into that situation you're totally on your own. A lot of my good friends were scared. A friend of mine, Kim, saw me once when I was high and she was so disgusted with my behaviour she just had to walk away. When you're a junkie you're useless. You're a useless piece of furniture, no good to anybody. All you do is make people miserable because you're totally self indulgent."

Like Oscar Wilde, George has been a spendthrift of his genius. Like Wilde too, he experienced being snubbed and slighted by people who were once proud to be considered his friends. If that happened to me I'd be very embittered, but not George. "I'm a Gemini, I don't hold grudges! You can't cut off from people, that's impossible. I have to be able to say 'I forgive Marilyn'. He came up to me recently for the first time in six months and it wasn't 'How are you, how've you been?' it was 'Can you lend me twenty quid?' I was furious, really angry that he didn't even bother to ask how I was. But I'm not going to let things like that make me embittered. I'm still as trusting and open as I always was. I still tend to give people the benefit of the doubt. My biggest problem in life is that I rely on other people. I need people desperately. I need them more than anything."

One recent bonus has been his dozen-strong new band, a group of people he's been working with since he's been back on his feet. "I've found the right bunch of people – they care about the show and they care about me. I'm not used to people being so supportive, and it's a real pleasure when one of the backing vocalists comes up to me and tells me off for partying the night before a gig! It makes me feel really secure, that people care enough to tell me off. I don't particularly like to be on my own at the moment because I don't much like myself at present. I like to be around friends who make me happy and remind me I'm a good person, because I've been through a very negative stage of feeling I was a bad person.

"You do after you've been a junkie. You tend to think you're bad dice, and it's taken me a very long time to get back to liking myself and saying to myself 'Yeah, you're alright'. That's why I like having somebody like Judy Blame the designer around, because he's witty and I need humour more than anything. Looking back on Culture Club I was very bossy in those days, and I'm still a bit of an organiser now. But I'm beginning to loosen up a little and nowadays if I screw up on stage – go off key or something – I'm learning to be able to laugh about it rather than torture myself.

"The hardest thing for me at the moment is facing normality, and it helps so much to feel secure with the people around me. Some of them were involved with my drug saga, but now they're out of it too. Judy and I used to get high together, but now we've both got the attitude 'Bollocks, let's work, let's get motivated, let's do things'. I was a very motivated person at one time and that's really important. If you're not motivated, what the fuck else have you got?"

By the look of his stage set – the "Eat The Rich And Steal Their Culture" slogans and the rip off McDonalds logo that towers above the band's heads – "The logo was just a joke on me being fat. I was saying 'I may be fat, but I'm not over rated... unfortunately'" – George still partakes of the punk ethic. "Yeah, I'm into people stealing ideas. Everything is theft. I'm an art terrorist and a perfume terrorist and a credit card junkie!

"When I was a teenager my whole life was a rehearsal. I'd go to clubs in the night, I'd sleep until four in the afternoon, then I'd get up and do my face and hair and go out and I was one of the beautiful people. Obviously I have other things to do now. I have a reason to exist – I have a job. My job is being a pop star, whereas before it wasn't a job, it was a lifestyle.

"But I still adhere to the theft ethic. I go round the world and I meet people who are clones of me; my ideas are being taken up and I like that. The collections that Judy Blame does are always being ripped off, but we don't cry about it – we just move on to the next thing. All my clothes are made of junk. I want those kids in the audience to stick Marlboro packets and safety pins and badges on their clothes. Our new collection is even called Filthy Rich, with the fake pearls and the champagne corks and the Möet labels and the Chanel badges. I always have been and always will be a magpie in every sense of the word."

And then there's the tour programme. "It's probably the bitchiest tour programme that's ever been printed! I gave it to the people who put it together and said 'Write something about me' and I told them what I thought of other pop stars – like how sleeping with George Michael would be like having sex with a groundhog. It's just a joke, and if he can't see that it's his problem. He's a very clever and talented guy and one of the best songwriters around, but it doesn't stop me from slagging him off for making such a no-neck dingleberry of himself. I could lose fans by saying I don't like him but I'm gonna say it. Because I don't like his attitude.

"I look at everything like a fan, and I like pop stars who are touchable. I don't dig all this shit about him launching his record at The Savoy, and I hate this attitude of being a Proper Pop Star – *only* having the right pictures going out, *only* talking to certain journalists, *only* having the right people around you. Actually, there's an almighty feud at the moment between George and myself because when I was a very bad heroin addict I got a message from Aretha Franklin via *The Evening Standard* saying she'd love to do a song with me. Then later, after she'd done the record with George Michael, they asked me if I thought she'd rung the wrong George and I said 'I think she banged on the wrong closet' and George got very upset about that.

"If you go around covering up your trail so heavily, people are going to start wondering; hide something behind your back and people will wonder what it is you've got to hide. That girl Pat Fernandez who he's with was my faghag for three years, and when I read the newspaper story of 'How Pat broke my heart' I was tempted to write one about 'How Pat broke my hoover'. Because the idea of her and George having a relationship is about as likely as my having sex with that door."

On the other hand, the Boy just *adores* Rick Astley. "I love him. I call him my little baby. Every time he comes on the TV I jump up and down. I met him in Holland and I was so excited I ran up to him and said 'I love your voice'. He was actually quite rude to me, but maybe he was just embarrassed. All he did was mumble. But he's got a great voice and he's so unpretentious. I don't know if he'll become pretentious like Tears For Fears did – they're the most pretentious no-necks in the world – but at the moment I just want to pick him up and cuddle him.

"Even though I've had all the screaming mobs and packed stadiums myself, I'm still a fan by nature. I love Nick Kamen and I have Morten from A-Ha on my jacket. Michael Jackson and Prince are fabulous. Madonna is fabulous. She can't sing, but she's still fabulous. I say she's got no talent, but maybe that's her talent – having no talent. I think that's what glamour is – a knowledge of oneself, and an understanding of oneself and one's capabilities. I'm fascinated by her. It's like Prince; I was sitting eating a meal in the same room as him recently and I was just transfixed. I couldn't believe I was in the same room with him. As for Larry Mullen of U2, he's just the horniest piece of shit in the world..."

George has an opinion about everybody, from puzzlement ("I met Morrissey and I don't understand his stand. I had lunch with him in Paris and I still don't know if he's just another gabbling Oscar Wilde clone or if he really has something to say") via adoration ("I love Marc Almond so much – I'm a big fan of his. Those lyrics...") to out and out loathing ("George Michael's macho-ness makes me want to gag"). But mention Bette Davis and he turns to jelly. "When I was on withdrawal I switched on the TV for the Oscars and she came on and I just burst into tears because I was feeling like shit and I thought 'There'll never be another Bette Davis'. So when she arrived in London I sent her a hundred red roses. She rang me to talk to me at the health farm but I never got round to calling her back because I was too scared. I was just petrified. But of all the people I want to meet, she's *the one*."

Stardom, fame, success, glamour. Even though they won't play his records on US radio anymore (because of the drugs) and the Japanese won't let him in the country for the next twenty five years (ditto) and his dummy has been in and out of Madame Tussaud's like a yoyo and he's had his fair share of flop records, George is still a star and he still loves being one. But he's well aware of the underside of it all, even when his post-cure come-back single rocketed to number one in the first week of release.

"It's funny, but I even had a negative response to 'Everything I own' going to number one. I was very ill at the time with going through a major withdrawal situation and I got up in the morning and switched on the radio and when they said it was number one I didn't know whether to piss, shit or fart, I was so happy. But then afterwards I got really miserable again, because I started wondering if people were buying it out of pity.

"The next couple of singles didn't do too well, but now I'm beginning to realise that maybe my career's always going to be up and down like that. And perhaps if I was going to be honest about it I'd have to admit maybe I'm a little jealous of George Michael and Madonna because their records *always* make it. When things are going well for me I tend to be a bit cocky and think 'Oh, everything's going to be great'. And then of course it isn't.

"But then you get surprises. Like I had no idea 'To be reborn' was going to be a big hit, and I'm really delighted because I'm very proud of that song. It's a real song about a real situation, not like 'Keep me in mind', which I wrote around the pool. All my best songs are about specific things and 'Reborn' is the last song I wrote about Jon Moss and it's real and truthful and so close to home it makes me cry when I sing it. And because I *feel* that, other people feel it too."

George, who keeps singing snatches of "Black coffee" and "Muleskinner blues" and other camp favourites to me, reckons he's not a pop star but an entertainer. "One of the band said to me yesterday, 'Why do all this bullshit pop star bit? Why not do what you're best at?' And I do love all that stuff with sophisticated lyrics, that's what I'm crying out to do. I want to be a crooner. I always want to be touching something new, both in other people and myself. I'm not just into grabbing money, you know. I'm not the richest person in the world. I have two houses that are worth quite a lot of money, and I've just bought a car, a secondhand one actually. But I'm not an extravagant pop star.

"The stuff I listen to at home includes Pearl Bailey and Ella Fitzgerald and 'The man that got away', because basically I'm into voices. Mick Hucknall of Simply Red slags me off all the time and says I make terrible music. But I don't slag him back because I think he's got a wonderful voice – even though he does look like a sack of Kiwi Fruit!" So do you relate to Garland as an entertainer? "Yeah, but I don't want to go down the same hole! I want to go with pizazz. I've decided what I want written on my tombstone is 'And Another Thing...' Either that or 'I used to be famous, but I'm all right now'."

And the difference between a pop star and an entertainer? "Pop stars closet themselves, everything's so calculated. George Michael is a pop star of the highest degree. Whereas entertainment can be at the bus stop or it can be being catty just for the sake of it. Like I'm doing a book called *Self-Defence For The Verbally Fragile*, which has lines in it like 'I love that outfit, I never get sick of seeing you in it' or 'You should be wearing glasses – beer glasses' or 'Why do you smell? So blind people can hate you too?' *That's* entertainment!"

Yet at one time there was *no one* so organised and calculated as you. "I'm so erratic and emotional I just can't be like that any more. I was like it with Culture Club. But because of what I've been through, my life is changing a lot at the moment and I'll never be the same as I was. It doesn't really matter if I have a flop now and then because the overall thing is that people like me, and I like people. My mum works in an old people's home and the people there used to say 'I wouldn't like him in my house, he's a disgusting creature'. But that's changed. Obviously I lost my Queen Mum image when I became a heroin addict. But I think people still like me and it comes down to more than the music. I read recently in *Time Out* a fan saying 'What did Spandau Ballet ever do apart from make records?' and I want that attitude from my fans. I want to make new fans all the time. Basically I want to be liked. I want to be loved. That's my biggest thing."

I suppose it always was ever thus. Frocking up, admits George, was "always a way of laying straight men. I used to think that all that people were interested in was Boy

George, but it wasn't that. I was always Boy George, even when I was going down the Beat Route and giving straight guys blow jobs in the toilets in my frocks. I don't think they'd have let me do it if I hadn't been dressed up. Partly they admired my bravery for looking the way I did, partly because I was like a surrogate woman – that somehow made it okay for them."

It was a similar kettle of fish with Spear of Destiny's Kirk Brandon: "I wrote 'Do you really want to hurt me' for Kirk. He's denying all knowledge of me at the moment, but we had three years of him going round telling people he thought I was a girl." And Jon Moss: "I learned a lot from Jon Moss. Like never to fall in love with someone who says they're heterosexual. *Ever.*"

And now there's Michael and monogamy. "He's the most temperamental sonofabitch in the world and yet he's also the most charming and adorable person I've ever met. I'm completely monogamous now. Not mentally – I refuse to be mentally monogamous. I think that's immoral and wrong and silly and self depriving. But though I always argue against monogamy in theory, for myself I've found it the most suitable thing. I always say 'Life's a bitch, and then you marry one...'"

As I leave, the Boy gives me a t-shirt; not the usual promo nonsense, but one that says 'NOTICE – You can't catch Aids by caring'. "I just want to make it a big issue in the future. I told my manager I wanted to do an Aids t-shirt for the tour and he said 'Why? We're doing a Boy George tour'. But I said I don't care, I want to do this, and I'll lend my name to anything to do with the Terrence Higgins Trust. All the people around me know what I'm trying to say. I'm an eternal optimist and I think people will have to start caring more because it's going to affect them in the end."

251

So you don't think the Moral Majority is actually the majority? "They might kid themselves they are, but they're not. They've only got to come across a nice person and it alters their perception. This thing about being a right on queen gets up people's noses and I really believe my way of doing it is much better. I think if I meet another right on queen I'll gag. I'm not interested in this gay liberation shit, because it doesn't mean anything. It means as much as black liberation or housewives' liberation or anything else – it doesn't really mean shit. You don't have to go up to somebody and say 'Hey everybody, take notice!' There are much subtler ways of doing things..."

Gay Times, January 1987

Also available

The Cruelty of Silence

Sebastian Beaumont

The Cruelty of Silence is the highly anticipated new novel from the author of *On the Edge, Heroes Are Hard to Find* and *Two*. This subtle and intensely atmospheric novel begins on the anniversary of the enigmatic disappearance of successful architect Alex Stern. His lover, Lol, has to spend a deeply distracted year looking for him – at the cost of both his job and of the comfortable home they shared. After much frustration and an inability to restart his life, Lol discovers that a large sum of money is missing and that a locked computer file may contain the vital clue to what really happened to Alex. Set in Edinburgh, Spain, Paris and Amsterdam, *The Cruelty of Silence* is a taut and compelling contemporary mystery. It is also a striking account of the rewards and tensions of family life, the confusion created by new love, of pop music and drugs . . .

ISBN 1-873741-30-8

£9.50

Thresholds

David Patrick Beavers

Set in early summer 1977, *Thresholds* is at once a claustrophobic and intensely sensual novel about three eighteen year olds idling away time as they decide what to do with their lives. Brian has been left Kehmeny Court, a house with rambling grounds, on the Pacific coast near San Francisco. Living with him are his fiancée Viola and his best friend Morgan. Everything should be idyllic – but discontent is about to bring change. Brian is falling out of love with Viola and, perhaps, in love with Morgan. Meanwhile Morgan, who has been in love with Brian since childhood, finds love now becomes sexual. David Patrick Beavers – author of *Jackal in the Dark* and *The Jackal Awakens* – focuses on the erotic turmoil that seems so much a part of late adolescence to produce a novel that is nostalgic, powerful and stimulating.

ISBN 1-873741-28-6

£8.50

Oddfellows

Jack Dickson

Oddfellows marks an auspicious debut for Scottish novelist Jack Dickson. This is the story of Joe Macdonald, dishonourably discharged from the army, who becomes a bouncer for – and lover to – nightclub owner and entrepreneur Billy King. Their relationship is all about power – Billy commands, Joe obeys. But when Joe intervenes after Billy commits a particularly brutal rape of a fourteen year old, things become more uncomfortable. And not just for Joe. Drawn into this web of double dealing, violence and murder are Joe's teenage nephew Sean and appealing policeman Andy Hunter. Located in Glasgow's gay and criminal underworlds and encompassing child abuse, drugs and sado-masochism, *Oddfellows* is a starkly delineated novel about aspects of gay life that many would rather ignore.

ISBN 1-873741-29-4

£9.99

Brutal

Aiden Shaw

Now in its third edition, *Brutal* is a raw and powerful debut novel which explores the life of a young man who makes a living as a prostitute. Paul, with the help of therapy, is trying to challenge what he has become – a person out of control on drugs and alcohol, desiring abusive and degrading sex, estranged from people he once loved. Moreover, he is facing his own mortality while living with H.I.V. Increasingly disappointed by the way men relate to each other, he discovers that there are women around him to whom he cam turn.

Set mainly in London's underground club scene – where drug use is commonplace and casual sex something of an inevitability -*Brutal* offers an extraordinary, sometimes bleak portrait of a lost generation for whom death is as much a companion as lovers, friends, and family. Yet this is far from being a dispirited novel, and although the subject matter may shock, the shining honesty of the writing will prove life-affirming and an inspiration.

ISBN 1-873741-24-3

£8.50

The Learning of Paul O'Neill

Graeme Woolaston

The Learning of Paul O'Neill follows the eponymous hero over nearly thirty years – from adolescence in Scotland in the mid-sixties to life in a South Coast seaside resort in the seventies and eighties and a return to a vibrant Glasgow in the early nineties. As the novel begins, fifteen year old Paul is learning fast about sexuality as his Scottish village childhood disintegrates around him. After many years in England, he returns to Scotland trying to come to terms with the sudden death of his lover and to establish himself as a writer. His return brings him face to face with the continuing effects of adolescent experiences he thought he had put behind him – some enriching, some of which have directly informed his sexual nature. And the influence of an ambiguous, handsome, married bisexual man raises new questions about the shape of Paul's life as he arrives at the threshold of middle-age. *The Learning of Paul O'Neill* is a compelling and adult novel about gay experience and aspects of sexuality which some may find shocking but which are written about with an honesty that is as refreshing as it is frank.

ISBN 1-873741-12-X

£7.50

The Biker Below the Downs

Graeme Woolaston

Another thought-provoking novel about aspects of gay life not usually explored in fiction. When John – a middle-aged and well heeled Scot on holiday in a small Sussex village – first sees his leather-clad biker neighbour he feels an immediate attraction. And both are aware of it. After an encounter with a naked youth in the neighbour's garden, John realises the two boys are lovers and that he is attracted to both. But a chance remark made by the biker leads John to make a set of discoveries which shock and move him. The story of a man discovering the son he didn't know he had and a boy discovering the father he'd never known, *The Biker Below the Downs* is compelling, richly comic and strongly erotic.

ISBN 1-873741-25-1

£8.50